Praise for BITTER BETRAYAL

WOW! This was such a fantastic read. Intriguing and captivating, I was hooked on the very first page! Amanda M. Thrasher pulled me in, and I couldn't put the book down. Bitter Betrayal is a must read for all teens, boys and girls alike. The message portrayed in this book is one that truly needs to be talked about. Kids need to learn to respect each other. Social media and bullies can ruin a kid's life and scar them forever. We all talk to our kids and tell them to never let someone touch you in a way that makes you feel uncomfortable. Amanda M. Thrasher brings it to an entirely different level. Two teens madly in love for two years, both great kids, who come from great families, but when you mix alcohol with teens who can't handle it, bad things happen, and events can change your life forever! This book could be the door to opening teens' eyes about bullying, social media, true friendship, and how important family is. I was super happy with the way the families handled the situation they were faced with. It will leave you wondering who to blame, though I believe that both teenagers were at fault. Unfortunately it's always the girl's reputation that suffers the most in this kind of situation. Having two teenage girls I have witnessed my share of bullying.

Congratulations Amanda M. Thrasher on a well written book. I can't wait to see the impact this has on teens and can only hope it helps them think before they act!

~ Felicia Scura Mazza
Talent Acquisition Manager at STA USA, Inc.

BITTER BETRAYAL

Amanda M. Thrasher

Text Copyright © 2017 Amanda M. Thrasher

All rights reserved. Published 2017 by Progressive Rising Phoenix Press, LLC
www.progressiverisingphoenix.com

ISBN: 978-1-946329-18-9

Printed in the U.S.A.
1st Printing

Edited by: Jody Amato

Cover photo: BigStockPhoto. ID:119500349
Copyright:altanaka-signed model release

Author photo: Jessica Prigg Murrah
Modern Studios Photography

Book interior design by William Speir
Visit: http://www.williamspeir.com

Book cover design by Kalpart.
Visit www.kalpart.com

Acknowledgments

I would like to thank my business partner and friend, Jannifer Powelson, for her belief in this project before I even wrote a single word. I'm certain one day we'll co-author a book together that will make us laugh, cry, and reflect on all the things that we've accomplished together.

Special thanks to my editor, Jody Amato, who read the manuscript and sent word that she thought this was an important piece, and for her invaluable advice, for which I'm grateful.

To Lynne Morton Groff, who read the roughest version of the manuscript, and still found it intriguing and captivating, thank you!

To Anne Dunigan, for your advice over the years, I appreciate it and haven't taken it for granted.

And last but certainly not least, to my family, Mike, Zack, Krista, and Lauren. Though at times you have no idea which book I'm writing, I appreciate your patience regarding the work I do.

Table of Contents

Preface

The purpose of this book is to demonstrate how the simplest actions in the name of fun can have devastating consequences. Some results are everlasting and can't be undone. And the circumstances and decisions themselves, due to the maturity level of impressionable teens, is often confusing and leaves lasting emotional scars that can take years to overcome, if ever. Consequences of reckless actions can put kids, families, friends, and communities at risk. My hope is that the story I've written triggers discussions, emotions, and allows teens—girls and boys—to make smart, intuitive decisions, and that they remember to respect each other's boundaries.

I understand that the Young Adult (YA) category covers the ages of thirteen through eighteen years. But I believe impressionable teens—thirteen through sixteen years old—aren't as emotionally mature as the older teens, yet they're in the same category. For this reason, I have intentionally kept the language and descriptive scenes clean so all teens could enjoy the book.

I sincerely hope you enjoy my work.
Amanda M. Thrasher

This book is dedicated to my dad, Martin Mulroy, who has been a hero to me my whole life. He took on that role and unintentionally became my children's hero as well. He has more faith in my work than I thought humanly possible and has read every piece I've ever written, published and unpublished.

Thank you, Dad,

Love you.

Chapter 1

Cover for Me

"They say there are two sides to every story and somewhere in the middle lies the truth; there's no exception to this one. But whose truth will you believe . . . his or hers?"

DTB CU there!
(Don't text back see you there)

The message flashed across her phone, and that's all it took. Not even a whole sentence and suddenly all she could think about was getting out of class. As her fingers frantically tapped away on her phone, Payton didn't hear a single word from the kid speaking nervously in front of the class. Looking back, what was she thinking?!?!

Payton: Cover for me
Aubrey: Seriously?
Payton: Problem?
Aubrey: Yah
Payton: Really? ☺
Aubrey: Nah
Payton: K

Aubrey: BTW 182
Payton: U don't hate me ☺ Luv u

Five, four, three, two, and the bell finally rang. Payton shot out the door. Aubrey, her best friend since sixth grade, shoved the books Payton had left behind in her own backpack. Payton's behavior, though frustrating at times, wasn't surprising. She was head crazy about that boy, Reece Townsend, and it helped that Aubrey liked him as well.

With less than ten minutes to freshen up, get across campus to her car, and make it to the dam in time to meet Reece, Payton didn't have time for small talk with anyone. Dodging in and out of students, she avoided eye contact with as many people as she possibly could. The boy's football coach, Coach Duncan, was headed her way. His voice, undeniably recognizable, bounced off the walls and echoed through the corridor before he was physically present. When finally in view, she purposely looked at her feet and rushed past him. No way did she want him stopping her and stalling her with questions about her brother and his playing time at college.

"Whoa girl, where's the fire?"

Coach grabbed her arm as she tried to rush past him and her whole body swung around, forcing her to face him. Arm still in his grasp, he shook his head.

"Slow it down, girl! If only my boys had moved half as fast this morning."

Managing a slight smile, she pointed toward the bathroom. Coach raised his hands in the air and shook them back and forth, stopping her from saying another single word. He wanted no part of what could pop out of that girl's mouth. She was liable to say something for the shock value alone. He didn't need to know, want to know, or care to know, for that matter. He let her on her way, no questions asked. A healthy spritz of perfume, lip gloss, duck-lip practice, and Payton climbed into her car. She must have sped, because she made it in record time.

"What took you so long?" he asked.

The love of Payton's life, well, at least to a sixteen-year-old, love-struck teen. One look at his smile and she melted. It was bad enough that they attended different schools, but he was a senior, in the process of narrowing down his college options, which meant she'd be stuck there without him. The thought of it made her cringe. On a daily basis she obsessed about him leaving, even when he asked her not to, but she couldn't help it. *Not today,* she told herself, pushing the thoughts out of her head.

The best part of his day was right then, as he watched her walk toward him. He was sitting on the back of his tailgate, swinging his legs back and forth, waiting for her to join him. He tapped the cool metal, her cue to jump up next to him. She grinned. So freaking hot! He always looked that way to her, and all she wanted to do was kiss that face of his! Her grin turned into a giggle.

"What's so funny?" he asked.

"Nothing."

"Whatever!" A cute smirk crossed his face. "Something, or you wouldn't be laughing."

She grabbed his face in her hands, laughed out loud, and kissed him before hopping up next to him on the tailgate. Right before she jumped up, Reece playfully pulled her back toward him instead. Now face-to-face, she brushed his sandy-brown hair to one side, revealing his green eyes. She could get lost in them; they were that pretty.

"What?" he asked.

"Nothing," Payton giggled. "You grabbed me, remember?"

"I did. But why are you staring at me like that?"

His breath hit her face. Truth be told, all she wanted at that moment was for him to kiss her, really kiss her. *Move, Payton. Move now*, she thought as she stepped back and took a deep breath.

"I'm just looking at you, that's all. You're kinda cute like that."

He rolled his eyes. But Payton could tell by the boyish grin on his face that her comment had pleased him. She loved that look on his face. He looked a few years younger, like a real kid. It was sweet. She stared a second too long, capturing that face a moment longer in her mind.

"You know I'm supposed to say that kinda stuff," he said as seriously as he could, but it wasn't working.

He tapped the tailgate again and held out his hand. *So thoughtful!* Payton thought, and this time she jumped up and joined him. The long cotton skirt she'd chosen to wear that day wrapped around her legs as she swung them back and forth off the back of the truck. Sandals, painted toes, and a T-shirt completed her outfit. Her long dark hair, with a delicate headband complimenting her outfit, finished off her look.

"You look hot. But I know you know that, so I'm not going to tell you!" He laughed. "Just kidding. You look amazing. Beautiful as usual!"

Payton's face lit up. She leaned in and kissed him gently on the lips. Funny thing, though, she thought Reece was the most beautiful thing she'd ever seen. They'd actually argued about that statement once. *Guys aren't beautiful,* he'd stated. They could be handsome. Good looking, sexy, dope, hot, or even cute, but not beautiful! Men were not beautiful. But it didn't matter what he thought. To Payton he was, and she could look at him all day long.

"Hey, you never did answer my question," he said.

"What question was that?"

"Why were you late?"

"You idiot!" She nudged him playfully. "I'm not late; you're early, and for the record, I'm the one who's usually waiting for you!"

He held her by the elbows, leaned in, and kissed her quickly on the lips. She would have kissed him back, but he'd already pulled away. Just as well, she wouldn't have wanted to stop, and that wouldn't have been good, since time wasn't on their side.

"Aubrey covering for you?" he asked as he rummaged through a sack next to him.

"Yep. Advisory. Shouldn't be too hard."

She was always late getting back when they met for lunch, but there was no way she was going to tell him that. He'd cut their time short for sure. Payton had never struggled with confidence before Reece, but he unknowingly made her question herself. She didn't need to worry, though; she was popular, a good student, considered hot, and well liked.

"Whole or half?" he asked, holding a sandwich in his hand.

"Half," she answered, knowing she couldn't eat in front of him anyway.

The breeze was cool but not cold, a perfect day for a picnic on the back of her boyfriend's truck. Why did they have to go back to school?

Reece's phone buzzed. She didn't glance at it, but she wanted to. It buzzed again. He didn't read the text, but did check the time. Pointing at the sandwich she hadn't touched, he nudged her to take a bite. She didn't think he'd noticed she hadn't eaten, but he had.

"We're going to be late if you don't hurry up. Eat."

She leaned into his arm. It felt good just being close to him. The feeling of closeness made her want to kiss him, and she had no idea if he knew that. It was so stupid and irritating that she felt this way every time they were together. Not to mention when it was time to head back to school. It made leaving incredibly difficult. Payton missed him before they'd even left. Surely this was normal for a teen like her, wasn't it? She looked at her sandwich just as Reece took a bite of his.

"I'm not really hungry." She hesitated for a second, opened up her mouth to speak, but closed it again.

"What is it?" he asked, knowing she wanted to say something.

The words unexpectedly flew out of her mouth,

surprising even her.

"We could cut class."

Reece's eyes darted toward her.

"Stay here and hang out a bit longer," she added.

Payton Phillips suggesting they cut class. Sweet! He wasn't sure if he was shocked, but he was definitely impressed that it was her idea. They'd been together nearly two years, but she'd never once insinuated they should cut class before. Grinning, he shook his head.

"I can't. I've got a test this afternoon. No pass, no play, remember?"

Even though she knew he was right, her heart sank.

"But I can't believe you just suggested that—it's something I might think of, *might*, but I didn't think you would." Reese took a drink of his Coke. "Um. OK then. I think you just kinda got yourself in a bind. I might hold you to it later!"

She didn't care. Hell, Advisory or Reece? Seriously . . . was that a real question? Worth the trouble if she got caught? Hell yeah! Reece jumped off the tailgate of his white dodge and stood in front of her. One arm wrapped around her neck, one around her waist, he kissed her, a real kiss, and she kissed him back. An incoming text interrupted them. Flushed cheeks, heart racing, and although Payton wouldn't have agreed in that moment, it was for the best that the text came in. They may not have left that spot for a while longer, and then they both would have been late. Not to mention Aubrey couldn't cover for that long. After all, Aubrey wasn't a miracle worker. Covering for lunch and half of sixth period, Advisory, was no problem, but more than that rose the red flags. Reece's phone buzzed again; this time he answered the text.

Reece: K CUS – DTB
(OK See you soon, don't text back)

"Hey, can I ask you a question?"

Reece shrugged his shoulders. "Sure."

"How come when you text me sometimes, and apparently others." Her raised eyebrows indicated she'd read his response.

"Yeah," he said hesitantly.

"You don't let me text you back?"

He looked puzzled.

"What are you talking about?"

"What's with the **DTB**, don't text back?" she asked.

Reece shoved his phone into his back pocket and packed up the trash. Payton waited for his response.

"What? Seriously?" He laughed. "That's your question?"

She nodded. "Yeah. That's it," she said, moving her foot in tiny circles in the dirt. "Like, if you text me first, why can't I text you a response back?"

He grabbed his phone and pointed to her texts. Now she wished she hadn't asked such a stupid question. It felt like she was invading his privacy or something, but a simple explanation hadn't seemed too much to ask for a second ago.

"Really, you want to know why?" He didn't wait for a response. "It's simple. Sometimes I'm in class. Sometimes I can't talk for various reasons. Like right now, I'm here with you, and dip-wad Walker is looking for me. Or sometimes I'm driving, at practice, whatever."

He glanced at his phone to check the time. "But right now I've gotta go, and so do you."

DTB. A way to communicate without communicating. Cute, wasn't it? Was it? Why was she suddenly questioning it?

Chapter 2

Sweet as Sugar, Bitter as Poison

Picking a college wasn't turning out to be as easy as Reece had hoped. The school he wanted to attend was out of state and hadn't made him any kind of offer yet. His coach had written letters of recommendation. His grades were good, game films highlighting his plays were in the hands of several recruiters, and services that assisted students and parents were working on his behalf. But the waiting part was no fun. His parents wanted him to stay in Texas, but agreed not to stand in his way if a school he liked came knocking.

Reece wanted two things: to attend a D1 school and receive an out-of-state offer. Truthfully, he hadn't thought too much about Payton or what she thought. There were 347 D1 schools that he was aware of, scattered across forty-nine different states. Some colleges were smaller, private schools and some larger universities, but the odds of Reece receiving a full scholarship were excellent. Coach had said a full ride was more than a realistic possibility; it was a probability, especially riding on his brother's reputation. Reece idolized his brother and wanted to follow in his footsteps, not easy to do, but he never once felt jealous or envious of his brother's success. Coach always bragged about Royce and Reece. Proud to have coached them both in their high school years.

"Just like Royce, son. You are capable of playing for a D1 program," Coach Duncan would say. "You know, those programs can generate millions of dollars in revenue annually for the schools. And like your brother, you could handle the pressure of performing and the expectations of winning."

Reece believed Coach and worked hard at proving him right. Payton cringed when Reece talked about the schools he wanted to attend, because she knew it meant the inevitable—he'd be leaving. He'd get so excited. His eyes would light up and he'd get animated as he talked. She was happy for him, but sad for herself. Despite the heaviness she felt weighing on her heart and in her head because she missed him already, she tried her best to encourage him. He called her to tell her about an email Coach had received asking about his eligibility. He could tell she was down by how quiet she got on the other end of the phone. Now he knew why he hated to call. He'd rather send her a text than talk.

"You know we'll stay in touch every day and hang out when I come home."

"Well, yeah," she replied, kinda shocked that he had to actually state it. Surely that was understood. Wasn't it?

"Just checking. You sound down or something."

Payton shook her head, and then realized she needed to answer. He couldn't see her through the phone.

"Sorry. I'm fine."

"I'm almost there. Are you ready?"

"I will be by the time you get here," she said. "If you let me off the phone!"

When Payton climbed in, Reece raised the console divider in the front seat so she could sit next to him. He'd crank the aux and she'd lay her hand on his leg, unless he was holding hers in his. She loved Friday nights, even more than Saturdays. It was the excitement of spending real time with him after being in school all week. They were going to the movies with Reece's friends. Aubrey didn't have a date and even though she could have joined them, she opted out. Payton didn't mind. All of her attention was on Reece anyway.

"You smell good," Reece said as soon as Payton climbed into the truck and turned to give him their customary kiss hello.

She knew the perfume she'd sprayed all over her clothes and neck was his favorite perfume; smiling coyly, she kissed him again.

"Trevor might bring some girl," Reece stated nonchalantly.

Payton laughed. "Like just some random girl, seriously?"

Reese shook his head. "Right! I didn't ask. He said he might bring some girl. I don't care who." He took a sip of Coke. "But I think her name begins with an S. Samantha, Sydney, Sophie, something like that. Chase is coming as well, but I doubt he'll bring anyone; no one will date that loser."

As they turned onto Trevor's street, they saw

Trevor outside, leaning against his car with a pretty girl standing next to him. She was tall, slim, and blond. Payton didn't recall seeing her before, but gave her a quick once-over as they walked toward the truck.

"This is Stacie," Trevor announced as they climbed into the back.

"Stacie," Reece repeated, glancing at Payton.

"Hi, Stacie, nice to meet you." Payton made the introductions for everyone.

Reece looked at Trevor as the girl climbed into the truck and gave him a nod of approval. How did Trevor score a date with that? Trevor looked as if he hadn't quite figured it out either; he seemed to know exactly what Reece meant as he grinned big, shrugged his shoulders, and threw up his hands. No complaints from him. They had met during one of his classes. She was a transfer. Totally used to rejection, Trevor was bold enough to ask her to go out with them that night. Shockingly she had said yes, and here they were. She was undeniably hot and he wasn't. Weird.

"You never know if you don't ask, bro," Trevor muttered as he patted Reece on the back.

Payton leaned over the back of the seat and spoke to the girl.

"You'll get used to it. They talk to each other as if we're not here, and they do a lot of things in groups." She laughed out loud. "They say girls are bad about doing everything together. OMG! These guys. Stick around, you'll see."

Trevor grabbed Stacie's hand, not sure if he'd actually see her again after that evening, but she didn't seem to mind. More of Reece's friends were waiting for them at the movies than they'd expected. Doug, Shane, Tristan, and Lisa. Additional introductions were made, tickets bought, and seats found. Sci-fi was not her thing, but Payton was just glad to be there. The boys enjoyed it, though; she knew because they were relatively quiet throughout the entire show. Unusual.

"Where to?" Payton asked as the credits rolled.

"Lake. Tiger's trail," Trevor suggested. "Denis said there's a party up there tonight."

Returning to the truck, Reece nodded, turned up the music, slipped his hand into Payton's, and they took off. Trevor was right. Trucks, cars, and kids were everywhere. There was no telling how long they had until someone called it in, but they were there now. The typical classic red plastic cups found at every teen get-together were being passed around. Beer was drunk by most, but others were slamming liquor brought by kids who could get their hands on it. Some of the kids pretended to drink it. Peer pressure. Payton was one of those kids. She held onto a cup that was handed to her and pretended to sip what was in it. Fake IDs were something else that kids seemed to have easy access to. Payton was dying to look into that, but hadn't quite been brave enough to attempt it yet. Reece didn't need one. If he needed anything, Royce took care of him. It was common knowledge that teens were able to get their hands on just about anything they wanted or needed if they had a few dollars. If the price was right, someone always seemed to know someone who could get it or whom to ask. At these parties vodka floated around because it looked like water, was easily found in most homes, and easily mixed with soda, juice, or just about anything else. Every time Payton was handed a drink with vodka in it, her mom's voice would ring in her head. ***Kids on booze: not only illegal, but lethal.*** Her mom had recited these words for years, hoping Payton would avoid the teen drinking scene. Payton was an observer and Reece for the most part was too, unless he was planted somewhere for the night and even then he didn't usually overdo. But he didn't mind enjoying the scene with his friends and usually he had fun no matter what, especially with his girl by his side. Handed a beer, Reece shook his head and pointed to his truck.

"Dude, I've got a full truck tonight."

His attention turned to Payton as he reached for the cup and handed it to her.

"Babe, yours is gone, you can have it."

She wanted to shake her head and decline as well, but against her better judgment she held out her hand. Noticing the hesitation on her face, Reece pulled her toward him and whispered in her ear.

"You're good, you're not driving. Plus, you're with me."

He put his arms around her waist, leaned forward, and kissed the back of her neck. She turned around to face him and he pulled her even closer, kissing her with such intensity that her stomach filled with butterflies. She kissed him back just as hard. As he pulled away from her, he whispered something so softly she wasn't quite sure what she'd heard. Were they *the* words, as in the real form and not a version of them, like he usually said, or number digits in his texts? That's what they sounded like; surely she hadn't missed *the* words? Tugging at his sleeve, she asked him to repeat what he had said.

"Wait. What? What did you say?"

"You heard me," he countered with a muffled voice so no one else would hear him.

"No, really. What did you say?"

"I love you, babe," he whispered again, bashfully the second time. He kissed her on the cheek and turned back toward his friends, joining their conversation as if he hadn't just said the most important words she'd ever heard.

Seriously, *the words*! First thing she wanted to do was say them back, but she couldn't because he was talking to his friends. Then she wanted to text her BFF, Aubrey, but she couldn't do that either, because Aubrey would want details. Super excited, madly in love, how could she have known what would happen next?

Chapter 3

Girl Talk

As soon as Payton hit her bed, she sent the text. She'd been dying to talk to Aubrey since Reece had said *the* words. Aubrey was still awake and had the response that any good girlfriend would have: excitement and asking for details.

> **Payton:** OMG he said 143
> (Oh my God, he said I love you)
> **Aubrey:** Seriously?!?
> **Payton:** Yes!!!! But properly, used real words, not digits. So happy could die. Love him that much!
> **Aubrey:** FaceTime now!!!!!!

"Details?" Aubrey asked as soon as they were connected.

Payton, giddy, didn't know where to start and was rambling. It had happened so fast, and she had loved him forever, so much longer it seemed than he had loved her. But hearing the real words, not a form of them, gave her a sense that this was without a doubt the real deal—to him as well. He wasn't even partying when he said it, which was good, because he meant it.

"I don't know where to start. It's insane. The whole

night was amazing!"

"Focus," Aubrey said, reeling her back in. "Details. Give me the details."

"It was lit. We went to the Trail and everyone was there, hanging out, and I really wasn't paying much attention to what they were all talking about. And Reece just kinda like kissed me, then pulled my arm, I think . . . I don't know. I'm still on freaking happy overload; but somewhere in there he kissed me and whispered the words, 'I love you, babe.' Real words, not a version of them, and that's what made it so special. Not like 'luv ya,' or 'love ya bunches,' or sarcastically or cutely like we do, but truly like you would want. 'I love you, babe,' he said. It was awesome."

Aubrey, happy for Payton, couldn't stop laughing. It was quite amusing, listening to Payton tell it over and over. If Aubrey could, which she couldn't since it wasn't hers to tell, she'd record her telling the story for the fifteenth time on her Snapchat. Such great material, wasted for sure.

"Well, I'm happy for you," Aubrey managed. "What was the girl like that Trevor brought?"

Payton burst out laughing. "Too hot for Trevor. I was like WTH, seriously? How did you pull that off?"

Their call was interrupted by a text from Reece. That would start their evening rituals of goodnights. This one was a little different, and Payton couldn't be happier.

Reece: Meant it, I love you.

Payton: I love you too. So happy, had a great time.

Reece: Me too, can't wait till tomorrow.

Reece: Talk in the morning. I love you for real.

Payton: I love you for real as well, OMG so happy!

Reece: Same girl, all is good.

Payton took a screenshot of her phone and sent it to Aubrey. It took forever for her to fall asleep. Excited and blissfully happy, she wouldn't allow herself to think about when he'd be leaving for school. She focused solely on *the* words. His words. "I love you, babe." They'd actually moved from digits, 143, the universal technology language that kids use for 'I love you,' to real words. He loved her! And with that one thought on her mind, she finally drifted off to sleep.

Chapter 4

Dinner with the Parents

It wasn't unusual for Payton to hang out at Reece's house or vice versa, for Reece to spend time with Mr. and Mrs. Phillips, especially on the weekends. It helped that Reece was well liked by her parents and his parents had indicated they enjoyed spending time with Payton as well. Since he'd said *I love you, babe*, Payton had been walking on cloud nine and jumped at any opportunity to spend extra time with him, even if it meant doing nothing but hanging with their parents. Reece sent her a text and asked if she wanted to eat dinner and hang out with his family; Royce, his brother, was home on break. It took her about three seconds to answer. Two of those seconds were actually spent counting down so she didn't respond too fast. Massive fail on that one! Certain her parents wouldn't object, she accepted before she'd even asked their permission.

Payton: Yes
Reece: Can't wait to C U
Payton: Same
Reece: 4:00
Payton: K

She wanted to text the words or the numbers, either one, but waited to see what he'd do. He didn't do it and her heart sank just a tad. Shaking it off, she texted her mom.

Payton: Can I go to Reece's for dinner?

Securing the deal and to make sure there weren't too many questions, she added a reason.

Payton: Royce is home. Break.

She received the standard preliminary answer. *Let me ask your dad.* Knowing she could go, Payton started to get ready. Her dad never seemed to mind, if Reece's parents were involved. At least he knew where they were, he'd say, and Payton was almost ready to go when her mom gave her the OK from her dad.

Mrs. Phillips: Your dad said yes. Is he picking you up or are you driving over?

She hadn't asked. Quick text. No answer. Another text. Nothing. She called him just as his text buzzed in her hand.

"Never mind. I'll see you when you get here," she said as he answered the phone, and then she hung up.

Payton: He's picking me up.

Payton stared at herself in the mirror. Was she too fat? She turned sideways and ran her hand over her stomach. Was it flat? She thought it was, but took another mirror and held it at several different angles to make sure. Her obsession to be perfect for Reece included her ideal weight. She couldn't stand the thought of not being perfect for him; crazy, because she had a cute little figure. Spritzing what had now become Reece's favorite perfume on her neck and wrists, dabbing her lips with gloss, she took one last glance in the mirror. Shorts, converse, and a pink T-shirt completed her casual-cute look. Her long dark hair was tied in a loose braid and pulled to one side. It was perfect for a stay-in day with your boyfriend's family, even if she did say so herself.

"How do I look?" she asked her mom.

"Beautiful as usual!"

She blew her a kiss and watched her daughter read a text as she walked out the back door.

Reece: Here

Payton: Coming

Royce, Reece's brother, was huge. Absolutely huge! Extra time in the weight room, no doubt, had paid off. The whole family was thrilled to have him home, including Reece. Everyone listened to his stories, locker-room talk, about the coach yelling at him, and what was going on in his head during certain plays of the games they'd watched. His mom doted on him, glad he was home, and his dad enjoyed a beer with his oldest boy. Payton noticed Royce refer to Reece as *little bro* or *little brother*, but Reece didn't seem to care.

"Yo, little bro, grab me and Dad another beer, will you?" He glanced at his dad, winked, and added, "Grab one for yourself if you want."

He knew Reece wouldn't, especially in front of his dad, but he liked to rile his dad up. Payton was trying to listen to the boys while politely answering Mrs. Townsend's small-talk questions. She heard Royce say something about a friendly game of flag football and Reece was already planning on texting his friends. Payton wanted to join them, but didn't want to leave Mrs. Townsend in the kitchen by herself. To her relief, she heard the following words: "Why don't we join the others now?"

Reece patted the cushion next to his on the floor and Payton happily flopped down beside him. Being close to him made her feel content. He slid his arm over her stomach and pulled her closer. Hesitantly she glanced at his parents. He caught her and laughed.

"We're not doing anything," he whispered, tickling her at the same time. "We're just semi-snuggling on the floor. And everyone's here."

He was right, and no one seemed to mind. Relaxing, she scooted closer into him and listened while everyone talked and laughed together. She wondered what it would be like laying that close to him in a room by themselves, but he was so happy visiting with his family that there was nowhere else she'd rather be. His laughter at his brother's stories made her laugh as well. Royce threw a cushion at Reece's head and Payton ducked just in time as Reece caught it. Their dad, Roger Townsend, playfully scolded them.

"Come on now, boys! Don't hit this beautiful young lady. Save it for the field."

"Time to eat," Mrs. Townsend announced.

Payton smiled and thanked her, and was surprised when Reece's mom asked her to call her by name.

"You can call me Reagan, not so formal is it?" She smiled and pointed toward the kitchen. "Come on, you two."

Reece kissed Payton on the cheek, jumped up, and helped her to her feet.

"After you," he said.

Most of the guests fit around the dining room table. Reece, Payton, and Tommie, Reece's cousin, sat in the family room. Mrs. Townsend had cooked Royce's favorite meal: brisket, beans, potato salad, rolls, and chocolate cake with ice cream for dessert. It smelled delicious, looked fantastic, and though Payton had put a little bit of everything on her plate, when she actually looked at the amount of food, she became overwhelmed with the fear of actually consuming it. The odd thing was that she was hungry. Even had hunger pangs. But the thought of eating in front of her boyfriend made her incredibly nervous. She pushed the food around on her plate, cornering it and making spaces between the meat, potatoes, and beans. The spaces made it look like she'd eaten a bit of everything, and every time Reece looked in her direction, she acted as if she were chewing or went as far as to put a small bite in her mouth. Once in her mouth, it became almost impossible to swallow. Feeling as if the food was sticking in her throat, driven by the fear of swallowing it, she grabbed her sweet tea to wash down the tiny morsel. She remembered thinking, as the ice tea washed the gritty meat down, *I'll eat when I get home, when no one is watching me.* Then she reminded herself to stop. That kind of thinking was crazy. Eat the food. In that moment she became aware and scared that she had to remind herself of something so mundane. She made a conscious effort to enjoy the food. She was startled by the buzzing sound of a text coming in, but it wasn't her phone. Reece checked his, but he didn't answer. It buzzed again. And a few minutes later it buzzed again. Finally he texted back. Sitting next to him on the couch with trays on their laps, Payton couldn't help but glance as he typed.

Reece: Same DTB
(Same don't text back)

Dying to ask but not wanting to seem to invade his privacy, Payton looked the other way. Reece leaned over, kissed her on the cheek, and said the four little words that made everything OK.

"I love you, babe."

And that was it, all it took. Everything was all right in Payton Phillips' world.

Chapter 5

All in Fun

Aubrey and Maddie drove up to Payton's house just as Reece pulled into her driveway. They tried not to look at them as Payton and Reece said their goodbyes; nothing worse than watching your best friend making out or kissing her boyfriend goodbye. It was Aubrey who playfully broke them up by opening the truck door on Payton's side.

"Seriously already, take a breath!"

Reece liked Aubrey. She was good for Payton and not bitchy like some of her other friends. Maddie he could take or leave. He kinda thought she was a snob, but Payton liked her. He tried not to judge her friends, since he had some who weren't Payton's favorites either.

"Jealous?" he joked.

"Hardly!" she retorted.

He pulled Payton toward him one last time, kissed her lightly on the lips and nudged her playfully toward the door.

"Go on then, get out of here! I'll text ya later."

The words slipped out before she could stop herself. "I love you."

Aubrey stood by awkwardly, not knowing what to do, and noticed the surprised look on Reece's face. Not embarrassed, but surprised. Payton closed the truck door.

"Hey," Reece hollered. "Back at ya!"

The girls went inside and immediately raided the kitchen. Sitting at the counter, laughing and talking about their evening. Payton nibbled on a handful of almonds, while Maddie and Aubrey snacked on pieces of cold pizza. Payton told them about the flag football game that had been arranged for the next day. It sounded like it could be fun; so many people going and all, and that's when she told them they were going.

"We're going to watch them play," she told them. "It will be fun."

"Fun for you," Maddie giggled. "But I'm in. I'll go."

Watching hot guys playing flag football sounded like a great way to kill time on a Sunday afternoon. Plus, what else did they have to do? Maddie brought up the new girl, Stacie; the one Payton had met at the movies. "I met her today," she said.

"So weird. I met her on Friday, at the movies. She was with Trevor." Payton took a sip of water and then asked, "How did you meet her?"

"She texted me."

"Whaaaat!" Payton and Aubrey asked at the same time.

"Yeah. It was crazy! She said she'd gotten my number from some kid at school, but she couldn't remember the guy's name. She went on to say that she'd spoken to you—guessing that was Friday night—and she knew I was friends with you."

"OK . . . this sounds jacked up already. What else

did she say and how did you end up meeting her?" Payton asked.

"It was really weird, but she was nice. She'd heard through this guy that I could catch her up on her physics because she was behind, with moving and all from a new school."

"Who worries about that stuff?" Aubrey asked. "Seriously. Don't you figure that stuff out at school? I mean, like, not on your own time?"

"True. True," Payton agreed.

"Yeah that is kinda weird. Anyway, I had all of my old work and since I've already taken the AP class she's taking, I said she could use it." Maddie took a bite of pizza.

"And?" Payton semi-screeched. "Then what?"

"She asked if she could get it, like now. It was kinda cool because she offered to pay for it, the work, but I didn't know how I felt about that . . . dealing schoolwork. Ha! And I didn't want to give her my address, so I met her at the mall." She took another bite of pizza and a sip of Coke. "I was going anyway. New converse. Anyway, she did talk about you a lot, though. Good things. Said she enjoyed meeting and hanging out with you guys at the movies. Really strange though, she seemed to genuinely like Trevor."

All the girls laughed. Trevor, who knew?

"That whole thing sounds weird, like a set-up, but whatever. I'm tired. Let's put on a movie and crash," Payton suggested.

She picked the movie and the girls went to bed.

***

It was a thrown-together flag football game, but who was going to turn one down with Royce in town? No one! The girls pulled up a piece of grass and sat down on the sidelines. There were enough players to form nice-sized teams. Royce picked Reece first. Reece was beaming.

"Little bro goes with me."

A coin toss determined which side would get the ball first, and the game was underway. The offense for Devon's team started first. The game moved along at a fast pace, with plenty of dirty plays, lots of laughter, and a few stolen kisses during breaks. An ice chest turned water breaks into beer breaks. Royce let Reece have sips of his beer when his father wasn't looking. Royce figured he wasn't driving, and it was all in fun.

"Damn bro, you're getting good at this game!" Royce patted Reece on the back and handed him his beer. "Not too much, now."

Reece beamed. For his idol to say that, his skills must be improving. Royce didn't hand out skill compliments just to make you feel good. He usually critiqued and coached him, but Reece didn't mind. He learned the most from his brother anyway. They watched film together, practiced together, tossed the ball back and forth to each other while they watched TV; that's what they did. Talk, think, and play football. Mr. Townsend clapped his hands and hollered for everyone to get back to the game.

"Last quarter," he hollered.

"Hut, hut," Royce's voice bellowed down the field.

He threw the ball and Reece caught it beautifully and ran as fast as he could to the end of the field. No one could catch him or even come close for that matter. He pelted the ball into the ground and raised his arms into the air.

"Townsends do it again!"

Covered in grass stains, smelling like sweat and mud, Reece jogged over to Payton and flopped down in front of her. She put her arms around his neck and pulled him back toward her. She didn't care, wet shirt and all. Kissing the top of his head, she was startled when Trevor suddenly yelled.

"Hey babe, glad you made it."

Everyone turned to see the new girl. She was smiling, waving, and walking toward them.

"Dude, you guys dating now?" Reece asked, shocked. "What?"

"I dunno, something like that," Trevor replied. "I know, right . . . what the hell!"

"Something like that, no offense."

"Ah dude, none taken. I still can't believe she stuck around myself." Trevor grinned from ear to ear. "Man, she's out of my league for sure."

"Sweeeeeet!" Reece said, holding up his hand to knuckle-bump Trevor's.

"Right!" Trevor agreed, proud of the hot girl who had her arm draped over his shoulder.

Payton smiled, but the word *sweet* stung a little. Why did Reece think it was sweet that Trevor had her? Should he really care if Trevor was dating the new girl, really? And come to think of it, why did it bother her? She'd never been the jealous type before, why now?

"Hi all," the new girl said.

And that was that. Payton wasn't sure she liked her. Ridiculous. The girl hadn't done a thing wrong. Not one thing. But in Payton's mind, surely she would.

Chapter 6

The New Girl

Who was this girl, anyway, and why was she here? Texas. Really! To Payton's disappointment, Mr. Townsend, Roger, introduced her to everyone. More than anything, that irritated Payton. Why did Reece's dad have to introduce her? She was Trevor's girlfriend; he should have introduced her to everyone. Roger was *her* boyfriend's dad. Logically she knew in her head Roger was being an adult and being polite. Illogically it pissed her off. Maddie was talking to her; how dare she! That was *her* friend. She knew better than that. Really! Come on already, girl code! Payton didn't like her, so why didn't one of best friends dislike her as well? Jealousy, new to Payton, wasn't pretty on her at all.

Reece had the audacity to ask Stacie if she'd like a bottle of water. She accepted, and he even jumped up and got it for her. Trevor didn't. Reece did. What in the *hell* was he thinking? Though she never said a word, Payton's irritation toward Reece showed in the form of short-answer responses and a lack of interest in conversation.

"Babe, are you OK?" Reece asked.

"Why wouldn't I be?" she responded harshly.

"Don't know. But you're acting as if you're pissed

off or something."

"Really?"

"Yeah. Really." He took a sip of water and walked toward the guys.

Stacie sat down—of all things—next to Payton and her friends. Awkward silence followed, until Stacie took it upon herself to break it.

"Looks like they're wrapping up," she said. "Hate that I missed it."

"Yeah. It was a good one," Aubrey added, followed by a question. "So are you and Trevor really dating?"

Stacie pulled the ball cap she was wearing down over her eyes; was she embarrassed or shy? Because she didn't really act either. *Just adjusting the cap, then,* thought Payton.

"I don't really know what we're doing, yet. Too early to tell; just having fun, I guess." Stacie replied.

No one said anything. Terrible words. *Just having fun.*

"Reece and Payton have been dating for nearly two years now," Maddie said, protectively pointing toward Payton.

Payton managed a half-hearted fake smile. Stacie nodded and picked at the grass in front of her.

"That's awesome." She hesitated. "Me and my boyfriend broke up when we moved. It was hard because we'd been together for a couple of years. But long-distance relationships, tough."

Payton felt a twinge of guilt. That would be awful, forced to break up because of a move you had no say about. The girls drilled Stacie, asking questions about her life and past, but she took it in stride and answered all of them. She was doing well until she mentioned she wanted to attend the same college that Reece had shown interest in. This made Payton's skin crawl, as if it was premeditated, and of course it wasn't. Disturbed that she was feeling this way, jealous, Payton tried to switch gears and be nice. Love wasn't supposed to feel like this; and the jealous feelings were unfamiliar to her. Was she jealous or insecure? Having never experienced the feeling before, she honestly didn't know. Had Reece really shown Stacie extra attention or was he just being nice, and why on earth couldn't Payton figure out the difference between the two? Payton instructed herself to get it together. *Pull yourself together and stop being ridiculous! Reece was just being nice. He merely handed her a bottle of water, and he was happy for his friend. That's all!*

"Hello, Earth to Payton."

Reece stood over her, holding out his hand. He pulled her to her feet and asked if she was OK. She assured him that she was and apologized for acting like an idiot. He didn't seem too bothered and didn't want the details anyway; she was glad, embarrassed that she'd gotten ticked off for no apparent reason. Stacie continued to make small talk with everyone, including the Townsends, and Payton was forced to push the negative feelings of jealousy that were rushing through her mind out of head.

You don't know her, Reece doesn't know her, she's with Trevor, and no one cares!

Trevor walked toward Stacie and laid a great big

kiss on her, and she kissed him back right in front of everyone. This actually made Payton feel a tad better. Reece glanced their way, but didn't mention the kiss. Payton waited to see if he would kiss her like that, in front of everyone, but he didn't. He wasn't usually big on PDA, public displays of affection, so she wasn't surprised. It just would've been nice. Why? So Stacie could see that Reece loved her, really loved her, like that too. She wasn't saying it was right, but it was a girl thing!

Chapter 7

Heating Up

Reece: Ditch ur squad and meet me @ the dam in 2hrs
   Payton: Yay. CW2CU
   (Can't wait to see you)
   Reece: We're going to our tree

"Want to a grab a bite to eat? I'm starving," asked Maddie.

That was going to be a "hell no!" After the game, Payton got rid of her friends, just like Reece had told her to do. Kinda weird, because she didn't really listen to anyone else but him. She had to eat with her parents, she told them, but promised to catch up with them later. She knew she wouldn't. If they had known she was meeting Reece, they would have known she was dumping them, which she was. It was starting to irritate her friends.

Now to leave the house without any drama from her parents, well, make that drama from her dad. His voice already ringing in her ears about how they hadn't seen her all weekend, she prepared reasonable explanations about why she should be able to leave again without an issue. She could tell them anything except where she was really going: to make out with her boyfriend, under a tree, at the lake. Now that wasn't exactly going to fly with the parental units.

The dam had become their usual meeting place. They'd leave one vehicle parked, usually hers because his truck had a lot more room, and drive out to their spot. Talking for hours at a time, occasionally sipping a swiped beer, even taking a walk wasn't unheard of, but ultimately they were going to kiss a little too long, touch each other the way teens typically do, and end up working themselves up to such a degree someone had to say stop and shut it down so that they could cool off. She never felt closer or more in love with Reece than when he couldn't wait to see her. It was written all over his face. In his eyes, she'd tell herself. They'd literally light up. The way he'd look at her right before he kissed her or when he stared at her in between kisses. Mesmerizing.

"How was the game, sweetheart?" her mom asked as soon as she walked in the door.

"Great!" Payton replied, waiting to announce that she was leaving again.

"I didn't expect you back so early."

Bingo! Great opening. "I'm really not, back, I mean."

Her mother stopped what she was doing and looked at her daughter for the infamous *rest of the story;* there always was one, and she couldn't wait to hear it.

"I mean that I'm not staying. I'm meeting Reece again, for a movie and bite to eat, if it's OK. I'm just cleaning up after the game, feeling kinda icky." She hesitated and then asked, "It is OK, right?"

"It's a school night, Payton. I'm not sure you'll have time for both, are you?"

"Well, I guess we could pick one or the other and I'm not hungry. I'll ask Reece what he wants to do."

Her mom accepted that as a reasonable compromise, one or the other. Payton grabbed a bottle of water and left the kitchen. Covering her hair, Payton took another shower. She didn't have time to redo that brown mop anyway. Touch it up, yes; wash and dry, no. Redid her makeup. Spritz of perfume and a change of clothes, which consisted of a plain, cute, slip dress and converse. She stared at herself in the mirror. Even Payton thought she looked presentable. Kinda cute, and she rarely gave herself any kind of seal of approval. Her body looked great, legs amazing, and the dress was perfect.

Reece was already waiting at the dam. He had the cooler in the back from the game earlier. He noticed she was looking at it, and he grinned.

"Yeah. I've got a kick-ass brother! Royce purposely left it in the truck for us. It's got a few beers in it."

He held up a sack: food as well! She grinned and pecked him on the cheek as she climbed into his truck. Anxiety and excitement rushed over her; she opted to ditch the anxiety. Seated next to Reece, she gave him a customary kiss on his lips. As she pulled away, he gently pulled her back toward him and kissed her again. Could she possibly be any happier than at that moment? Hell no! Sitting next to her boyfriend, windows rolled down, aux turned up, and headed to their tree. Yep, they'd claimed it and made it their own. Reece and

Payton had a tree!

"Let's roll," Reece said as he backed up his truck.

Their tree was located by the lake in a secluded spot off the main road, but still had a clear view of any passing cars. Reece parked in the same place every time. Pulling his truck under a large oak, its big branches acted like an umbrella, shading the truck from the Texas heat. All the windows were rolled down, and a gentle breeze blew across the water and through the truck. It felt wonderful on Payton's bare legs and arms. Their routine was comfortable. Reece opened a beer, wrapped a napkin around his, and poured hers into a red plastic cup. They didn't always have beer, never took liquor, but today Reece was quite proud of the fact that Royce had scored him a few. Payton climbed into the back seat and waited for Reece to join her. She propped her legs onto the back of the seat as he handed her the infamous red cup.

"Nice legs," he stated.

She didn't reply. No need. Her face was beaming. Proud he'd noticed, his comment made her feel ridiculously warm and fuzzy. Between the heat, the excitement, and the beer being ice cold, it went down relatively easily, considering Payton didn't typically like the taste of beer. They shared a sandwich and under his watchful eye she managed to choke down a few bites, but for some reason the beer was going down easier than the food.

"You don't eat enough," he stated.

At which she replied, "I'm working on that; but the beer is tasting better than the food right now!"

He didn't mind that answer and took it upon himself to open another beer, splitting it between the two of them. He sat back and put his arm around his girl and relaxed. It took less than fifteen minutes for that to change, and the two to be all over each other. It started with a little kiss, but that kiss led to full-fledged tongue on tongue. In between breaths, her hands wrapped around his neck, his wrapped around her waist, they continued to kiss, losing themselves in each other. As their kisses became increasingly deeper and intense, they wouldn't have heard a car pull up if it had. Reece slowly moved his hand up her rib cage, testing the waters, seeing how far he could go. Touching her, she didn't object; it wasn't the first time he'd touched her there. They'd been that far before. She was nervous, excited, and madly in love, or at least as much as a sixteen-year-old girl could be. Reece knew if she moved his hand, it was his cue to be respectful and to remove his hand from that area of her body. It worked. It was their unspoken system. For that she was grateful. She didn't believe she was ready for other things, yet, certainly not all the way, but when she was ready she wanted it to be with Reece. *I'm going to marry that boy,* she'd tell herself, just like all sixteen-year-old girls in love do. As exciting as the thought at times seemed, it was also scary and intimidating. She wasn't ready, and she knew it.

Reece had been with another girl, all the way, but Payton didn't ask questions. Many boys in their circle had. Payton even knew several girls in their school who had done everything as well. Part of her wanted to know about Reece's experience, but the other part didn't want to know. For some reason it hurt her feelings and made her feel jealous, but she didn't understand why. He hadn't even been with her then, so why should she care who he'd been with? That's what she'd tell herself. Jealousy, so frustrating!

Reece still hadn't pushed her past her comfort zone. But it didn't stop him from trying to slide his hand a little higher up her thigh or try each time to get that shirt or top of her dress all the way off. But even in the heat of the moment, he wouldn't resist when she'd gently move his hand away. Heart pounding, cheeks flushed, body jumping out of her skin with excitement, she'd move his hand down her leg or lower back. Not once did she stop kissing him, and not once did he object that she'd carefully replaced his hand to a spot on her body that she was comfortable with. She could feel his body under hers; he was as excited as she was, and between the two of them there wasn't going to be anything but trouble if they didn't stop. Someone had to have some sense. Payton pulled back away from him, face flushed beet red, and took a sip of beer. She handed the cup to Reece, who accepted and willingly finished off the rest.

"Guess we should take a break," Payton giggled.

"You're probably right, but I'd rather not," Reece replied.

Payton won. It was almost time to dump the evidence—beer cans—and head back anyway. They straightened up their clothes, gave each other one last intense kiss, and drove back hand in hand.

Chapter 8

Separation Sucks

The closer Payton and Reece became, the more unbearable attending separate schools became for Payton. Focusing became an issue, as her mind wandered in class. What was Reece doing and who was he with? Was he having fun and did he miss her? It didn't seem to matter that she had his schedule down pat, the fact she couldn't just text or talk to him at will drove her crazy. Most of it, she knew, she had brought upon herself. He had practice, physics, English, electives, and lunch as usual, but it didn't stop her from fretting over him.

> **Payton:** Call when you can
> **Reece:** K
> **Payton:** 143 babe
> **Reece:** Same
> **Payton:** I made it easy. Sent digits. ☺
> **Reece:** What?
> **Payton:** Just messing with ya
> **Reece:** K

Payton wanted 143s back from Reece, but didn't panic because she didn't get them. The numbers weren't the real deal, but they still made her feel special. She hung on to what they supposedly meant. Code for *I love you*.

Reece shoved his phone back into his pocket, not once giving the conversation a second thought. He'd had a rough workout that morning, two-a-days during summer had continued during school, with their season about to start. Coach worked them before and after school, weights and film in the evening, and then he went over everything again with his dad once he got home. But he loved it. Sometimes he'd even put a call into Royce just to discuss plays or fill him in on games. Payton had been with him during his junior year. He figured she was used to it, but they hadn't been as close as they were now. His phone buzzed again, but he didn't bother to pull it out of his pocket. He'd just talked to Payton; if she was texting again, then she'd have to wait. He was distracted. Running late. If it wasn't her, then he didn't care who it was anyway. Trevor and his hot new girl, Stacie, walked up next to him. He guessed they were starting to really date after all, not a fluke, but weird.

"Trev." They knuckle-bumped each other and then Reece turned to the blond and said, "Hello, Sophie," purposely saying her name wrong.

"Stacie," Trevor corrected him, but she rolled her eyes and laughed.

"That's right. Sorry. Slipped my mind."

"No, it didn't slip your mind, idiot!" Stacie retorted.

But that just made them all laugh, Reece included. Hell, all the guys liked this girl. She was funny. Down to earth. Too hot for Trevor, who looked like a cat that just ate a mouse, and she was holding her own. Reece liked that. But there had to be something wrong with her; she was, after all, dating Trevor. *He was holding her hand in his, stupid*, Reece thought. He barely knew her and was walking her to class holding her hand. Just weird. That was it; she must be kinda weird as well. He'd figured it out! Reece was about to text Payton and tell her about Stacie being in his class, but as soon as he pulled out his phone the message he'd received earlier was staring at him instead. It made him smile.

Payton: TOY oh yeah, DTB. HA!
(Thinking of you and yeah... don't text back)

Witty girl. He started tapping away, ending with the text message that said the following:

Reece: Same TOY and 143 . . . Yes, I love you.

That made her morning, and Reece had lunch next. Who didn't love lunch?

It was hard to feel sorry for Payton, being in a different school, when she was happy most of the time. Her boyfriend was hot, was an athlete, made great grades, had a kick-ass brother, nice family, was well liked by just about everyone, and had a great truck. She was cute, and together they were damn near a perfect couple. Reece called her at lunch, but they didn't talk as long as usual. Payton grabbed her water and sat down with her friends, feeling a combination of disappointed and pissed.

"I hate being in a different prison than him!"

"Right!" Aubrey agreed, not knowing what else to say.

"Everything OK?" Maddie asked.

It was. Reece had mentioned lunch with his friends, including Trevor and Stacie. What he hadn't mentioned was that Trevor and Stacie were riding with him, and of course Stacie rode in the middle. Where else would she have sat? There wasn't a reason to mention it, and with the way Payton had been acting, or overreacting, he wasn't taking any chances.

Chapter 9

She's One of Us

Several of them met at their usual Mexican restaurant for lunch. It was good, but more importantly, it was cheap. Trevor was the only guy who brought his girl, the new girl, Stacie. The boys gave him a hard time at first, but after a few minutes no one seemed to care, and she didn't mind that they were harassing her boyfriend. She just kept eating; everyone noticed that, refreshing. She ate like them; she didn't pick at her food, she actually ate it. And she didn't turn up her nose at how much or what they ate. She even slouched just a bit. Most girls Reece knew, including Payton, were hesitant about eating in front of the guys. This girl couldn't care less. He hadn't counted them all, but he'd seen her put away four tacos while they were sitting there. She also contributed to their conversation. Real stuff. Trevor hadn't mentioned she was the outdoor type, but she talked football, deer season opener and, of all things, trucks. She held her own when they talked about their last game, and even bitched about Trevor's truck for all the right reasons! Clearly she had brothers, or her dad wanted a boy and got stuck with her. Witty, hot, ate like a horse but didn't look like one, liked sports, had a great laugh, and didn't seem to notice that she was way out of

Trevor's league. Damn! That girl was a keeper. She had all the boys mesmerized, not just Reese, but part of her charm was that she didn't know it, nor care. Her mannerisms reminded Reece of Royce's girl, Jenna; she was hot. A text brought him back to his girlfriend, Payton.

Payton: TOY 143
(Thinking of you, I love you)
Reece: love ya babe

Straight to the words he knew she wanted him to say. Cut it short so he could finish eating and listening to everyone else. Just as he slipped his phone back into his pocket, the table erupted into laughter. Everyone was staring at Stacie's screen, a clip she'd been describing, and she'd pulled it up.

"I know, right? Who would've believed it?" She laughed.

"I'm trying to get it to go viral, see how many hits it's got already?" Her face beamed.

"Damn!" Duncan screeched. "No freaking way! How'd you capture that?"

Trevor replayed the video again, realizing his friends were stunned. Reece reached out his hand and took the phone. Trevor didn't object.

"What is it?" Reece asked.

"Dude, check this pass out and who caught it." Trevor pointed to the phone. "It's freaking awesome!'

They weren't kidding. Reece had the same reaction they did.

"Whoa! Seriously!"

"Hell yeah," Stacie hollered. "That's exactly who you think it is!" She laughed. "That's my boy, right there, doing it!"

"How'd you capture that?" Reece asked. "Looks like you're right there, on the side lines." Puzzled, he asked, "Why are you there?"

Stacie took a bite out of her taco and did something Payton would never do: spoke with her mouth full, kinda gross, but funny.

"Cause I was, there, hanging with my dad."

"Wait, what?" Reece looked shocked. "Hanging with your dad. How's that possible, what does he do?"

Stacie swallowed her food and started to laugh. "Fool, how may people in this town do you think have the name Wiggins?"

"You're kidding me! You're the kid of the new defense coach they brought in?" Reece asked, and then stared at Trevor. "Trev! C'mon man!"

"Dude, she didn't want me to say anything. Figured ya'll would figure it out."

"I was wrong." She laughed.

That wasn't a small deal. No one thought to mention that crap?! Hell, if Reece didn't want to leave Texas as badly as he wanted to, he'd consider playing for them. The guy, evidently her dad, had been all over the media for months. Recruited for the university when they didn't renew the contract of their last defensive coordinator. They had high expectations for Coach Wiggins; his reputation preceded him, he had an exceptional record.

"Wow! That's cool!" Reece stated and he really

meant it. "Really cool!"

"Hey Stacie, can we meet him, Coach? I guess your dad," Shane asked, grinned and added, "you don't know if you don't ask, right?"

"Yes, I'll introduce you morons to him." She grinned. "No, he won't care, and yes he'll let you hang at the field with me sometime."

Trevor had just elevated his position to a level he couldn't begin to imagine with his friends. He was proud of his new girl. No wonder she was so confident around guys; she'd been around *him* her whole life, not to mention all the players over the years she must've hung out with. Everyone knew the coach was coming, but they didn't know much about his family. Now his daughter was their new best friend, at least to them. Hanging with *the* coach's kid. Trevor, of all people—now she was one of them!

Half in fun and half dead serious, Shane playfully shoved his friend, Trevor, knocked his cap off his head and asked Stacie a question.

"How come you're with this joker right here? I'm available!"

Trevor placed his ball cap back on his head and waited to see what she'd say. He was as surprised as they were that this girl had actually said yes and gone out with him, let alone stuck around. Reece's ear perked up. Why was a girl like that with Trevor? He liked Trevor, but seriously. Stacie had their attention as they walked back to the truck. The ridiculous seriousness of the question they were trying to get an answer to caused her to burst out laughing.

"OMG, you idiots. What do you expect me to say? He's Trevor." She grabbed his arm. "He's nice, why not?"

"Well hell, you're not gonna hear me complain!" Trevor said, throwing up his arms.

"Hail Trevor!" Chase laughed.

"Will you let us know when we can go to practice, then?" Shane asked. "I can't wait to meet Dustin Miller."

She nodded. "But I think I should have everyone over first, like a meet-and-greet of my new friends." She laughed. "I swear, you better be on your best behavior. All of you!"

Reece couldn't wait to tell his dad and Royce he was going to Coach's house. She'd even said Payton could go. He wasn't sure how thrilled Payton would be, but she'd have to deal. The question was, how quickly could she plan it? They were all ready!

Chapter 10

Coach's Daughter

Even though they talked and texted daily, sometimes even managing to pull off a picnic lunch during the week, Payton lived for the weekends. Football season would take Reece away most of the time, and he'd be leaving for school after that. She did enjoy watching him play and listening to him talk about the game, especially after a win. It made her happy hearing him relive his plays as he explained to her why he'd done what he had during the game. And often, though she didn't always care about the reason he'd made those choices on the field, she acted as if she did. Payton had not been informed that Stacie was Coach's daughter or that she'd hung out with the guys most of the time, but that was about to change. Reece wasn't quite sure how to break it to her without ticking her off. He definitely got the feeling Payton already disliked Stacie; he didn't know why, because it hadn't started out that way, but girls didn't hide their feelings very well. Stacie was new, hot, and well liked by all the guys. Not for the reasons the girls thought; she was just well liked. But that seemed to be all it took to piss off most girls, but not usually Payton, till now. He liked Stacie. Therein lay the problem. Not wanting to set her off unnecessarily, he tread carefully.

> **Reece:** Can't wait to CU
> **Payton:** YAS
> **Reece:** We'll chill
> **Payton:** YAS
> **Reece:** CU at 8
> **Reece:** 143
> **Payton:** 143 back

Watching how Payton acted after the 143s nauseated Aubrey, but even she recognized that she would likely feel the same way if someone were texting her that message. Admittedly, Aubrey needed a boyfriend! The last guy she'd dated lasted for about six months; he was nice, but she really wasn't overly attracted to him. When they split, she was more relieved than sad. He wasn't worth the hassle, and clearly wasn't boyfriend material.

"Crap! I need a boyfriend."

Payton hugged her. "Want me to set you up with one of his Reece's friends?"

"OMG! That is so random. Hell no!"

"Why not?" Payton laughed. "Why? We could all hang out. It doesn't have to mean anything, could just be fun." She strung out her words. "Annnnnnnd you may just find the rigggght one or temporary right one."

"Right one. What's that supposed to mean?"

"You know. The guy. The one you're supposed to be with."

"Bump your head today, did you Payton?" Aubrey grabbed Payton's shoulders and shook her gently. "I'm going to graduate, go to college, and become a criminal psychologist." She let Payton go. "I want a dang boyfriend just to hang out with, that's all. You know, so I don't look like your loser girlfriend." She laughed. "Third wheel and all that."

Rolling her eyes, Payton flopped down on the bed. "I haven't thought that far ahead. College. I know I should, but I can't think about all of that stuff yet." She stared at a photo of her and Reece on her phone. "I do know I'm going to marry this guy right here though, got that down."

She tried again to persuade Aubrey to let them set her up. "I'm seeing Reece tonight, but we could double-date tomorrow night. You, me, Reece, and one of his friends. We'd have so much fun!"

She grabbed Aubrey's phone and held it in front of her face. "Come on. What else do you have to do, seriously?"

She had a point there, and she could be very convincing. Aubrey knew she'd give in for no other reason than to hang out on a Saturday night with her best friend. That would be better than sitting at home alone. If Reece brought some guy with him, well, so be it.

"Fine, whatever." She pointed to Payton's phone. "Doooo it!"

Turned out Reece had the perfect guy for Aubrey after all: Cody Mickle. His girlfriend had just dumped him, and he wasn't out looking for anyone serious to date. It was a perfect scenario.

Reece: Sup

Cody: Chillaxin

Reece: Wanna hang out Sat. Payton and her friend?

Cody: Nah man, not ready for that nonsense.

Reece: C'mon man. It'll be something to do. Not serious. Just hanging.

Cody: True. Who is it?

Reece: Aubrey. Nice girl

Cody: Nice girls are often ugly. She ugly? JK

Reece: Hahahah. Nah, cute girl. Drive around and hang out or something.

Cody: K

***

Friday night, Payton got Reece all to herself. She loved it. He was picking her up and most of the time she wasn't sure what they'd be doing, but she didn't care. She'd seen his text telling her he was on his way. A moment of panic, a quick reply, a change of clothes, and finally the outfit she'd wear. They'd been on too many dates to count, but her nerves still kicked in and got the best of her. She settled on a cute shirt and denim shorts. The familiar sound of Reece's truck pulling into the driveway could be heard from her bedroom window. Spritzing his favorite perfume on her neck, chest, and wrists, she ran down the stairs just as her dad welcomed him in.

"Hey, come on in, Reece. How's the training coming?" he asked.

They talked football for a few minutes, even discussed the new coach in town.

"Funny you should mention him, sir. I actually go

to school with his daughter. In fact, Payton's met her, and we're going to meet him, Coach, and hang out at his house pretty soon."

Payton's eyes flashed toward Reece. What the hell was he talking about? Coach's daughter, the new coach, and no they didn't. Why would he lie to her dad like that? Reece immediately grabbed her hand and squeezed it tightly, signaling he wasn't done.

"You remember Stacie, right?" he asked. "The new coach at the university, that's his daughter."

Payton cocked her head. What did he just say? Surely not! Her eyes were humongous. Reece continued talking to her dad, as he held onto her hand as tightly as he could so she couldn't snatch it out of his. Yep, the girl wasn't happy. She was trying to pull it away.

"Girlfriends included," he added quickly, but she didn't seem to care. "Trevor is dating her, sir. Stacie Wiggins. Coach Wiggin's daughter."

"Well, son, that's fantastic!" Perry Phillips said proudly. "I know that will be a real treat for you, visiting with him." He glanced at Payton's sour face and cautiously added, "But clearly you've got the prettier gal!"

"Clearly!" Reece agreed. Knowing there was no way in hell he'd say anything else.

"I think a bunch of us are going out tomorrow night. Even setting up Aubrey. It should be fun. Me, Payton, Cody, Aubrey, Trevor, and Stacie." He waited to see what Payton would say.

Payton glared at him, but didn't speak. Her dad pointed both of them to the door.

"You know the rules. Be home by midnight. There's nothing going on after midnight that's any good. Twelve, be home."

Reece felt pretty good about the way he'd broken the news. Killed two birds with one stone. Impressed her dad and broke the news about Stacie and Trevor joining them Saturday night. Worked in his favor. Besides, it was her BFF that he was doing it for; they were just tagging along. Now, if he could get Payton's mind back on their date and not Stacie, he'd say he'd have one heck of a night to look forward to. She looked great! But Payton bombarded him with questions as soon as she climbed into the truck. Answering a few of them, dodging some, he leaned toward her and planted a great big kiss on her lips. She couldn't help but notice the cute smirk that wiped across his face once he pulled away. Opening her mouth to speak, he leaned in and kissed her again. This made her laugh and broke up the questioning, but she knew it was a deflection from the interrogation.

"But *why* do you have to go to her house?" She grabbed his hand. "You don't have to go."

"It's a party. I'm invited, but so are you," he responded. "Could we just not do this?" he asked, but sounded a tad irritated.

"Not do what?" Payton snapped defensively. "What? Talk?"

"You know what I mean. Make it something when it's not. It's a party. We're invited, and that's that. Besides, I have a surprise for you."

Payton's face lit up. One mention of a surprise and

she'd forgotten she was trying to be difficult.

"I love surprises." Moving closer toward him she asked, "What is it?"

"No way. But don't get overly excited. It's not that cool."

Reece grabbed her hand as he drove, but they hadn't been driving very long when she recognized where they were going. For a second her heart sank. Loving his parents was one thing, but sharing her time with Reece, on a Friday night, well, that was quite another.

"Surprise. They're not here!"

Now that was the best surprise ever! She loved her time alone time with Reece, but alone time in a private place was heaven to teens. They couldn't get out of the truck fast enough. It took less than ten minutes for them to fall into each other, and they landed in the game room on the big leather couch. Shoes kicked off, door locked, and their favorite playlist playing in the background, they were oblivious to anything going on around them. His body weight on top of her felt comforting. Odd. He never felt heavy. One arm wrapped around his waist, pulling him even closer, the other softly grasped his face, as she tried to control her breathing. It wasn't working. She couldn't get enough of his intense kisses, and he couldn't get enough of hers. His hands explored her body as far as she would let him. He'd touch her up until the moment she'd stop him by gently moving his hands or shifting in such a way that he'd be forced to move his hand on his own. This *I'm not quite ready* statement, without actually saying a word, was all it took. Though Reece attempted to explore the undiscovered areas of her body, when Payton put up her silent barriers, he respectfully responded and moved away. His body uncontrollably responding to her kisses and his soft touches pleased her. Knowing she turned him on made her feel wanted and loved by him. She felt sexy and beautiful, having no idea that her body could even feel that way. Hormones raging for both of them, the discussion they'd had on previous occasions came to both of their minds. When would it be time for them to go all the way? Payton didn't know when she'd be ready, but she did know with one hundred percent certainty that she wanted Reece to be her first and in her mind planned for him to be her last. She also knew that, despite how badly she wanted to be ready for that moment, she just wasn't ready yet. She was scared. Nervous she'd do it wrong. And in the back of her mind thought that she was supposed to wait, but a small part of her wouldn't allow her to share that much of herself with even him just yet. Payton simply wasn't ready.

In the midst of those tangled, heated moments, madly in love, Reese wrapped around her, her body and heart were on board with most of Reese's moves. Following his lead, thank goodness for that nagging voice that raged in her head. Reluctantly she worked her way from underneath the weight of him. Flushed cheeks, hair a mess, she fanned her face with her hand, rolled her eyes, and indicated that they needed a cool-down break. Reece didn't want to stop, but he respectfully did as she asked. Breathing hard, trying to catch his breath, he sat up.

"Damn, girl. You'll be the death of me."

He jumped up, looked down at his pants, pointed to his predicament, and they burst out laughing.

"Cool-down time for sure! I'll grab us a beer, Royce hid some, or Coke if you'd rather."

"Water, please," she replied.

She sipped water, and he slammed a beer. Royce had shown him years ago how to disguise a missing beer or two, and he always stashed his little bro a couple, thinking he was doing him a favor. Time always flew when Payton and Reece were together. They'd been alone for three hours already. Starving, they straightened their semi-jumbled appearance, making themselves presentable again and made plans for the rest of the evening.

"Let's grab a bite to eat and figure out our double- or triple-date night for tomorrow."

Though not thrilled about the extra intrusion on their double-date the following night, Stacie and Trevor, Payton was starving, and even though she knew she wouldn't eat much, food was the perfect distraction.

Chapter 11

Triple Duos

Texts were flying back and forth between Payton and Aubrey as they were getting dressed to go out for the evening. Though Aubrey liked the idea of finding a boyfriend, the thought of impressing a guy she knew nothing about had zero appeal to her. Her texts in response to Payton's were super short.

Aubrey: Fine
Aubrey: OK
Aubrey: Don't care
Aubrey: See you soon

She threw on her favorite pair of jeans, a T-shirt, and her black converse shoes. Her hair, straightened, hung over her shoulders, and the makeup she'd applied, natural, completed her look. Her overstuffed bag included the usual: a toothbrush, something to sleep in, make-up wipes, and her phone charger. She said her goodbyes to the parental units, threw her bag onto the seat beside her, and drove to Payton's house. Claudette Phillips let her in.

"You know the drill. Help yourself to anything you need or want," she said as soon as she opened the door.

Pointing to the stairs, she added, "Payton's in her room."

"Thank you!" Aubrey replied and headed up the stairs.

It wasn't unusual for Payton to take a lot longer to perfect her look than Aubrey. If she didn't have other plans on Saturdays, making an event of it was her thing, dragging out her date-night process. Extra-long shower, leave a towel on her hair too long, flip through a magazine while her hair air-dried. Eat a snack. Finish blowing out her hair and straighten it. Scroll social media, and then it was time to pick out her outfit. Picking her clothes became an ordeal. What hadn't she worn for a while? Did that outfit make her look fat? Did this one show off her butt? Did her thighs look thick? Flicking through the hangers in her closet, she pulled out several outfits, tried on a few, but usually didn't decide until the last minute what she would wear. The last step of the ritual: makeup application, natural of course. Before Aubrey could throw down her bag, Payton asked a question about her hair.

"Is my hair straight?"

Aubrey glanced at it, but there was no need. It was straight as a board. Perfect as usual. Just like her makeup, flawless.

"Yes it is," Aubrey replied. "And yes, that looks good as well!"

"What?" Payton asked, surprised.

"Your makeup looks good as well."

The jeans she had chosen fit her figure perfectly. She looked cute, but polished. Aubrey didn't ever seem to pull off that kind of look. Polished. There was definitely a knack to it, and Aubrey wasn't gifted with fashion skills. Hers was more thrown together and voila. As good as it was going to get.

"You look cute!"

"Awe, thank you." Payton turned around to look at her rear in the mirror, and then did the best friend compliment reciprocation. "So do you!"

"What do you think of Stacie?" Payton asked, sitting down on the edge of the bed.

"Stacie. The new girl?"

"Yeah, that girl!" Payton rolled her eyes. "I don't know how I feel about her yet. I don't dislike her, but I'm not sure I like her. Does that make sense? She hasn't really done anything, but I get a weird vibe when I'm around her."

"Any particular reason?" asked Aubrey. "Anything at all?"

"Do I need a reason?" Payton snapped.

Aubrey shook her head. "Nope. I guess not. It's just not like you to dislike anyone, without a reason, I mean."

Aubrey was right. Payton was pretty easy to get along with and well liked. And truth be told, Stacie hadn't done anything to her, or anyone else for that matter. She wasn't sure why she felt that way or any way about her. Not worth thinking about, especially now. Date night. Aubrey opened her mouth to speak, but shut it again, as if she'd rather not. Too late! Payton knew her too well.

"What?" Payton asked. "Spit it out."

Aubrey's cheeks flushed, knowing for certain she

didn't want to say what she had intended; now she tried to change the subject. Muttering under her breath, she said something lame about the outfit Stacie might wear. It didn't work. Payton knew Stacie would look cute as usual and insisted Aubrey repeat what she was originally going to say.

Aubrey sighed and spat out the words. "I said, do you think you dislike her because all the guys seem to like her?"

If looks could kill, Aubrey might not have lived another second. Payton's eyes flashed toward her friend. "Just what in the hell is that supposed to mean?"

She stood in front of Aubrey, flailed her arms in the air, and shook her head, shocked that Aubrey had said something so stupid. Even if it were true, Payton wasn't about to admit such a thing. Reece liking anyone but her, even platonically, wasn't something she'd allow her mind to think about.

"Aubrey, really?" She stepped back and flopped down in a chair. "I can't believe you just said that!"

"Whoa, wait a minute, not like that! I don't mean as in *like* her, *like* her. But as in like her, you know, as a friend type of thing?"

It was Aubrey who had her arms in the air now, waving them in an upward movement as if trying to stop Payton from leaving, when she wasn't going anywhere. "She's the coach's daughter and kinda acts like, well you know, one of them. That's all I'm saying."

Payton wasn't buying it. "I don't know what it is, but I get a weird vibe from her. But I don't know why and it bothers me. She's too nice or something."

Payton stood up and paced the bedroom floor. "Maybe it's because she looks that good and is really nice. Too nice."

Aubrey grinned. "You think you have a problem with the new kid because she's nice?"

"Well that didn't sound too stupid, did it?" Payton muttered.

Laughter broke the awkwardness and once again Payton shoved it out of her mind and shook it off. Stacie hadn't done anything. Insecurity or jealousy was an ugly trait, and she knew Reece hated both those things. No one liked a jealous, insecure girl, and she refused to become that one—the girl everyone noticed because she acted like a bitch. If Reece and the guys talked football with Stacie and admired her dad, so be it. But now wasn't the time to focus on that, triple duo night and all.

"I hope this Cody guy is nice. What are we doing, anyway?" Aubrey asked.

It just occurred to Payton she had absolutely no idea. Reece hadn't mentioned it. Probably because she had insisted that he find a date for Aubrey and that had kinda thrown things. She picked up her phone and sent a text.

> **Payton:** What are we doing tonight?
> **Reece:** Dunno
> **Payton:** Well what should I wear?
> **Reece:** Whatever you want. U always look great
> **Payton:** ☺ thank you babe 143
> **Reece:** love you too

"Oh my God, he's so sweet!" Payton held up her

phone and let Aubrey read the message.

"But that was a waste. I still don't know what we're doing." She read it one more time, then put down the phone.

"Tell me about this Cody guy," Aubrey said. "Do you at least know if he's cute?"

Payton didn't know him very well. She'd seen him in passing with the guys. He and his girlfriend had broken up, and she found that out from Reece. But she assured Aubrey that most of Reece's friends were decent looking. They heard Reece's truck before he pulled into the driveway. Royce, always working on it when he was home, seemed to make it louder every time he touched it. One of the projects the boys did together, working on the truck. Running down the stairs, the girls quickly shouted goodbye to Payton's parents and ran out the door. To Payton's dismay, Stacie, Trevor, and Cody were already seated and waiting for them. *You're kidding me, right?* Despite her thoughts, Payton managed to bite her tongue and keep the vibe positive. Not to mention she was smart enough to know anything negative that she said or did would only make Stacie look twice as nice. Ugh! Not on her time.

"Hey there, this is Aubrey," Payton forced herself to make the introductions with a smile.

Cody nodded. "Hey."

"Hi." Aubrey's cheeks turned beet red, which she hid rather well as she climbed into the truck.

Introductions, awkward, but at least that part was over. Turning toward the window, Aubrey tried to deflect the attention from herself and allowed Payton to take over. It didn't work. To her dismay, he started talking to her.

"Do you like bowling?"

Was that a real question? Payton wondered. *Bowling? Seriously? They were going bowling.* The thought of putting her feet in shoes that someone else had worn grossed her out. OMG!

"Actually, I do," Aubrey replied. "I'm not great at it, but it is fun. And I haven't been in forever, though, but yes, it sounds like a blast."

Aubrey did not just say that! Payton shot Aubrey the what-in-the-hell-did-you-just-say friend look.

"Ah, cool. I love bowling!" Cody was pleased. Bowling gave you something to do and you didn't have to talk a whole lot. "That's where we're headed."

Of course we are . . . freaking bowling . . . cause you look like an idiot who would wear another person's shoes, thought Payton. Checking herself; after all, the entire triple-duo thing was her idea, she forced herself to join in the conversation. It wasn't without a snide remark.

"I didn't know you bowled, Aubrey, like ever!" Payton didn't wait for a response; she turned her attention toward Stacie and smiled. "Do you like to bowl, Stacie?"

"Yeah, actually I do. My dad, believe it or not, bowls to relax." She grinned. "Funny, right? But that's where he'd drag us growing up, bowling allies. Still does."

Of course he did, thought Payton, but kept her mouth shut.

"That's kinda cool actually; family stuff," Cody interjected. "My mom and dad are split. Growing up I spent a weekend here, weekend there, and can't really remember fun family stuff; I mean like that. The dumb stuff seems to be the best."

He flicked Reece playfully on the back of the head. "Now my boy here, he's got a great family. I used to hang there quite a bit when we were little. Hell, everyone did."

Payton grabbed Reece's hand as he drove. He did have a great family, and she felt lucky to be included in it. The sport thing tied them together, but it was more than that; they all respected each other as members of the family. Cody was right: friends were extensions of the family in the Townsend home. She knew she needed to get out of her funk and over herself or she was going to ruin the night. Stacie hadn't done anything. Bowling might be fun, and she could disinfect her feet when she got home. Hell, if necessary, summer was over and she could throw away the shoes she was wearing if the bowling shoes were really that nasty.

The bowling alley was packed, but that didn't stop them from getting a lane without having to wait too long. The kid behind the counter recognized Reece as Royce's brother and bumped them to the top of the line. Good to have friends in a small town. To Payton's surprise, the shoes weren't as bad as she thought they'd be. She insisted the guy behind the counter allow her to spray her pair herself with the disinfectant they used prior to touching them. He thought she was crazy, but because of Reece, he handed her the can. The shoes were drenched, but she didn't care. It made her feel as if they were disinfected more so than the others in the alley.

"He's got connections. Nice!" Stacie grinned, nudging Trevor.

"Yeah. Safe to say most people know the Townsend boys or their dad. Good peeps."

"Reece seems nice, and I've actually heard my dad talk about Royce," Stacie whispered. "Talented twosome, he called them."

Trevor nodded. No argument from him; they were both talented, and he felt fortunate to know them both. Cody entered everyone's names, and it was decided they'd play as couple teams, and in order of the couples. Reece and Payton, Trevor and Stacie, and last but not least, Cody and Aubrey. Cody was polite, which Aubrey noticed. He spoke softly and had a knack for talking to everyone in the group, including Aubrey, and making them feel as if they'd all been friends for years. She felt oddly comfortable and was grateful for that. Admittedly even Payton was having fun, gutter balls and all. Giving it their best shot, the boys tried to order a pitcher of beer. Declined, but worth the try. They washed down a soggy pizza with flat soda, but couldn't help but try to place the order one last time. Didn't work. Stacie stood up and pointed toward the bathroom.

"Anyone gotta go?"

"I do. Hang on." Payton grabbed her wallet and walked with Stacie to the restroom.

Stacie was standing in the same spot that she had been when Payton went into the stall. A smirk covered her face. Not quite a grin, but definitely a smirk. Grabbing Payton's arm, she motioned toward the woman who was about to leave. Puzzled, Payton waited. As soon as the woman left, Stacie stepped into an open stall and pulled Payton inside with her. Startled, Payton's words tumbled out of her mouth.

"What the hell?"

"Shush!" Stacie put a finger to her lips.

Pulling a travel-sized vodka bottle out of her pocket, she removed the lid and took a swig like a pro.

Payton pointed to the bottle. "You are kidding, right?"

It wasn't really a question. Nervously she cracked open the door and looked out. People were coming in and out, and she knew it would look suspicious if they didn't hurry up and leave. All things considered, the coast was relatively clear. Teens, younger than them, were washing their hands at the sinks.

"Girl, please." Stacie laughed. "Do you want a shot or not?" Stacie took another swig and held out the bottle toward Payton. "You don't have to on my account, just so you know. I judge not, actually couldn't care less if you do or don't. Personal choice." She hesitated. "And of course this is to protect me, at our age, it's illegal . . . so remember that, I'm *not* forcing you. My brothers taught me to say that, don't know if it would hold up under an MIP, minor in possession, or if we got busted, but I don't want anyone to think I force my choices on them." Stacie laughed. "Gotta be your decision."

Payton couldn't exactly say why she gave into peer pressure, because Stacie couldn't care less if she joined in or not, but Payton sure didn't want to be outdone by the new girl. Although it was unlike her to be so impulsive, Payton stuck out her hand.

"Kinda hard to say no when the bottle is so cute."

"Right," Stacie agreed and handed it to Payton.

OMG. I'm a freaking idiot. Self-inflicted, reversed peer pressure put upon myself, just because a girl handed me a cute bottle, Payton thought. After the terrible taste, Payton felt embarrassed. She wasn't being goaded or made to feel childish if she didn't take a sip, yet she had, all on her own. Adding insult to injury, she instinctively accepted the bottle and took another sip. At the very same time she took the sip, running through her head were the words, *What am I doing?* It was the weirdest feeling. Contradicting herself. Payton took a deep breath, and focused on getting back to the table.

"What took ya'll so long?" Reece asked as soon as she rejoined them. "I bowled for you, strike, and you're welcome!"

"Thanks, babe, that's awesome!" Payton jumped, literally, onto his back and kissed the side of his cheek.

Aubrey snapped their pic and immediately added it to her story. They could be so cute sometimes that she didn't mind documenting their relationship, especially for Payton's sake.

"You guys want to go again?" Cody asked as he stared at the scoreboard. "I know you losers suck at bowling, but me and Aubrey happen to kick ass at it!"

Aubrey knew they were teammates, but she couldn't help but like the way it sounded when he said her name alongside his. Sweet. Cody cleared the scoreboard, knowing they likely weren't playing again, and he was right. They were ready to split and with good reason.

"Nope. Think we're good," Stacie answered, but added for good measure, "unless of course ya'll want to bowl again?"

Bowling was fun, but Payton was ready to get out of there and spend time with Reece, and she didn't care if Stacie and Trevor were there with Aubrey and Cody, as long as they were all having fun.

"Well if no one has any objections, we could swing by my house, meet my parents, then sit out back," Stacie offered.

"Hell yeah!" Reece yelled, literally jumping to his feet.

Trevor grabbed her hand and pulled her toward him. "Are you sure, babe, your dad won't mind?"

Stacie shook her head. "Trust me. He wants to know where I am at all times. If I'm at home, it makes it super easy for him." She pushed the hair that had fallen into her face behind her ear and hesitated before she spoke again.

"You look like you have something else to say," Reece said, noticing the pause. "What? Rules. The way we should address your dad. Things we shouldn't say?"

Stacie couldn't help but laugh. "OMG, stop! No! He's like the nicest guy ever, at least to me and my friends." She opened up her purse, revealing the tiny bottle of vodka. "It's just that I've got access to liquor there. You don't have to drink it, but I've got it." Closing her purse, she started to walk toward the exit.

"My brothers bring that stuff in the house all the time, and their friends leave stuff all over the game room when they get together. I fill bottles up and stash it. I've literally got a secret stash going." Stacie turned around and walked backwards so she could face them. "You don't have to drink it, you really don't, but of course it goes without saying that you can't mention it."

"Fair enough," Aubrey giggled. "Now turn around before you fall down and you don't make it out of here except on a stretcher. We'd actually like to meet your parents."

"Well, hell yeah!" Cody said, thrilled at the opportunity of meeting Coach. "Time to meet the parents."

Chapter 12

Meet the Parents

It took less than fifteen minutes to get to Stacie's house. The boys were more excited than the girls. They were about to meet someone they'd admired and heard a lot about over the past few years. The girls took it in stride; Payton happy to be anywhere as long as it was with Reece, and Aubrey actually enjoying the group date and getting to know Cody. Stacie lived in a gated community not far from the college campus. It was as they'd all expected, exclusive. Needless to say, Reece's loud truck wouldn't go unnoticed, but Stacie didn't seem to care. She grew up with two brothers; they went through the same phase. And her dad, regardless of the neighbors that they had at the time, always got stuck in with the boys and worked on their trucks as well. It definitely seemed to be a Texas thing.

"Right here," Stacie said, pointing to a massive two-story, white colonial sitting on a large corner lot.

"Wow! Didn't picture Coach in a house like that, a big house, yes, but more of a um, what can I say . . ."

Cody didn't finish his sentence. Stacie's laughter interrupted him as she interjected what she knew he was about to blurt out anyway.

"Like a ranch style or more rock-and-wood type

thing, you know, manly?"

"Yes!" Several voices rang out, followed by laughter.

"No offense," Cody added.

"Mom's pick. The house." Stacie was still giggling. "No compromise. Sick of moving, she made Dad promise to buy her dream house." She pointed to the house again. "And that's it."

"It's beautiful. Your mom has great taste." Payton acknowledged. "It's huge!"

Piling out of the truck, Stacie motioned, and they followed her around to the back of the house. They couldn't help but notice multiple cars parked in the driveway; the Wiggins had company, but no one who would interest them, Stacie had said. Nervous energy consumed them all as they entered the house through the back door and found themselves in the Wiggin's kitchen. The house actually had two kitchens: a gourmet kitchen and a regular kitchen area. Cody hadn't been in a house with two kitchens before. He nudged Aubrey, leaned toward her, and whispered in her ear, "Is this sick or what?"

She nodded, but thought how good his breath felt on her neck. He was still standing close to her, as if he were afraid to move his feet for fear of knocking something off the granite countertops, which actually looked as if they could be marble. Stunned herself by the magnificent house, Aubrey waited to see where Payton and the others were supposed to go. Stacie led them through the kitchen, into a foyer area, and then down a hallway and into a large game room.

"Wait here. I'll be right back," Stacie said as she turned and left the room.

The room, filled with large leather chairs and couches, contained multiple flat screen TVs. One of them, the largest any of the teens had ever seen in a house, was mounted on the wall above a large leather sofa. The room was so big that a pool table, located on the left side of the room, didn't look big at all. And a loaded bar, located by the pool table, had another flat screen above it. There were deer head and boar mounted on the walls, hunters for sure, very cool, and too many football photos of players with and without Coach to count were scattered around the room. There was also sports memorabilia of famous athletes placed on the wall. Reece couldn't help but think how much his dad and Royce would love and appreciate the room that he was standing in.

"Well, hey there, guys," a voice suddenly boomed from behind them. "What's going on?"

Everyone turned around and suddenly came face-to-face with Coach for the first time. He was every bit as intimidating as they'd feared, but not in stature. It was his presence, and he hadn't done anything except walk into the room and introduce himself. Stacie made the official introductions, just as her mom appeared and politely offered everyone snacks and drinks. They all declined. They made small talk about sports, but mostly they all listened, until Stacie started to walk toward the back door, waving her hand as she did.

"We're going to hang out back for a while. That's OK, right?"

"Well sure it is, you know that. You don't have to ask."

Coach looked at each one of the boys as he spoke. "You're all going to be gentleman with these fine young ladies because you're good boys, right?"

"Yes, sir!" they said in unison.

"Dad, stop. Oh my God. Seriously. You're so embarrassing!"

Coach chuckled, patting Reece on the back as he walked by. "Girls. Can't live with them, can't live without them." He ignored his daughter's dirty look.

"If you need anything, help yourself. Our guests will be leaving shortly." He turned to walk away and added, "Stacie, make sure your friends get what they need." He chuckled again and pointed at the boys. "Except, it goes without saying, the beer and liquor out there, don't touch that!"

"Yes, sir!" the boys said politely, as if they'd dare do anything so stupid in Coach's house.

"Thank you," the girls replied, smiling sweetly as they walked past him and out the back door to go outside.

Out back was as impressive in its own unique way. Past the pool, complete with a loaded bar, outside kitchen, and pool house, Stacie led them to an outdoor sitting area. It was nestled in between several large oaks and a beautiful rock fire pit away from the pool house.

"Light it, babe."

She threw Trevor a lighter and within minutes the crackling sound of wood and the wonderful smell of smoke filled the air. They all sat down around the pit, enjoying the slight chill in the air.

"I'll be right back," Stacie said as she ran back toward the pool house.

Music suddenly blasted all around them. Reece pointed toward the rocks scattered around the fire pit area. Hidden speakers, disguised as rocks. They were actually scattered all around the sitting area, pool area, in fact, all of the outside area. This place had everything.

"Way cool!" Reece said to Payton as he grabbed her hand, pulling her up out of her chair and onto his lap.

Stacie appeared, dragging a cooler on wheels behind her. Inside were a variety of drinks, but she pointed to several soda bottles.

"These have either liquor or beer in them, from the keg, we have a keg. It's up to you, and this one is vodka. It's marked KA." Stacie lifted it up. "Last two letters of the word."

"Are you crazy?" Reece snapped, stunned she'd pull such a stupid stunt at Coach's house, even if it were her dad. "Really?"

"Hey, I happen to live here as well. And my two older brothers live here, when they're home." She was quite amused that Reece freaked out. "You've gotta chill, he's my dad."

"Stacie. No way. Put it up. Not here. Not today." Reece wasn't giving in. Nervous her dad would venture out to check on them, he jumped out of his chair, practically knocking Payton off his lap.

"Reece. You don't have to drink it. But I live here.

He's Coach to you, but he's Dad to me."

Defiant, Stacie held out a beer and offered it to Reece.

"Hell no. I don't have a death wish! Put it up Stacie, or we're leaving!" He grabbed Payton's hand. "Look, I'm all for a great party, good time and all that, but come on. There's a time and a place, and this ain't it."

Stacie stood next to Trevor and slipped her arm through his. Seeing Reece so nervous made her laugh. It was amusing to her.

"Reece, I think I know my dad better than you. He's not coming out here! But you don't have to drink. No one does. There's regular soda in there as well." She handed him a Coke. "Relax."

She took the lid off the soda bottle containing the vodka and took a large gulp. "Trust me, I don't give him a reason to check on me fifty thousand times. I do everything right, most of the time. If I didn't, I wouldn't have a life."

Trevor, shocking Reece, reached for a beer. To Aubrey's surprise, Cody did as well. Stacie acted cool as a cucumber. No sign of nerves at all; clearly she'd done this before.

"Dude, we do this out here all the time. We can tell if someone's coming, but they never do," Trevor said convincingly. "See how far away the house is from here?"

Stacie turned to Payton.

"You?"

"What?" Payton asked.

"You want another shot or are you going to pass?"

"Another one?" Reece asked, surprised. "What's she talking about?"

"I'm with him. I'll pass," Payton answered and whispered, "I had a shot in the restroom at the bowling alley."

Stacie didn't continue to press them or put them on the spot, but she did keep moving on down the line.

"I've got vodka, Aubrey, if you don't want a beer."

Aubrey shook her head. "Nah, I'm good. But go head."

Stacie had a shot of vodka, slammed two beers, and switched back to vodka. Cody drank one, sipped another. Trevor finished one and switched to soda. Nervous, Reece wanted to leave. He pulled Payton back into his lap, kissed the back of her neck.

"Let's leave. Do you want to?"

She did. Problem: he was driving everyone. That little fact brought them both back to reality. Stacie was laughing and talking with the guys. Reece was listening, but wasn't joining in. Trevor offered him another beer, but Reece stood firm and refused to drink at Coach's house. Payton grabbed a bottle of water; Reece tapped her on the rear, grabbed her hand, and pulled her back into his lap. Though she didn't say a word, it made her feel loved, wanted, and special. It would take years for her to realize that those types of actions really weren't the things that made her special or loved at all.

"This would be a sick place to have a party," Cody blurted out. "I mean, if you didn't have to worry about

Coach."

"Yeah," agreed Reece. "But who in their right mind would try to pull that, here I mean, at Coaches house!"

It would be great but a death sentence—unless you were his daughter. Stacie grinned from ear to ear. She had seen her brothers try and fail many a time. They'd pulled off a couple parties over the years, but not at that house. She'd watched from afar, the planning, and had even been to one or two. She was well aware of the risk, but had full confidence in herself that when the time was right, she could pull off a party—maybe not there, but definitely at the lake house. Her party would go down in history. It would be the party that everyone should've been at, and people will have wished they were lucky enough to have been invited. That was it! Stacie made up her mind right then and there: she was going to throw a party at her parents' lake house! It would be epic.

Chapter 13

It's the Real Deal

Reece: When can I see you again?

    Payton: Wait. What? Aren't we hanging out tomorrow?

    Reece: No, babe. We're going down to visit Royce. Well, meeting him halfway really. Hang out and eat. Family thing. Remember?"

She hadn't remembered that, but if he said he mentioned it, he probably did. Disappointment set in. She missed him already; that was dumb, he wasn't really going anywhere.

    Payton: That sucks! Not like that, glad you're seeing Royce. Tell him I said hi. Just wanted to see you, that's all.

    Reece: Me too. Hey was Coach's, I mean Stacie's house, lit or what!

    Payton: Yeah, not what I expected, but wow!

    Reece: Right!

    Reece: You surprised me when you told me about that drink, bathroom.

Throwing her head in her pillow, embarrassed,

Payton tried to blow it off.

> **Payton:** YOLO right.
> **Reece:** True. True.
> **Payton:** I wished that we didn't have to take everyone home though; we could've had   more time to hang out.
> **Reece:** Make out you mean, and yeah!

Who was she trying to kid? He was right. Dropping off Cody and Trevor cut into their time, not to mention the fact that Aubrey was staying over, which she never failed to keep pointing out by reminding them that she was still in the truck. As if they didn't know. Please! Thirty minutes later, in her jammies, she was on the phone FaceTiming her boyfriend. Aubrey was in bed, texting with Cody. Not a bad night for either one of them. For some reason, Payton felt the need to let Reece know that one day she would be ready. It was odd, since that particular subject came out of the blue, or so he thought. But Payton had been conflicted about when she'd be ready to have sex, and when he'd want her to be ready. It had been needlessly weighing on her mind.

> **Payton:** You know it will happen. I just don't know when.
> **Reece:** What will happen?
> **Payton:** That, you know.

Reece had to think for a second. Confused. Then it hit him what she was referring to; must have been his make-out comment. His tone came through on the text message soft and sweet when he responded.

Reece: Babe, this is the real deal. We can wait. I love you.

Payton screenshot the thread. Proud that he was her boyfriend. She was filled with a desire to please him, but no idea why. She came to the conclusion that being a teen in love was incredibly complicated. She didn't have to please him; they had to get along and respect each other. Have fun and make great grades. His words ran through her mind over and over. She didn't doubt him for one second. His words were true. He did love her, and this was the real deal.

Payton: You have no idea how much that means to me. Thank you. I love you too, babe.
Reece: Baby you're crazy. Love you. Goodnight.
Payton: Thanks ☺ Crazy part. Love you too.

Aubrey texted Cody until the early hours of the morning, Payton next to her sound asleep. Reversed. Usually Aubrey was crashed. Payton had fallen asleep with Reece on her mind, already planning what she'd wear the next time she'd see him. Right before she fell asleep, she wondered what it would be like, to do that with him. Was it possible, could she screw it up if they were together? Fear snuck in her head, but it didn't matter anyway, she had nothing but time.

Reece had taken pictures of Coach's game room for Royce. As soon as he could, he hit send. Smiled. And put his phone on the table by the side of his bed. It had been a great night. He'd gotten to hang out with his girlfriend and his friends, meet the new coach, and even manage to sneak a beer when he got home, thanks to Royce and his stash. His phone vibrated. He read the text. He was right. Royce wanted a room like Coach's game room. As soon as he responded, he rolled over and crashed.

Chapter 14

Awe C'mon

The undeniable aroma of bacon filled the house, but neither Payton nor Aubrey stirred. Payton's mom stuck her head in the bedroom: they were out, and she didn't dare wake them. Teen girls, she knew better; woken up before they were ready and the entire day would go downhill from there. Payton's brother, Parker, didn't care. He ran up and down the stairs numerous times trying to wake them up.

"Let them sleep," his mom whispered. "If you wake your sister, she'll be a bear."

If he couldn't wake her up, maybe he could get by drawing his new tattoo design with a sharpie on her ankle or arm. If he could pull that off on his sleeping sister, sleepovers with his buddies would be a blast. To his dismay, Payton was curled up in her usual position. Buried deep under her blanket, and the only way he could tell it was his sister and not her friend was the mass of her dark hair that poked out of the top. His eyes darted toward Aubrey. No chance for menace there either. Aubrey was buried just as deep under her blanket, with a pillow pulled tightly toward her stomach. Giving up, Parker went back downstairs to eat breakfast and irritate his mom.

"You'd think they'd be up by now."

Mrs. Phillips, with a raised eyebrow, handed him a hot buttered biscuit.

"Don't you have better things to do than aggravate two teen girls?"

He shook his head. But it was Sunday morning, and he'd find something to do before his dad found him a chore or two to do instead. Shoving the last bite of biscuit in his mouth, he jumped up and grabbed his football from the bottom of the stairs.

"Is Reece coming over today?"

"I don't know," his mom answered. "Payton didn't say."

"I hope so. Maybe he'll throw with me."

"Ask your dad to throw with you," she suggested.

His look said it all. Dad certainly wasn't Reece. Reece Townsend was cool. At least to a twelve-year-old wanna-be football player. His brother, Royce, well, he was even cooler, and on the rare occasion Royce was in the truck when Reece picked up his sister, that was a selfie day.

"Suit yourself."

Payton finally stirred a tad after noon. Before she went to the bathroom, she did what most teens do: checked her phone. Reece had texted her good morning and told her they were on their way to visit Royce. He said he'd FaceTime her later. He ended his message perfectly with a *love ya babe*. Her fingers instinctively tapped away on her phone as she messaged him back.

Payton: Miss you like crazy already. Can't wait to talk to you. I love you!

He texted her few minutes later; it was short, one word, followed by the dreaded three letters she had learned to hate. And though she'd never admit it to him, after reading the message her heart sank.

Reece: Same DTB

Aubrey stirred and Payton needed a distraction. Leaning on top of her best friend, she pulled the blanket off Aubrey, exposing a sleepy teen. Aubrey pulled it back and the tugging match began. Payton won; Aubrey was up. Aubrey pushed her tangled hair out of her face, rubbed the sleep out of her eyes, and asked Payton how she slept. They talked for a few minutes while Aubrey checked her phone. She was smiling. Cody had sent a text first thing, nothing major. He'd had fun and wanted to know if she wanted to hang out again some time. She did. Quick response back, filled Payton in, and thanked her friend for the hook up. Payton managed a slight smile.

"Let's go eat. I'm starving and need to get out of here for a while."

"Sure. No arguments from me." Aubrey grabbed her bag. "I'm not dressing up, sweats it is."

Aubrey's phone buzzed. Cody had already texted back. She responded. Thrilled, she shared with Payton. Payton did her best to act excited about the text. There wasn't anything to it, but it was a new phase and Aubrey was happy. Payton was hiding how she really felt, but evidently not very well. Aubrey caught on immediately.

"Did I miss something last night?"

"What do you mean?" Payton replied, puzzled by the question.

"You're acting weird, that's all."

"What do you mean?"

Aubrey shook her head. "C'mon. What's going on?"

Payton flopped down on the bed next to Aubrey. She started to talk, but her eyes inexplicably filled with tears. Barely able to talk, embarrassed she felt so emotional, she had to stop talking before she started crying.

"OMG, don't cry. It's OK, let's go eat and we'll talk there, OK?" Aubrey suggested.

Payton agreed, though she had no idea what she was supposed to say. Experiencing emotions and feelings that she didn't understand or know how to deal with were making her feel vulnerable and exposed. She could honestly say she had never in her life felt so blissfully happy at times, heartbroken at others, and emotional at the drop of a hat. And yet all it took to cheer her up could be something as simple as a text that required no response. **Reece:** *Love ya babe.* What in the hell was wrong with her? What was she supposed to say to her best friend? My boyfriend sent me a text that I didn't like and it upset me? But the text wasn't bad and he doesn't even know he did anything wrong? She felt like she was falling apart, for no reason, and that was ridiculous. It was a text. Yes. Talking it through would be a good thing!

Less than twenty minutes later, they pulled into their favorite burger restaurant and placed their usual order. Even if Payton only picked at it, at least she ordered the meal and was going to make herself try to eat it. Aubrey dove right in, as Payton picked at her food. Waiting for an opening, Aubrey asked the question she thought was weighing on Payton's mind.

"Did you and Reece have a fight before he left or something?"

Payton shook her head. First time ever she'd wished it were that; fights were easy, you made up. But it was nothing like that; in fact, it was just the opposite. She'd had a great night. Reece, her friends, even being at Stacie's house wasn't bad. Taking a deep breath, exhaling, and taking another, she tried to explain, but it was harder than she expected because she felt embarrassed for feeling so stupid.

"Don't judge me or think I'm crazy."

Aubrey shook her head. "Awe c'mon, you know I would never do that!"

They were truly like sisters, but this was ridiculous. Surely it wasn't even worth talking about. Payton didn't even know where to begin. She pushed her burger to one side and opened her mouth to speak, only to shut it again. Tears filled her eyes. She blinked to ensure they wouldn't fall, and then started to speak again.

"I don't think I've ever felt so stupid in my entire life. I honestly don't even know what to say or how to explain what I'm feeling."

Aubrey waited, nervous, not sure what to do except to wait and listen. Payton started to open up.

"I do miss Reece, but that's not it. He sent a text

with such a short response; it actually hurt my feelings. That's what set this off, me acting so weird. He's done it before, and when he does that, those types of texts, it makes me feel as if he doesn't feel the same way I do."

She took a sip of her shake and a great big tear rolled down her cheek. Aubrey handed her a napkin. It wasn't making sense yet, why Payton was so upset. Maybe she was on her period, emotional, hormonal—she didn't know. But she kept her thoughts to herself and allowed Payton to continue.

"We've been discussing some pretty intimate things lately, you know, like when I'm ready to do that . . . *the* that. And I know it will be with him. But this is the part where I feel stupid. He responds to a text I send, sweet text, and I feel that he should have answered it differently and because he didn't, it makes me feel like crap for the rest of the day. I'm not saying it's right, but it makes me feel like he's not on the same page as me. That he doesn't care about me like I do him."

She wiped her face with the napkin and added, "Like he's dismissing me; that's it, being dismissive and I feel like crap."

Her cheeks were flushed, embarrassed about the words that had just tumbled out of her mouth. Saying them sounded ridiculous and hearing them out loud didn't seem nearly as bad as how she actually felt. Text. Text response and feeling like crap. But to her it felt far more complicated than that; her feelings weren't matching the simplicity of how it sounded. Her heart and head were clashing. Logically she wasn't sure if

Reece had even done anything wrong. But her heart felt as if it were sinking. That feeling, emotionally, that made her question his love for her, was driving the sixteen-year-old kid crazy. Payton handed Aubrey her phone to read the conversation for herself. Aubrey read the message and chose her words carefully. Best friends rarely trumped boyfriends, and she was smart enough to know whatever she said could be held against her when Payton was feeling madly in love again.

"You know, it's possible he was in the middle of lunch and had been told to put up his phone, I don't know. Or it could just be a guy thing; guys and texts, they suck at it."

She paused, and then gingerly added, "But if you feel like crap over this incident, short-answer texts, how would you feel if you shared *that*, you know, with him and you thought he was being dismissive? Payton, how would you deal?"

Putting her head down, digging back into her food and avoiding eye contact, Aubrey softly added, "Could be a red flag you're not ready, emotionally, I mean. To even talk about going down that road. No offense intended."

To her surprise, Payton didn't deny it.

Chapter 15

Will This Day Ever End?

Payton slept through her alarm the next morning. Reece hadn't texted until late that night, and even then it was only a couple lines. That only added to her anxiety that something wasn't right. Her mind raced with questions and she had no one to ask, not even a friend to bounce off scenarios since it was so late. He wasn't driving, so how come he couldn't text? Did he just not want to talk to her? Was he texting someone else? Damn it! Her mind was going crazy, and she couldn't seem to turn it off. It took forever for her to finally drift off to sleep. Her mom's voice, calling out her name, travelled up the stairs. It was the first sound that alerted her she'd overslept. Before climbing out of bed, she checked her phone. A wave of relief swept over her as she read Reece's good-morning text. She replied instantly, even though she knew he was on the field at practice and wouldn't read it until later. Her head was pounding and she felt nauseous; lack of sleep and worry had done a number on her. Glad she'd showered the night before; deodorant, bra, underwear, jeans, T-shirt, converse, that was all she could bother with at the moment. There wasn't enough concealer in her makeup bag to hide the dark circles that had formed under her eyes. Base, powder, mascara, and gloss were all she could manage that morning. Hair, forget it! A loose braid pulled to the side would have do.

"Toast or a bagel?" her mom asked.

Payton shook her head, made a face as if she were going to throw up, and headed toward the door. Her mom grabbed her arm and felt her forehead. She didn't feel warm, but she didn't quite look like her normal self, either. Asking if Payton was all right, assured that she was, her mom gave her a hug and a kiss, and sent her on her way.

"Hey, wait for me."

Parker grabbed his backpack, Payton's slice of toast, and ran to the car after her. He could tell she wasn't in a good mood, so he kept conversation to a minimum and ate his toast. But that didn't stop Payton from taking her frustration out on him.

"We're going to be late!"

"That's OK!"

"It's not, you idiot! I've got a test."

"Well, you're the one who's an idiot. You overslept!"

He had her there; it was her fault. She dropped Parker at the curb in front of the school. He climbed out without saying a word. As he walked toward the door she called out his name, and when he turned around she apologized for being rude to him for no reason.

"If you want to wait for me this afternoon, I'll pick you up."

He nodded and went on his way. By the time she parked and got to her AP English class, she was ten minutes late. One look at the teacher and she knew she wasn't going to get by without a pass. She turned around and walked to the office. A few minutes later she was back, tardy pass in hand. No explanation needed. She was late and that was that; the teacher didn't care why. Relieved to see a seat close to Maddie still open, she sat down. The test hadn't started and she needed to catch up with her anyway; they'd barely talked all weekend.

Payton propped her bag up by the leg of her desk, wide open, with her phone sitting on top of her books. Positioned where she could see the screen clearly, she glanced downward every second she could steal. If Reece texted, she wanted to read it immediately. She couldn't stand the thought of missing a text from Reece, even *if* it came in while Mr. Caldwell was walking between the rows of desks. He was already irritated that Payton had shown up late, she didn't dare give him another reason to be angry with her by getting caught on her phone; he'd take it, for sure. *Resist the urge to look right now, he's too close,* she told herself as he stood next to her desk. Head still pounding, she forced herself to focus on the lesson instead. She was struggling and she *liked* poetry. She was having difficulty concentrating; her mind raced and she found herself spending more time focusing on getting focused than hearing a word the teacher said. The only thing on her mind was Reece. Thankfully, Mr. Caldwell hadn't paid any attention to her doodling and had moved on down the row. The only way to calm her nerves was going to be to talk to Reece; she knew herself well enough to know that. That's what it would take to put her mind at ease. All that fretting over a few texts or lack of them—crazy!

Usually his texts and snaps kept her smiling during the day, but she couldn't shake the funk she was in and was doing a terrible job of faking it. Hearing his voice would put her mind at ease, but seeing his face and looking at that beautiful smile would definitely fix it. He likely didn't have a clue anything was wrong, but for her, it would ease her mind. Thinking about his smile alone made her heart melt. Payton promised herself that she'd calm down; all was well, and she was panicking for nothing.

Aubrey: OK?

Aubrey didn't understand why Payton felt the way that she did; being crazy in love played with your emotions, for sure, but to her own credit she was still trying to be supportive and that seemed to help. Payton lied, knowing Aubrey really didn't get it anyway.

Payton: Yeah. Thanks for checking on me.

Embarrassed and confused that she felt the way she did, she ended the conversation. Part of her knew it didn't seem rational that she'd be so upset over a short text, but the other part of her couldn't help but feel something wasn't quite right. She was a smart girl: honor roll, popular, and well liked. So why she felt the need to have an immediate response from a guy just because he was her boyfriend was ridiculous, even to her. *Note to self,* she thought, *ask the other girls if this is normal.*

It felt like an eternity, but her phone finally flashed. Snap notification lit up the screen: Reece goofing off with guys in the locker room. Still in his dirty jersey, pads, and smiling, sitting on a bench in front of his locker, and the dark cloud that had been floating above Payton's head immediately disappeared. Her whole demeanor changed: her eyes lit up, and a smile crossed her face. She acted like a completely different person than an hour earlier. One snap pic had done all that! She posed and snapped a pic right then. Aubrey grinned, thankful that he'd finally sent something and, at least for now, all was well again. The dismissive nature of the text messages that Payton had told her about hadn't been addressed, but maybe Payton wouldn't even bring them up. Who knew? The Payton in front of her right now acted as if nothing had happened at all, and maybe that was for the best. The bell rang and they met up with Maddie. Every detail of the weekend was discussed again.

"OMG! So hard to keep up!" Maddie laughed as Payton explained their triple date over the weekend.

"Right!" agreed Payton as she rolled her eyes.

"Are you going to mention the texts or how they made you feel?" Aubrey asked.

Payton shrugged her shoulders, uncertain what to do. Things right now were good; scared to rock the boat, maybe she'd wait and feel him out. It was possible she was overreacting; she didn't know yet. All she knew was that as soon as she had communicated with him, even for a second, she felt content.

"You know how dense some guys are, regardless of

their intelligence level, when it comes to texting," Maddie said. "He may not know he's done anything wrong."

"True," Payton agreed. "We'd already thought about that."

Cody, on the other hand, was getting pretty good at it, a fact that Aubrey had shared with the girls. The bell finally rang. Biology was next. A class they all dreaded. Aubrey gathered her things and pointed toward the door.

"Meet ya outside." She grinned. "I've gotta call Cody."

Payton checked her phone. Reece had sent her a text confirming that they'd talk during lunch. She could feel her nerves starting to settle. Girl talk with her friends took over her thoughts for a few minutes, but her mind soon wandered. What was Reece doing right now? Who did he sit next to in class? Did cute girls surround him? Did he secretly like any of them? Was he talking to them as well as talking to her? Did he go to lunch with them or drive them home? She realized she was asking herself fifty million ridiculous questions. The last one scared her the most. *What, if anything, was wrong with her?*

Maddie kicked Payton under the table. Mr. Brown stood directly over them, and to say Payton was unprepared would have been an understatement. He made a sarcastic comment about his class and their lack of participation and then, to her relief, moved on. Payton knew it was time to call it a day. She couldn't concentrate, had just started her period, felt like crap, and needed to sleep.

"I'm sorry. I didn't sleep well, I've just started my period, feel like I'm about to puke, and I don't think I need to be here today," she confided to Maddie.

"Go home sick," Maddie suggested. "You don't look well. It's not like they won't believe you."

It felt as if the day simply wouldn't end. Bad way to start off the week, but maybe if she went home she could get up the next day and start over. A do-over day in the morning! She raised her hand and asked Mr. Brown if she could be excused. He denied her request. She raised her hand again and sat there, hand raised, until he acknowledged her.

"What is it this time, Ms. Phillips?"

"I don't feel well. I think I'm going to throw up."

Frustrated, he let out a deep sigh, pointed to his desk at the hall passes, and sent her on her way. A phone call to her mom completed the process, and she agreed with her mom that, if she felt up to it, she'd still pick up Parker so he wouldn't be disappointed by having to ride the bus later. Reece actually sent his first real text during her drive home. Great! Just her luck; driving. She pulled over. She didn't tell him she was ill, likely mostly unjustified worry, or that she was on her way home. She simply responded as if nothing had been wrong with her at all.

Payton: Can't wait to talk to you. Love you, babe

What am I thinking?!?! she wondered. But that was the trouble: she wasn't.

Chapter 16

Selfish, Right?!

The boys' locker room was like any other high school locker room during football season: decked out and decorated for game week. After football practice it stunk. Once the coaches were done with their speeches, motivational talks, instructions or chew-outs, depending on how practice had gone, the boys were turned loose. They talked trash about their pending opponent and each other; they often had their favorite playlist blaring, and the entire atmosphere felt festive and a tad chaotic. Coaches had said everything they'd needed to say, and it was time for the boys to bond and have a little fun. It wasn't unusual for the coaches to look the other way while they horsed around, unless it was necessary for them to step in.

"No broken bones, no blood, and always remember to treat each other the way you expect to be treated—with respect! Pick up your mess and hit the showers!" Coach's closing words at the end of every locker-room speech.

Reece sat on a bench between Trevor and Cody, watching a clip of Royce's game on his phone. Coach stopped, glanced down at the phone, and made a comment about Royce's play.

"Did you see how he cut to the left, then right, before he did that?"

"Yes, sir."

"That's what you boys need to do out there, just like that—anticipate and execute!"

"Yes, sir," they responded again.

It was one heck of a move. Reece had seen the game in person and watched it twice via DVR since. Evidently Coach had watched the game himself a few times, which pleased Reece. He made a mental note to himself to tell his dad. It would please him as well, knowing Coach was keeping up with Royce.

The boys were always starving after practice. Volunteers provided snacks, which often got them by, but nothing seemed to fill them up. Reece pulled a protein bar out of his locker and slammed down a power-aid drink. He was still hungry.

"Speaking of lunch, where are we going today?"

"Man, I'm craving barbeque for some reason. Specifically chopped brisket," Trevor answered. "But I've gotta see if Stacie's willing to eat barbecue. She'll eat just about anything, but I haven't taken her for barbecue yet."

Barbecue did sound pretty good, especially right then. Cody didn't care. Reece was in, and plans were made: get through the rest of the morning and meet at the restaurant a little after noon. Physics was next on Reece's schedule. He checked his assignment one last time. All he could do was hope it was right; he wasn't getting most of it, but he didn't understand the problem. His stomach rumbled. He looked at the problem one last time. Shook his head. Thank God this class was almost over! It was doing his head in!

He shook his head and put his book away. He needed more time to grasp what he was supposed to do, let alone finish his homework. He was trying to concentrate on his schoolwork, but the Friday night football game kept popping into his head. It was a big one, a rivalry game, and it was possible, since it was Royce's bi-week, that he might make it home. He wasn't holding him to it though, but was hopeful, fingers crossed and everything. A snap notification hit his phone. Zoe. A friend. No big deal, cute pic. Cody glanced at his phone.

"That girl, right there . . . ," Cody paused, then added, "yeahhhh . . . she's so *not* hot enough for me!"

Reece and Cody burst out laughing. Zoe, every bit an easy ten, possibly a twelve, was beautiful for sure! Long dark hair and steel-blue eyes; she was kinda like Payton, only cooler. She was mysterious. Quiet but not rude, and kept to herself unless she was with her usual small click of girls. Liked, but not overly well known, which was really weird because she was a cheerleader. Zoe was smart but not obnoxious, confident but not arrogant, and definitely hot, hot, hot!

"Why don't you set me up with her?" Cody asked. "Nah, just kidding. I think this Aubrey girl is about right, if you know what I mean! You know what I mean? Besides, like I said, that Zoe girl, way too ugly for me."

Reece took a pic of his shoes and snapped it back. He looked at Cody and laughed.

"What? We have a streak going!"

Zoe had been in one of Reece's classes for the past two years, but he'd always seen her at the games since she was part of the cheer squad. Though few words were said, it was enough to strike up a friendship. Getting through AP English before leaving for lunch was painful, but at least the random snaps and texts killed time. London, Zoe's best friend, was actually in Reece's class. She was pretty. Thin, tall, dark blond with blue eyes, cute girl. London was dating Gavin, one of their friends, who played football with the boys. London poked Reece with her pen.

"Did you say lunch? Cause I'm starving!"

"Yeah, me too. Getting ready to eat some barbecue with Trevor."

"Oh my God, that sounds so good right now!" She pulled out her phone and started texting.

"Ugh. Gavin has to take a test." She put her phone down on the desk.

"You can go with us if you want," Reece offered.

She reached for her phone again.

London: Since you can't go, we're going with Reece and them. Do you want anything?
Gavin: No. But thanks for asking. Sorry about that, next time.
London: No worries.

Her next text was to Zoe.

London: Let's eat brisket for lunch. Reece driving. Meet you at his truck.
Zoe: K

"Are you sure you don't care if we tag along?" London asked.

Reece shook his head. It was just lunch. He'd call Payton right after that, no big deal.

"Oh, by the way, do you care if Zoe joins us?" she laughed. "Cause she is."

He shook his head again. "Nope. No big deal."

Cody was already at the truck, and to Reece's surprise, Zoe was there with him. He was dying because she made him nervous and he'd run out of small talk. Funny, he didn't get nervous around Aubrey. Trevor pulled up next to the truck; Stacie was sitting in the passenger seat next to him with a great big smile on her face. She glanced at Zoe and London, smiled, and hollered out the window as loud as she could.

"See you there losers!"

Reece grinned, opened his door, and let the girls climb in first. Cody leaned over the back seat, making sure the girls weren't offended.

"You do know Stacie, right?" he asked. "Cause that's just her, Stacie."

"She was talking to us, by the way." Reece laughed. "She's a trip. Looks like a girl, acts like a guy, and dating our bud Trevor. She's C-R-A-Z-Y, but you gotta like her."

"Yeah, we know Stacie. We've hung out with her several times, and she definitely likes to have fun, Coach's daughter or not." London laughed.

"Has she mentioned the party she's having at her parents' lake house?" Zoe asked nonchalantly as she dug through her backpack for money.

Reece glanced in his rearview mirror. She'd mentioned wanting to plan a party in passing the night they were at her house, but no, she hadn't confirmed anything. Cody said the same thing. She'd talked about it, but hadn't told them anything definite.

"Why, has she planned one, definitely I mean?" Reece laughed. "We might not be invited."

"Yeah, right!" Zoe flicked Reece on the back of the head. "Betting she mentions it at lunch. But to answer your question, yes. It seems she's nailed down a date or at least the proximity of a date."

"Awesome!" Cody hollered. "Love to party!"

Reece's phone vibrated in his pocket. He didn't pull it out to check to see who it was. There was no need; he'd call her back after he ate. He didn't have enough time to talk anyway, plus too many people in his truck.

Zoe and London were right. Once they were all seated, talk about the party began. Between bites of food, Stacie politely threw out the invites. Coolest part, it wasn't going to be at her house. Reece felt better about that, knowing he could never relax at Coach's house. Holding it at her parents' lake house didn't feel quite as intrusive as actually being at her parents' house.

"So are you in? Can ya'll make it?"

"One question, cause I don't feel like dying or jacking up my entire life over a party, even a kick-ass one." Reece set his sandwich down. "How in the hell do you, meaning Coach's daughter, expect to pull a party off at your parents' lake house without being busted?" Reece eagerly waited for her to respond.

"Parental units are going to an out-of-town game. I'm going to Sophie's. Sophie is supposedly coming to my house. But of course we're going to the lake house." She took a sip of Coke, dabbed her mouth, and waited for the next round of interrogation.

"Nah. Not enough. Your parents will check with Sophie's parents before they leave," Reece stated. "You know. Chaperone-type thing."

He took a bite of his brisket sandwich and added, "Hell, even my parents confirm stuff like that, and I'm not even a girl."

A smirk that a parent of any teen girl would dread crossed Stacie's face. Clearly she'd already anticipated that; her parents, like any parents who loved and worried about their teens, had several safety measures in place. But Stacie had thought of all of them. Naturally, to pull it off, the master plan required manipulation, effort, and teamwork.

"So who's your partner in crime?" Zoe asked. "The so-called adult who is currently missing in the picture, you know, the go-to one you need to help pull this off?"

Without hesitation Stacie answered. "Sophie's aunt. She's more like Sophie's older sister because she's only six years older. Her voice sounds way older when she's on the phone, and she is actually an adult." She took a sip of her drink and a bite of her sandwich. "Anyway, for a tank of gas, which I'll put on my gas card, she'll act like Sophie's mom *if we need her*. But of course she'll deny it and she's not using her phone and she really doesn't want to do it, but she will."

Stacie was one hundred percent confident that she

could pull it off without Sophie's aunt if they were prepared in advance. She hadn't given her parents a single reason to doubt her, even when she'd done things that they wouldn't necessarily approve of; topping that off, she'd never been caught doing those questionable things. She chose to leave out the part about turning off the security system, complete with video cameras, knowing that Reece was already nervous. The whole "Coach's daughter" thing was throwing him. No point in riling him up. Who knows what his brother's advice might be, and if he were nervous, as much as he idolized Royce, surely Reece would ask him. He might advise his little bro to snitch, which was doubtful, or bail and not go. Either way, Reece Townsend needed to relax.

"Seriously, it's not a big deal. Likely it will be a text confirmation. And if it is a call, I know it will take less than a minute and Sophie's aunt can pull it off." Stacie sounded dead spot-on believable.

London had the same calm demeanor that Stacie had. Not bothered at all about being caught, just excited at the thought of a party. Zoe's steel-blue eyes lit up. Reece wondered if Gavin knew what was going down yet; they were all on the same team, and he hadn't even heard a rumor until on the way over to the restaurant. Stacie announced that all girlfriends or boyfriends were welcome, so now it was understood he could take Payton. Reece had mixed feelings; but the more Stacie talked, the more she was starting to calm his nerves.

"It's not going to be tooooooo big," she said. "I can't afford for anything to get trashed. We'd be busted for sure and I'd be dead!"

"Who's going? I mean, other than the obvious," Cody asked.

"Trevor's friends." She pointed to the guys. "My friends." She pointed to Zoe and London. "Some who are mutual friends, and of course you can invite Payton, and Cody, you can invite Aubrey."

She wadded up her trash, aimed at the trash can, and missed. Reluctantly she got up and put it in the trash. When she sat down, she placed her arm around Trevor's shoulders while he finished eating. For a moment Reese wished Payton went to the same school as him. Reece, who wasn't huge on PDA, thought Stacie letting her boyfriend know that she was there with him, in a subtle way in front of all of them, was kinda cool. Stacie threw out one last thing; talk about saving the best for last.

"Instead of leaving, everyone should stay and camp, literally. We could cook out; we've got a great grill out there, and a dock for fishing. I'm not going to risk taking out the boat, so don't ask, but camping would be a blast. Think about how much fun it will be if we really don't have to worry about driving back. You know, if peeps do drink."

"Like, everyone spend the night?" London confirmed. "Just crash wherever we can find a piece of floor?"

"Well, I was kinda hoping everyone could bring a tent or crash in the back of their trucks; you know, real camping," Stacie suggested. "I don't know who will drink, but if they do, then they're not driving."

Reece had grown up camping; most of his friends

did. Camping, hunting, fishing with a group of friends, guys and girls, sounded like a blast.

Reece glanced at his phone as a text flashed across the screen. One word. Not good.

Payton: Hellllllllo.

His mind now on Payton, he knew he had no choice but to make the call, but at least he had great news. Was it even possible for her to get out and spend the night at the lake house? If they planned far enough in advance, could they pull it off? How cool would that be! They'd never even come close to having an opportunity like this before. He excused himself from the table and stepped outside.

"Hey, I've got to make a phone call." He waved his phone in the air and headed toward the door.

"Hey babe, what's going on?"

She had picked up, he had heard her say hello, but then came the semi-silent treatment after that—really? WTH? Why did he bother calling her at all?!

Chapter 17

He Said, She Said

He got it. He hadn't called her right away, but he was calling her now. Was she really that ticked off? Their conversation went south before it even started. He tried again.

"Something wrong, babe?"

Was there something wrong? Payton's heart sank. Of course there was something wrong! How did he not understand that she was irritated—no, pissed off—at him? It was after one o'clock! His lunch was almost over and she'd sat there, like an idiot, and waited since noon for him to call. As relieved as she was when she saw his name flash across her screen, her emotions switched from happy to disappointment within seconds of each other. To be honest, she was hurt; maybe she was overreacting, but the fact that he didn't get why she was so upset crushed her even more.

Payton knew Reece could tell something was wrong, but with only a few minutes left to talk, she couldn't relay all the things she wanted to say. Still upset from the weekend, mad at herself for feeling that way, she fought back tears, which pissed her off even more. Payton had no idea why something had evoked such strong emotions—enough to produce tears in the first place. Disappointed, yes, tear-worthy, surely not. Payton smudged mascara across her face and pulled her long dark hair aside and placed it on top of her head. She took a deep breath and gathered herself for a second. As his girlfriend, didn't she have the right to ask a simple question? She thought she did.

"Why are you just now calling?" she asked, adding, "you got out for lunch at noon and now your lunch is almost over, it's after one."

He knew it. He should have called earlier and for some reason figured he could call after he ate, and that's what he told her as he started to explain. Purposely omitting certain parts of lunch, mainly Zoe and London joining them, and the part about him offering to drive them. He spoke confidently, knowing he hadn't actually done anything wrong. Maybe he shouldn't have driven the girls, but it was innocent, and he didn't feel like fighting over something that was nothing. See. She had already made him question his decision without saying a word. Best not to mention the party yet. Leave it till later, likely when they were together in person. Better chance of getting her to say yes and to work on a plan to stay over with him if he could sweet-talk a little bit first—*that* he did know how to do. Reece had already made up his mind. He was going to the party with or without her. It sounded like a blast. Stacie's party was going to be stellar, and he really didn't want to miss it. Admittedly it would be awesome if she could go; but he wasn't asking, not right then. Change the conversation; get the heat off him, distraction.

"What did you and Aubrey do yesterday?"

Wrong question. He unknowingly stepped into the fight that he didn't know was coming. It was the one that he had no idea he was supposed to avoid in the first place! This teen-dating-love thing . . . OMG!

"Well, babe, not trying to be mean or anything, but if you'd bothered to send that text, which takes all of two seconds, or had called instead of being so dismissive, I would have filled you in."

Reece bit his tongue, knowing anything out of his mouth right then would only fuel the fire. Payton, however, couldn't help herself: one more dig at him.

"Two seconds. 'Thinking of you.' Send."

She waited to see what excuse he had, but he didn't offer one. He'd already tuned her out. Irritated that he called her and this was where the conversation was going, he was ready to get off the phone. That irritated Payton. And the tension increased.

"It's almost time for you to go, and I had so much to tell you," Payton complained. "Now we can't even talk."

"We are talking," he interrupted before she could say anything else. "I don't know what else to say, Payton. I was with my family on Sunday, and you know that. Royce brought his girlfriend. There were several people at lunch, not just me. I couldn't stay on my phone. First, my dad won't allow it. Second, I like listening to Royce. I enjoy his stories and his girlfriend's pretty cool as well." He took a breath. "And while I'm at it, after lunch we went to Royce's apartment for dessert, which his girlfriend made, by the way. We'd been up early, so driving back I fell asleep. Because yes, Payton,

I was tired!"

OMG, great! Now he was getting mad at her, and she couldn't be mad at him. This conversation was going from bad to worse, but Reece wasn't finished.

"I had practice all week long, school, game, and we went out before I left, remember? By the time I got home, all I wanted was to shower and go to bed." He took a moment, and then added, "I even sent you a text before I fell asleep."

Payton hoped he was done, but he added one more thing. "I didn't want to say this, Payton, but the truth was I really didn't want to talk to you. Nothing against you, but I was just tired. If you can't get that, then I don't know what else to tell ya; but right now I gotta go!"

His explanation made her feel as if her worrying had been ridiculous. Why had she freaked out and assumed something was wrong? Everything he said sounded totally logical, but her reasoning in the moment for being so upset had made total sense to her. Payton didn't know if she was overreacting or going plain crazy. In that moment, she thought she was losing her mind!

"Sorry for overreacting. No idea what's going on with me right now." Payton blinked away her tears. "I thought you were selfish, but I guess it's me."

Reece shook his head, but she couldn't see on the other end of the phone. "Let's call this one a massive communication fail. Deal?"

He was done with it and wanted Payton to be over it as well. She wanted him to understand why she was upset, but she had the feeling that he really couldn't care less. The difference between teen guys and girls: emotions, and the way they look at things. His head had already shut down. He wasn't going to talk about it anymore. Reece noticed everyone walking toward him, including the girls. The last thing he needed was for Payton to hear them talking and cutting up and having fun. He hadn't done anything wrong, had he? He was feeling the heat from not calling her earlier, now he hadn't mentioned there were girls with them at lunch, and no way was he going to mention that he'd been their taxi driver as well. That was more trouble than he needed or wanted to deal with, especially after this conversation.

"I'll call you back as soon as I get out of class today?"

"OK. I'm going to take a nap anyway."

"Wait, what? You sick?" Reece asked.

"I came home early. Headache. Tired."

"Man, wish I was with you."

She couldn't help but smile when he spoke like that, hit her soft spot every time. Reece put a finger to his lips and pointed to the phone. Everyone quieted down and climbed into the truck.

"OK, I'll talk to you later. Love you, babe."

"Love you too, babe," Payton responded. "Hey, Reece. I'm sorry. I love you."

"It's all good. Love you too."

"Awe, that's so sweet," Zoe cooed as Reece climbed into the truck.

Glancing into the rearview mirror, he smiled, but didn't acknowledge her comment. Knowing Payton went home sick made him feel bad for not calling earlier, but he already had a plan to make it up to her. Stacie's lake party was the topic of conversation on the way back to campus. London knew that she and Zoe would use each other as a cover, no problem there, and Gavin could be with any one of the boys at any given time and it wouldn't be suspicious. Reece wasn't worried about being able to pull off a cover for the night, and he was already planning on Payton making it happen as well. It would be the only time to spend an extended period of time together unsupervised. Camping out with all of your best friends, except no one would probably sleep. They'd never come close to pulling off anything remotely like the party she was planning—or even had the opportunity before. Reece was determined to make it happen.

It was the sound of muffled voices that woke Payton. She'd been asleep for a while, longer than she thought. She must've drifted off right after she and Reece had gotten off the phone. As she stirred, she realized her headache had eased. Footsteps climbing the stairs, along with the sound of her mom calling out her name, caused her to sit straight up in bed and gather her wits. Did her mom say what she'd thought she had said? She waited for her mom to approach her room; within seconds the door swung open.

"How are you feeling, sleepyhead?" her mom asked.

"Better. Funny, I could've sworn I heard you say something about Reece."

Her mom smiled and handed Payton her favorite

hairbrush.

"You might want to run this through your hair, and yes, you did. Reece stopped by to check on you; wasn't that nice of him?" She walked back toward the door. "I'll tell him you'll be down in a few then, unless you're still not feeling well?"

Payton climbed out of bed, splashed water on her face, ran the brush through her hair, and spritzed on Reece's favorite perfume. She didn't look great, but she wasn't supposed to; after all, she'd been semi-sick. She could see him watching for her as she topped the stairs. He looked so damn cute! Jeans, boots, T-shirt, and a baseball cap; the boy could wear anything and look amazing.

"Hey, how are you feeling?"

She didn't really answer his question. Happy to see him, her face lit up.

"I had no idea you were coming over!"

"Surprise! Just checking on you."

His green eyes lit up as he spoke and that beautiful smile, the one that always melted her, spread across his face. He walked toward her, pulled her close, hugged her, and kissed the top of her forehead. Mrs. Phillips exited toward the kitchen, but not before offering snacks and drinks, which they both declined. They didn't need to turn on the TV when they were together, they had plenty to talk about, and TV was a distraction. Reece asked her again how she felt, waiting for the perfect time to mention Stacie's party. He filled her in on his day, left out a few details, some of the events during practice, and even discussed some of the conversation they'd had with Royce about the rivals they were about to play. Payton hung onto every single word that poured from his mouth. From time to time she'd interject her thoughts or ask a question that she didn't really care if he answered or not, but asking made her feel as if she were showing interest in what he did and loved. Didn't matter, he didn't mind and didn't seem to notice the difference. Her dad came home from work and Reece still hadn't mentioned the party. If he didn't hurry up, he'd run out of time before he'd have to leave for the evening.

"Hey Reece, are you joining us for dinner?"

Reece shook his head. He thanked Mr. Phillips for asking, but assured him if he didn't get home soon, his mom would kill him. Family dinner was a big deal at the Townsend home. Payton leaned into Reece as she sat next to him on the couch, knowing he'd be leaving soon. He pulled her closer to him and whispered into her ear.

"We've got the best opportunity ever to hang out like nearly all night, if not all night, right around the corner."

Payton bolted straight up.

"What? How? And more importantly, when?"

Mr. Phillips walked back into the living room. Sure enough, Reece's phone vibrated in his pocket. "Be here in ten," the message said, and he showed it to her. It was time for Reece to head home for dinner himself. He waved his phone in the air, indicating he had to go and would text later. Color back in her cheeks, barely able to contain her excitement, still not knowing all the details surrounding this opportunity to spend a whole night with Reece, Payton literally bounced to the door and kissed him goodbye.

Chapter 18

Start Planning

Every kid who planned to attend Stacie's lake party was preparing the necessary groundwork, in order to avoid complications for when the actual event rolled around. Stacie had already discussed her plan with her partner in crime, Sophie, working out every detail to a tee. Sophie would spend the night at Stacie's, then Stacie would go to Sophie's; they'd make a routine out of it for the next few weeks. The night in question, party night, there shouldn't be any red flags at all. And if there were, they had a plan for that as well. Sophie's Aunt Chloe would put in a text on their behalf and if the text wasn't enough, a call would be placed as backup. Patterns. Stacie had learned from her brothers that patterns didn't raise red flags, but sudden changes in behaviors did. Stick with the pattern and, worst-case scenario, her parents might make a comment about her staying at her friend's home too much, but it wouldn't be weird or out-of-the-norm behavior for her.

"That's a great idea!" Sophie agreed.

"Right!" Stacie said proudly. "It's practically a no-fail plan if we start getting them used to it now. They'll think we're just taking it in turns, yours, mine, yours, mine, sometimes yours, and then mine, and we're home free!"

Sophie took a sip of her Coke and tried to calculate how many people would show up. Imagining each face of those they'd invited and had said they'd be there, she quit counting after thirty.

"Dang, girl, it's going to get too big if we're not careful."

Stacie wasn't worried. She had every intention of making sure everyone stayed out of the house as much as possible. There was plenty of room, no need really for anyone to go in and out of the cabin, except maybe the girls to use the bathroom. The guys, hell, she'd seen her brothers disappear behind a tree on numerous occasions out there in the woods. Her mind was focused on food, as in snacks, and alcohol, as in beer and whatever else they could get away with that night.

"I'm already nervous, about your dad, I mean. And the beer part; not sure about that."

"Don't talk like that," Stacie said somberly. "You'll make me second-guess myself. I don't need to envision him and what he'd do to me if he had any idea what I'm planning. He'd absolutely freaking kill me!"

Sophie hesitated, and then asked Stacie a question she wasn't sure her friend would answer. "Then why do it, Stacie, the risk? It's crazy. You know what I mean."

"Do what?" Stacie purposely avoided the question, knowing exactly what Sophie wanted to know.

"Why risk him finding out? You get away with so much; I mean, really, compared to most kids. Let someone else throw a party. You could let someone else take that kind of risk."

Stacie stared out her bedroom window. She thought about the question that Sophie had just asked. Why did she take such stupid risks? This one was, by far, the worst she'd ever contemplated taking, and if she pulled it off, what next? But why risk literally making her father so furious? She could lose her car, be grounded for life, have her brothers hate her for embarrassing them, her dad the *Coach*, and her mother would look at her with such disappointment in her eyes that it would hurt. *Why?* She thought about all the times they had moved. All the tricks and stunts she had pulled over the years, no one had asked her this question before. Being asked such a question head-on irritated her and made her feel uncomfortable. She didn't have an acceptable answer, because there wasn't one. Taking the risk made her feel like she was in control of something, and that certainly was an unacceptable, selfish answer. Stretching out onto her bed, she finally answered Sophie. She said the most shocking thing she could think of, but her answer didn't surprise Sophie, though she'd hoped for something different. Her answer was chilling and convincing.

"I guess because I can."

Sophie's phone buzzed, and she held it up to show Stacie the message. Her mom's response was "yes." Stacie could spend the night, but she had to pick up her clothes. Phase one was in motion; phase two, start stockpiling snacks; phase three, work on possibly hiding beer and a bottle of liquor. She could swipe beer from the fridge in the garage, a few from the house, and find a spot to hide them from her parents, and brothers when they came home. Oh and don't forget the housekeeper—she'd have to think about that one; she'd need a secure hiding place. But that was going to be the easy part. Phase four, getting everything to the lake house unnoticed: that was going to be difficult.

"I don't want people to feel like they have to drink it, though, the beer and stuff, you know what I mean?" Stacie stated. "I do know I don't want to be responsible for that, pushing alcohol on anyone. That I know is way bad, off limits. Gotta be their choice."

Sophie started to laugh and interjected something for Stacie to consider. "Yes. I get it! Can I make a suggestion?"

Stacie nodded. "Shoot."

"I don't think you should supply it at all—liquor or beer. Or even suggest or recommend it. In fact, I don't think you should insinuate it's OK to bring it or anything at all relating to it, if you know what I mean." She raised her hands to silence Stacie when she tried to object. "Let me finish. Look, you're already risking the party. But if you supply the alcohol or say it's OK that people bring it and someone gets sick or worse, and your parents or their parents find out, can you seriously even imagine? Stacie . . . your dad is the new coach."

Surprisingly, Stacie didn't object. "I could just say bring what they want to drink. Then it's up to them, not me." She smirked. "Because I already know they'll bring it. It's what they do. Right! No worries; there will be plenty of booze."

"That's a great way out of it. That way you're supplying the venue, but not any alcohol. Who knows what they'll bring, but you're not the one who's supplying it." Sophie lowered her voice, as if she shouldn't say it for fear of upsetting her friend. "If we're lucky, there really won't be a bunch of alcohol there. We don't need the trouble."

It was decided right then and there: that's what they would do. When the time came, they'd announce that everyone coming to the party would bring their own beverage. Stacie would never admit it, but she felt one hundred percent relieved about that scenario. Why couldn't she just tell her friend the truth: she didn't want to be responsible for kids on booze anyway. It made her feel semi-responsible, while being completely irresponsible. She pushed the irresponsible part out of her head. Who didn't have parties at their age? It's just that hers would be ten times better than everyone else's. *Keep blocking out the negative, focus on the positive,* she told herself. At least there would be no drinking and driving, and no trashing the house or damaging property. Think of it like a great big camping trip for teens. That was responsible, wasn't it? That was the theme. Camping party for teens, with no mention of alcohol at all. They would focus on cooking, hanging out, and fun for everyone!

***

Reece couldn't wait to text Payton. Surely she was over being disappointed and mad at him; the excitement of spending extended time together had seemed to help. Not to mention they still had plenty of regular date time to hang out, prepare, and anticipate the big party ahead. It was all everyone in their circle was talking about—a night at the lake, all night.

> **Reece:** Can't wait to see you. Picnic?

Payton had a test, but when it came to that boy, she couldn't say no, and without hesitation she texted back.

> **Payton:** OMG Yes. Can't wait!
> **Reece:** love ya DTB

She didn't try to analyze why she couldn't text him back. Maybe he was driving or was about to hit the locker-room shower. Who knew? All she cared about right then was that in a few hours she'd be meeting that boy at the dam. From there, she knew she'd hop into his truck, plant a great big kiss on that beautiful face, and they'd head to their tree by the lake. Texts to Aubrey to make sure she'd cover her during lunch and Advisory, no problem. Quick text to Maddie; she'd know how to get out of the make-up test that she was scheduled to take after she'd been sick. A great knack that Maddie had was thinking on her feet. She was always good with coming up with excuses if someone needed one—plus an added benefit, the teachers loved her!

> **Maddie:** Easy peasy. Tell her you're double-booked for tests due to being out sick, but immediately ask if you can come back by after school to take it. Chances are she doesn't want to stay late and will reschedule for lunch tomorrow.

Great idea. Payton recognized that asking the teacher if she could come back the same day after school and take the test showed that she was sincerely sorry for missing it in the first place, booking two tests during the same lunch period, and she was trying to keep up her grade. Again, Maddie had come up with another great idea on the spot!

> **Payton:** Do you think she'll check with Ms. Taylor?
> **Maddie:** Nah. Why would she?
> **Payton:** True.
> **Payton:** Thanks.
> **Maddie:** No problem.

As soon as the bell rang, Payton ditched her friends and literally ran to her car. Reece was already waiting for her when she arrived at the dam. Pulling up next to him, he rolled down his window as she parked and climbed out of her car. His smile radiated across his face, making Payton smile too. She couldn't see his pretty green eyes, because his shades covered them. Hopping into his truck, she leaned over, held his face in her hands and kissed him hello. He reciprocated, kissing her back just as sweetly. As soon as they pulled up to their spot, Reece parked under the branches of their tree.

"Let's eat," he insisted, pointing to two brown paper sacks on the floorboard.

They jumped out of the truck and perched themselves on the back of his tailgate. Perfect picnic weather: clear, with lots of sunshine and a cool breeze. Rummaging through the sack, Reece handed Payton her favorite sandwich. He smiled, knowing he'd done a good job with his restaurant selection. Pleasing her pleased him.

"I want you to eat that, now, ya hear?" he mocked playfully.

"Thanks, Dad, I will," she replied, knowing he was watching her eat.

She'd never been so relieved that she accidently looked decent. Her outfits were typically planned, but she'd half-haphazardly thrown together something that morning. Jeans and a light sweatshirt that she'd pulled out of her closet complimented her casual look, with black, low-top converse, and she looked cute.

It didn't take long for the conversation to turn to Stacie's party. Surprisingly, Payton brought it up first.

"Give me the details. I can't stand it."

Recce took a bite of his sandwich, washed it down with a swallow of water, and dove into his bag of chips. Making her wait for information was fun. Payton wasn't good at being patient, and knowing he had information she wanted made him laugh. She asked him again, only this time she had that whiney girlfriend-working-it voice, not quite irritating, but almost.

"Seriously. C'mon, babe. I'm dying here. Give me details!"

"You already know most of them," Reece said. "Stacie's throwing a party at her parents' lake house, we're invited, and it's going to last all night due to location. The real question is, how are we going to pull it off?"

Payton's entire face lit up. She didn't even care that it was at Stacie's parents' lake house. She heard two things: "all night" and "Reece." Her eyes sparkled, and she tried to contain her excitement. She already knew, just like Stacie, that she was going to pull her friends Aubrey and Maddie into her plan. Schedule a sleepover night, but one without raising any concerns. It wasn't unusual for them to spend the night at each other's houses, but Payton felt the need to secure that date. She thought if she had a viable reason in place for being gone, and her parents checked up on her, all would pan out.

"I feel like I should come up with something more than a sleepover, like a sleepover for a reason, to ensure that the date is blocked."

"Whatever you think will work, do it. Anything in particular in mind?" Reece asked.

"Maybe an opening of a movie, like we plan a sleepover specifically because we're going to said movie." Payton looked down at her legs, which were swinging back and forth as she sat on the edge of the tailgate.

"I think you're way overthinking it," Reece stated. "Just stick with the sleeping at Maddie's or Aubrey's and have them do the same. Worst-case scenario, you can always say miscommunication and you ended up at the wrong house."

Payton agreed that might the best way to go, if she couldn't come up with a viable excuse for the date in question. Lying to her parents made her nervous. But going to the party and spending extra time with Reece suddenly seemed worth it. She couldn't believe she'd have a whole night with him. The excitement and anticipation of being with him for so long was consuming her every thought. He was excited as well, but showed it differently than she did.

He'd already prepared his own groundwork. He'd be going fishing and four-wheeling for the weekend at Trevor's Dad's place, with Cody and a few other guys. If a group of boys were going, his dad would probably talk openly with the boys. They all had the same story and Reece had even pulled in Royce as backup. As an added bonus, Trevor had asked his dad if he would take them out hunting or at least to fish and ride the four-wheelers in the next few weeks. His dad not only agreed, but started making plans as well. Only downside that they could see, which wasn't a downside at all, was they'd be taking a boys' trip!

Reece's phone vibrated and a message flashed across the screen. Payton never asked who it was, but she was dying to find out. He never mentioned it, but tapped away, ending with the infamous DTB. They wrapped up lunch and sat and visited for a few minutes in the bed of his truck. She didn't want to leave, and truth be told, he didn't either. Sitting in between his legs, his arms wrapped around her, she wished the party was already here. His warm breath hit the back of her neck. She took her hands and ran them softly through the back of his hair. Turning around to face him, she stared into his green eyes. He pulled her closer and kissed her. She kissed him back. Her phone broke the momentum this time; alarm, time was up. She had to go. Seeing him during the week always made her happy, but leaving him was always hard. She never dreamed, at her age, she could feel the way she did. One last kiss and another, and then one more, before Reece finally peeled himself away and said goodbye.

Chapter 19

Party Buzz

All over campus, everyone was whispering about Stacie's party. Who was going, how they were going to cover, what they'd take, and how lit it would be. It was going to be the go-to party of the year, and if you were invited and weren't going, you should, and if you weren't invited, you were a loser. The plan Stacie and Sophie had put in place was in motion. Stacie's parents had mentioned on more than one occasion that they didn't mind if Sophie stayed over again, but had also asked if Sophie's parents had missed her yet, since she'd been at their house so often lately.

"It seems like she's never at home. Don't get me wrong; I love it when you're home. I just want Sophie to clear it with her parents, that's all," Stacie's mom had mentioned more than once.

Sophie's parents were starting to quiz her as well.

"Isn't Stacie's mom going to wonder why you're always over there? Why don't you guys take a break this weekend from each other? You were there last weekend."

"Nah, mom. We don't want to take a break, and yes, I was over there, but to be fair, Stacie was here as well. We broke it up, remember?"

It was true. The girls had been taking turns. On occasion they'd stayed at Stacie's twice in a row, but by and large it had been spread out between the two households.

"Well, as long as her mom doesn't mind, I'm all right with it," Sophie's mother had replied to yet another request for a sleepover. "Just don't overstay your welcome!"

Time dragged by at first as they waited for the night of the party, but the last few weeks seemed to fly by. Stacie didn't quite feel prepared. Nerves maybe? Sophie wasn't nervous at all, just excited. She was throwing her first party without adult supervision; her parents would absolutely kill her if they knew, but there was no reason for them to find out. For a brief second she felt guilty, but pushed the guilt and thoughts of disappointing her parents out of her head. The buzz and excitement was contagious. Payton, Aubrey, and Maddie couldn't contain themselves either, especially since they had learned to tolerate Stacie.

Everyone had noticed that Aubrey was in an amazing mood. It wasn't too hard to figure out why, and asking her confirmed it. Cody either texted or called her on a regular basis, and they had now been on multiple dates. He'd already asked her if she would go with him to Stacie's lake party. She was beside herself and w*ell duh, yeah, of course* she was going with him! Though it had never officially been discussed, and she hadn't said it out loud, they were clearly officially dating. No one needed to say anything anyway; it was understood. Aubrey, who was finally blissfully happy for the first time ever, felt zero guilt about what she was doing, party-wise, as long as Cody was doing it with her. Payton and Maddie were happy for her. She deserved to have a good guy in her life. Maddie was just along for the ride. Keeping her options open, she'd say. Dating, but not anyone serious. That was code for "didn't have a boyfriend but really wanted one." Who knew, maybe she'd meet someone at the party. Stranger things had happened. Look at Aubrey and Cody; there was hope for her as well!

"Whose house are we sleeping at tonight?" Aubrey asked. "I'm getting confused and can't keep up. Do you want to crash at mine?"

"Let's do yours tomorrow. We could double-date. That's easy and would actually help with our cover for later. Maddie, you can join us if you like, we could go eat and hit a movie," Payton offered.

"I hate being the third freaking wheel!" Maddie whined. "I don't know."

"Do you want me to see if Cody can bring someone with him?"

"Hell no, Aubrey! Sorry, not snapping at you, that just makes me feel like a dating loser."

"Don't knock those blind dates; look at Aubrey now." Payton pointed to their friend, grinning from ear to ear. "She's got her man!"

"True. True." Aubrey laughed. "It's all good."

"I'm not ready for a blind date, but maybe if they want to bring some single dudes to the party, that will work." Maddie sat down on Payton's bed next to Aubrey. "I am happy for you. Slightly jealous, but happy."

"Awe, thanks friend," Aubrey replied, hugging her around the neck. "We'll get you hooked up, no worries."

"I think I might like to work that out for myself, kinda. I think. I don't know, maybe."

Payton jumped in between the two of them on the bed, pushing them both over. "Girl power. What are friends for? We'll find you the perfect guy and make it happen!"

Mrs. Phillips stopped at Payton's bedroom door and smiled. At times the girls still looked so young, and at others they seemed so mature. Girl power. She hadn't heard her girl say that in so long. It warmed her heart to hear those words come out of her daughter's mouth. The three had been friends forever it seemed, and here they were, teens, and still getting along.

"Can I get you girls anything?" she finally asked.

Payton thought about it for a second. "Actually, if it's not too much trouble, if you're cooking, can we have your lasagna for dinner and some of that awesome banana pudding?"

Mrs. Phillips looked surprised. "Sure. I'd love to make you that. Just like old times." She turned to walk away, but stopped and asked a question first. "You're not going out tonight with Reece, date night and all?"

Payton threw her arms around her friends. She knew Royce was in town and Reece was going to dinner with his family, but her mother did not know that yet— a perfect opportunity to help execute and further the plan while pleasing everyone.

"Actually, Mom, we thought we'd have a girls' night in. Can the girls stay over?"

She almost didn't need to ask in moments like these; the answer was automatically a yes. Mrs. Phillips could hardly stand it. A house full of girls, how fun! Parker, on the other hand, who had suddenly appeared by her side, rolled his eyes, shook his head, and took off down the stairs.

"Lasagna and banana pudding, then. Perfect!" Mrs. Phillips grinned from ear to ear as she turned and followed him down the stairs.

Chapter 20

Party Jitters

The night before the party had finally arrived, and everyone's nerves were on edge with the anticipation of pulling off their plans, not getting caught, and wanting to have a great time. Payton lay in bed tossing and turning, counting sheep in her head, and when that didn't work, she counted them backwards. But in between the sheep, images of Reece popped in her head and all she could think about was how much fun they'd have spending so much time together—a first, for sure. Nothing could calm her down enough to sleep. Great! She'd look like crap. Tired and dark circles under her eyes were going to be a given. *Note to self,* she thought, *work in a nap before going to Aubrey's.* Feelings of guilt about deceiving her parents started to sneak into her head again; they weren't being pushed aside as easily as before, and this bothered her conscience. Since she'd never given them a reason to doubt her, they didn't act concerned at all that she'd be sleeping over at Aubrey's the next night. Knowing that she was blatantly lying to them was weighing heavily on her. Payton convinced herself it would be the only time that she would do such a thing; it was a special occasion, and this type of opportunity to spend the whole evening with your boyfriend and friends rarely occurred. This lie was a one-time deal. Payton told herself whatever she needed to in the moment to justify her actions and make herself feel better. It wasn't working. Nerves were starting to get to her. She needed a distraction, and reached for her phone.

Payton: U up?

Nothing from Reece; he must be sleeping. She went to the next person on her panic list, Aubrey.

Payton: U up?

To her relief, she received a response almost immediately.

Aubrey: Thought I heard my phone. Yes. U OK?
Payton: Can't sleep. Too excited.
Aubrey: I'm awake now ☺
Payton: Was feeling nervous for a second. So stupid!
Aubrey: I know, right.
Payton: But I'm over it.
Aubrey: It will be fun.
Payton: True.
Aubrey: Seriously though, we don't have to go.
Payton: Are you CRAZY? ☺ ☺ ☺
Aubrey: Right! What am I thinking?
Aubrey: I've been stashing snacks.
Payton: I haven't done that yet.
Payton: But have cash for store.
Aubrey: Cash is good.

Aubrey: Do you want me to grab an extra ice chest?

Payton: No, we're good.

Aubrey: OK. Get some rest. Think of Reece.

Payton: Thanks. You too.

Aubrey was right. It was going to be fun. She wasn't going to get caught, and she didn't ever have to do it again, at least that's what she kept telling herself. If it was going to be so much fun, then why was she so scared?

Payton calmed herself down enough that she started to feel better, less anxious and worried. As soon as she thought about Reece holding her and laughing with her, she knew she wanted to go to that party more than anything else in the world. She didn't want him going there without her, that was for sure! Reece, girls, party, beer, oh no way. She wanted to be the one by his side, as she should be, she was his girl! That crazy thing called love; they didn't call it crazy young love for nothing. It made you do things you wouldn't normally do, like lie to your parents, cut class, worry constantly about your looks, have your friends cover for you, and worry over texts, phone calls, and when you weren't together. Now, with an opportunity like this coming up, Payton could fix the tension they'd had over the miscommunication with the texts and phone calls that also had been weighing on her mind. That was it, the peace she needed to finally fall asleep. Fixing the tension between her and Reece. She had the perfect opportunity to cement their relationship. Who knew what a night like that night could hold? Unlimited possibilities. Payton lay back down, pulled the covers over her head, and finally drifted off to sleep.

Reece: Good morning babe, love you. Can't wait to see you today!

Payton read the message on her phone as soon as she woke up. Her fingers tapped away the same type of response, love and excitement about seeing him. She felt groggy. Tired. She lay back down for another half hour. Her mom stuck her head in the door to check on her. She was still under the blanket, breathing, not moving, but alive. Forcing herself out of bed, she reached for her phone a second time. Reece had texted again. Short but sweet. His messages made her smile and reminded her of how excited she really was about the party. Cody had texted Aubrey, pretty much the same type of message, and she had sent a screen shot of the text to Payton. *Perfect,* thought Payton. She'd show her mom a portion of Cody's text. Knowing that Aubrey was giddy, her mom would think they were doing the double-date and girl talk thing, and would give Payton one more thing to convince her mom not to check on them later that evening. Payton emerged in the kitchen.

"I was beginning to wonder if you were coming down," Mrs. Phillips said softly.

Handing her mom her phone, Payton pointed to the screen shot of Cody's message.

"Is this not the cutest thing ever?" She giggled. "I think Aubrey is in love."

Waiting for her mom to read it, she added, "I'm so glad we're double-dating tonight. And yes, I know, text you when we get back to Aubrey's."

Mrs. Phillips' grin spread over her face. She was happy for Aubrey. She had a boy she liked who seemed like a good kid. She topped off their coffee and asked about Maddie.

"Isn't Maddie going to Aubrey's this evening as well? Won't she be uncomfortable, third wheel and all that?"

Payton had already thought of that. "Nah, mom, it's not like that anymore. Everyone goes out in groups. She'll be in our group. Plus Cody had mentioned that some of his friends were joining us at the movies. We're just going to a movie and to eat." She took a sip of coffee, but it was too hot and she spat it back into her cup.

"Now that was gross!" Her mom laughed.

"Sorry. Burnt myself!" Putting the final touch on the conversation, she mentioned something else. "You never know, one of Cody's friends might hit it off with Maddie. Wouldn't that be something?!"

The conversation turned to the movie, who was starring in it, and the author who wrote the book. Payton was feeling confident that her preplanning to pull off the fake sleepover would be enough. Fortunately a phone call took her mom out of the kitchen. She was home free!

***

Stacie's mom had quizzed her extensively about her plans, especially since they were going to be gone and Stacie would be at her friend's house for two nights. Did Sophie's parents mind? She insisted on verifying, but Sophie showed Mrs. Wiggins a text from her mom. It said: *Stacie is welcome any time. It's not a problem at all; we never know she's here. Have fun at the game. Go Bucks!* It was a real text, but Sophie didn't mention it pertained to Friday night; the party was going to be held on Saturday night. Mrs. Wiggins assumed it was for both nights and the girls didn't correct her.

> **Pattie Wiggins**: Thank you so much! You have my cell if you need me. Stacie has money and knows the rules. She knows how to reach us, as do you. I owe you one!

Stacie and Sophie had said their goodbyes to the Wiggins and headed to Sophie's house to spend the night. Their night had been long and restless as well. Excitement and nerves had consumed them. Stacie had decided she'd impose two mandatory rules or there would be no entry to the property: one, all keys were to be handed over once their vehicles were parked, and no one could leave once they'd arrived; and two, no social media pictures unless it was Finsta (a secret, not-so-secret social media site). How she would enforce that, the social media part, she didn't have a clue.

"That's going to be impossible to monitor," Sophie argued.

"Well, they're not going to have a choice," Stacie insisted. "Can you imagine what my brothers would do if a pic slipped out and they saw it? Or someone they knew got wind of this party? OMG. I can't even think about that!" She brushed her hair out of her face. "The pics would show we were here; the roads, out there, are so dangerous—twisty and winding all the way up the hills."

"What if you make a deal with them: don't post pictures except to your private accounts or leave?" Sophie suggested.

"I don't know. Maybe. But what if they don't listen? We may not have a choice but to take them or they can't come in. I'd be DEAD, no kidding, DEAD, if this leaks. I don't feel like dying yet. You?"

Sophie shook her head. Stacie was right. But how do you enforce a no-pic rule except to certain sites? They packed their overnight bags for Laurel's house. Laurel had been over to Sophie's house a few times, knew her aunt, and was actually going to the party. They could all cover for each other if needed. They loaded up a bag of snacks and their cash so they could stop at the store on the way to buy more junk food.

"We need a semi-nice thug." Stacie laughed. "Is there such a thing? Maybe an oversized dope, nice, but threatening, like one of my brothers!"

Sitting on the bed, Stacie wracked her brain. Butterflies were starting to fill her stomach. Her brothers' faces flashed in her mind's eye, and she could hear her dad's voice from time to time. The party would be a blast, she told herself. The best of the year! Why was she having doubts? Sophie sat down on the bed next to her and put an arm around her shoulder.

"It's not too late, you know. We can cancel this thing, tell people your dad or your mom came back sick, something like that."

It was so tempting to bail, but there was no way

Stacie was going to back out now. Her reputation was on the line. Too many people were talking about the party; it was going to be lit, and she knew she'd have fun once she got going! Relax. Just relax, she told herself. Her phone buzzed. Perfect timing.

> **Trevor**: OMG babe, you ready?
> **Stacie:** Oh yeah!
> **Trevor:** It will be epic. Love you
> **Stacie:** Yes it will! Love you too!

"Well that's that, then." Stacie put her phone in her purse. "We've got a lot to do. Let's go!"

Chapter 21

Party Time

It took nearly two-and-a-half hours to get to the lake. Nice and secluded, no locals to worry about. Everyone invited knew that they had to stay for the night, no exceptions, and upon arrival Stacie had decided that Trevor or Cody would stand with a bucket and all keys would have to be turned in as soon as vehicles were parked. Safety measures: ensuring that once they arrived, they didn't drive. The girls had stuck to their plan, providing food and sodas, but hadn't provided alcohol. However, they weren't stupid, knowing kids would show up with alcohol all by themselves. Private invitations on social media with the rules and directions had been axed at the last minute. If they were leaked, she'd be busted for sure; a paper trail wasn't worth the risk. Everyone relied on word of mouth, coded texts, and phone calls. They climbed higher and higher as they drove up the long, twisted driveway to the cabin. Between the trees, the height of the location, and the lake below them, the view was spectacular. The lake house, a massive stone-and-log cabin, was two stories, complete with a wraparound porch that extended all the way around the house. Picnic areas were located on the east and west sides of the cabin, complete with fire pit and grills, and both sides had views overlooking the lake. A rock path led down the bluff to the dock and boat ramp. A covered area housed the boats and water toys, too many to count, and a boathouse sat to the left of it. Impressive to say the least, especially for a secondary home; most people never lived in anything as beautiful in their whole lives, let alone vacationed at home in such luxury.

"It's beautiful up here," Sophie said as they pulled up to the house. "Absolutely beautiful."

"Thanks." Stacie knew it was a one-in-a-million location. It was her dad's future retirement home. "This is my dad's dream place. Not so much my mom's."

"She doesn't like this place?" Sophie asked, shocked. "Really?"

"She likes to vacation here, but not so much live. Too far away from town, she says."

As soon as she entered the house, Stacie disarmed the security system. Unlike their main residence, her parents couldn't access the system from their devices. Nor were they notified if something was amiss. Just an old-style, regular system had come with the property when they had purchased it. Advanced for then, it had cameras, but not like the ones at their main house, where when the alarm went off the security company was notified, and they received *the call*. Her dad had said on numerous occasions that he'd like to have the alarm system at the lake house updated. Fortunately for Stacie, he hadn't done it yet. Once the alarm was dismantled, Stacie opened the wooden shutters and the windows, and cool air immediately rushed through the house. For the first time, Stacie was glad she hadn't listened to her nerves and bailed on the party.

"Surely they'll stay out of here, right?" It wasn't a real question. Stacie was praying people wouldn't trash her parents' cabin.

"We know these guys, they're our friends," Sophie reassured her. "There's really no reason for them to come in the house."

"Well, let's put our stuff in our rooms." Stacie smiled. "I'm taking the master, but you can pick any other room you like."

Each room had a fireplace and its own bathroom. It didn't matter which room Sophie picked; she would be more than comfortable. Both girls sent random texts to their parental units. They each waited for responses. Once they received them, breathing easier, they cranked up the music and started to prepare for the party. Sheets pulled off the furniture, counters wiped down, sodas iced, and extra chests filled with ice for whatever people brought with them to drink. Snacks were ready to be put into bowls, wood placed in the fire pits outside, and chairs set out around sitting areas. It was safe to say that things were coming together nicely. A truck pulled into the driveway, startling both girls. Trevor and Cody had shown up early to help. Stacie had never been happier to see that face. Somehow he made her feel safe.

"Wow! You can't hide money," Cody joked.

"Hey babe, looks great, what can we do to help?" Trevor asked.

Trevor picked her up, held her at eye level and

kissed her on the lips before setting her back down again. Cody, still shocked that Trevor had a girl like that, shook his head and walked over to the top of the bluff to look at the view. Sophie joined him.

"Bet there's some good fishing out there!"

"Yeah. That's what Stacie says," Sophie agreed.

"Now I wish Ryan or Reece were here already, but they'll be here later." He smirked. "You know we love to fish."

Cody took his cap off and scratched his head. "How long have you and Ryan been dating, anyway?"

"Almost a year." Sophie grinned. "And yes, I do, the fishing part. You? Bringing someone or meeting someone?"

A smile crossed Cody's face. "Meeting someone here. Aubrey. Do you know her?"

Sophie nodded. She had met Aubrey several times and liked her. Aubrey was easy to get along with and was cute. Trevor and Stacie joined them. Trevor also made a comment about the fishing. Stacie offered to have them over when her dad was there, take them out on the boat and fish to their hearts' content.

"How did you get this girl?" Cody joked. "Hot. Likes football, Dad's *the* Coach, and she's a dudes' dude. Too good to be true."

"Well, he won't have me for long if I'm dead!" Stacie flopped down in Trevor's lap. "We've got to pull this off with no hitches. None!"

Getting back to work, they finished setting up. Stereo outside worked. Didn't matter anyway, they'd pull a truck over and attach an aux cord to play their own music. The ice chests were placed by the fire pits and outside sitting areas. Stacie hoped this would help keep people out of the house. Trevor and Cody set up two tents in the area to show everyone where to start setting up their tents. It was going so well; nothing could go wrong!

"Grab that bucket over there, the big one from under the outside faucet on the left," Stacie instructed. "It's for everyone's keys. No exceptions."

"How are we going to do that?" Sophie asked.

"I'll do it," Trevor offered. "As soon as they park, I'll take their keys. Have them put them in the bowl themselves."

Perfect. They were all on the same page. They went through the cabin with a checklist and confirmed everything had been done. It was about that time, party time, and everything was ready. The boys picked a bedroom and hit the shower, and the girls went to their rooms and did the same. Casual attire, yes, but hair and makeup still needed to be perfect; after all, girls will still be girls. A call from her mom couldn't have come at a more perfect time. Stacie was as calm as could be. Small talk and lots of questions about the game, complete with a request for her dad to text the final score, sealed the conversation as a success. No nerves to be found. Excitement and adrenaline rushed through Stacie's body. Now ready, she couldn't wait for the party to begin!

Pouring food into the bowls, Sophie placed the snacks on the tables outside, another deterrent from the house. Texts were coming in left and right. Were they on the right track? Did they miss the turn? Should they bring anything special? Stacie finally handed her phone to Sophie.

"Unless my dad or mom texts, please handle these."

"Got it!"

Cody set up by the main gate. As cars pulled in, he directed them over to Trevor and the parking area. Once parked, Trevor stuck out the bowl. Keys in the bowl or don't stay, that was the rule. Surprisingly, no one seemed to object. Once parked, most put up tents or makeshift tents. Some more like windbreakers for ball games, but once a sleeping bag was thrown inside, all looked like they were functional. Others set up pallets in the beds of their trucks, and some said they'd sleep in the back seat of their cars. It was coming together better than Stacie had even imagined. It was starting to look like a camping resort by eight p.m. By nine p.m. it was hard to find a parking place. It was apparent that more people than had been invited had shown up. Payton, Aubrey, and Maddie, had followed Reece. Reece had a cab full of guys, Dustin, Gavin, Larry, Dolton, Ryan, and Mick; they all played football together. London and Zoe arrived shortly after Payton and Reece. Gavin was waiting nervously for her. Needless to say, they all arrived safely.

"I thought you got lost. Scared me." Gavin leaned into her window and kissed her cheek.

"You are the sweetest!" London grabbed his face and placed a kiss on his lips.

Gavin jumped into the back seat of her car and

rode with her over to the parking area. Stacie checked her watch. Surely arrivals would start to slow down. Trevor jumped up on the tailgate of Reece's truck and made an announcement.

"Guys, find a tree."

Everyone laughed.

"Girls. You can use the bathroom, lower level, by the kitchen on the right, in the house. That's the visitors' or guests' powder room." He raised his hands in the air and quieted everyone down. "Seriously. Have a good time, but don't do anything stupid. You break it, you pay for it and you'll have answer to her dad for damages and we all know who that is . . . Coach." Trevor took a breath. "My advice, stay out of the house."

"Thank you, babe, appreciate you looking out for me," Stacie whispered. "Glad you handled that."

"No problem. It's what I do." Trevor pecked her on the lips, popped a can, and handed it to her. "Here ya go. Ladies first."

Stacie reached out and took the beer. She didn't ask where it had come from or if Trevor had brought it with him. The truth was, she didn't want to know. She hadn't brought it, right? She was only going to sip it. Payton and Reece walked over to where Trevor, Stacie, Sophie, Ryan, Gavin, and London had gathered around one of the fire pits by the bluff. Aubrey and Cody soon joined them. Teens were in small groups all over the property, having fun and talking among themselves. Music was blasting, but no one cared. There were no neighbors to be had. Sophie was right. People managed to bring their own liquor and beer in, and no one said a word. That wasn't her problem; she didn't bring it, buy it, suggest it, or even say it was OK. Drinks of all kinds were flowing and despite having soda available, the only time they seemed to drink it was with the liquor. Some of the boys had made a drinking game out of throwing horseshoes, and a round of beer pong was next. A team of girls, including Payton and her friends, challenged them to a round. Drinking. Laughing. Seemed like fun, at first.

"Every time we're supposed to drink, let's not," Payton giggled.

"Sounds like a deal to me." Stacie laughed, enjoying the challenge and the thought of tricking the guys.

Beers were opened, and Gavin explained the rules. The boys allowed the girls to go first. It didn't go as planned. They couldn't fake taking the sips of drinks; they got caught up in the fun, and the boys had marked the cans with sharpies. Time was flying by. And after a while Stacie had no idea who was outside, who was in the cabin, or what was going on at her own party anymore. A drinking game consumed the whole group, which turned into a game of truth or dare. Laughter, sometimes bitterness, and the occasional temper flared. Payton didn't care. It was late, she was feeling ecstatic, and Reece hadn't left her side. He slipped his arm around her waist and kissed the back of her neck. Nestling into him, she felt the warmth of his body on hers. She'd been sipping more than she'd realized. Between the laugher and the fun, she hadn't been keeping track of how easily it could go down. Reece sat down in a chair and pulled her into his lap. Payton didn't question it, automatically sitting down on his knee. The music blared out across the bluff, and the louder it got, the more fun they seemed to have, as the kids' voices echoed the words of all the rappers and the artists that they played. The no-pic rule didn't last; but looking back, why had Stacie thought that it would? Teens and their phones; inevitable they'd start pulling out their phones and snapping pics for their streaks and social media favorites. #litparty #beerdoesabodygood #litnight #whereru #bestnightever

A trash can full of party punch had finally surfaced. A concoction of whatever liquor, juices or sodas they could find, a bad deal for everyone. No one really knew what was in it; they never did. Disguised with anything to make the flavor doable, most of them downed it. Sophie poured plastic cups and left them on the table, but soon Zeke was handing them out. Payton's hand reached for one of the infamous plastic red cups. It tasted like cotton candy and went down like Kool-Aid. She had never felt so happy and in love in her life. Invincible. Guilt—what's that? No adult supervision. Feeling intoxicated without knowing it. Sitting in her hot boyfriend's lap, while he whispered how much he loved her and wanted her, all at a party she was invited to with him. The Coach's daughter's party at that . . . Payton never wanted to go home. Stacie's favorite song came on, and a group of girls jumped up and started dancing in a big circle. Reece and the others were watching and hollering, egging them on. Some of the guys joined them, but most just watched. Payton stood up to join in, but Reece pulled her back onto his lap.

"No. Stay here with me," he said. "I want to do this."

She never asked what. He slipped his hand up inside of her shirt and rubbed her back. Payton smiled and leaned back into him, glad she'd sat back down. The air was nice and cool, feeling good on her skin as he rubbed her back. Happy, Payton turned around and kissed Reece. He kissed her back just as hard. Their mouths locked together as they kissed in sync with each other effortlessly, barely able to breathe. Reece's hands started to roam. Payton grabbed his hand, stopped him, and whispered in his ear.

"A lot of PDA. Not right here."

Reece kissed her again and then checked his watch. It was still a tad early to disappear unnoticed. Holding her face in his hands and staring into her beautiful brown eyes, he took a deep breath and pushed her out of his lap. Puzzled, she stood up. He ran his fingers through her hair, kissed the back of her neck, and whispered in her ear.

"In a bit, we'll disappear and do whatever we want. OK?"

Payton, not thinking about the words he was actually saying, immediately nodded. She couldn't wait to spend alone time with Reece, but wasn't thinking literally about a thing. Here they were, only an hour away from her usual curfew, and she still had all night. Any nervousness she had about breaking rules had long disappeared. Blissfully in love, she couldn't wait to slip away.

Cody cracked open another beer, and everyone gathered around their host. Laughter and voices continued to echo around the bluff, but no one cared, no noise violation to worry about that night. Trevor lifted his cup and kissed his girl.

"Can I have your attention please?" He laughed. "Hey, for just a second," he yelled again when no one seemed to stop talking the first time.

Reece offered his assistance. "He's trying to saying something here, shut up!"

One by one the voices lowered, and all eyes were upon Trevor.

"I just want to thank my girl for pulling off this amazing night. Is this fun or what?"

Everyone hollered and cheered, and applause broke out for Stacie. People were truly enjoying themselves, and for the most part no one seemed to be acting like an idiot; no fights to be had. Drinking, yeah, they were doing that, but Stacie had convinced herself they were doing that responsibly. She was wrong. Not one of them thought twice about being a minor and breaking the law, deceiving people, let alone the effects of the alcohol itself. The party, in her mind and everyone else's, was a huge success. They'd gotten away with it; pulled it off. If only they'd known.

Chapter 22

Stay Out of the House

No matter how hard Stacie, Trevor, Sophie, or Ryan tried to keep people from lingering in the house, it wasn't working. Kids were everywhere, and that included upstairs. Most were just talking and hanging out, but some were looking for areas of the house where they could hook up; hardly unusual for teen gatherings, but even Stacie didn't want to deal with any of that in her parents' cabin. Something inside her allowed her to block out what they might be doing if she knew they were outside and she didn't have to deal with it. But in her parents' house, different story, get out. Things out of place or damages were constantly on her mind, knowing she couldn't possibly duplicate everything in time the way her mom had left it. The housekeeper wouldn't be back until her mom called her, and if she noticed too many things out of order, Stacie's mom could expect a call from her. Stacie needed them out of the house. She went from room to room and told them they had to go outside; some listened, some couldn't care less. It seemed that every time teens gathered, there were always people who brought people. Those were the ones who didn't care; they didn't really know anyone anyway, except the person they tagged along with in the first place.

Payton didn't have to worry about hooking up or hanging out with guys or finding a boyfriend; she was with her boyfriend, and her best friend Aubrey had Cody by her side. Maddie was hanging with them as well, talking to Dustin. The fire pits were awesome since the air had chilled, perfect for a camp night, and another round of truth or dare had been started. Stacie was freaking out as she tried to monitor the house. The thought of locking it up crossed her mind, but the girls were running in and out of the bathroom, and the kitchen and her bedroom were in there, and she decided against it.

"I wish they'd at least stay the hell out of the house, that's all!" she snapped. "It's not a lot to ask!"

Cody handed her a drink of something in a cup. Lifting the cup to her nose, she drew in a big whiff of something sweet: trash-can punch.

"Relax. It's your party. Remember?" He laughed.

Stacie threw her head back and downed the sweet-tasting punch. It went down with ease.

Cody pulled Aubrey closer and asked if she'd like some as well.

"What is it?" Aubrey asked.

"Honestly, I don't know. Some concoction that Justin threw together—trash-can punch. You know, anything they were able to get their hands on. Taste it, it's good."

Aubrey shook her head and pointed to the half drank, warm beer in her hand. She'd made that one last for over an hour. Not liking the taste, but trying to fit in, she hung on to it. She knew better. Trash-can punch: good going in, nasty coming out and that was only one-way—puking.

"No thanks, still drinking," she held up her beer.

Cody didn't pressure her to try it, and she was grateful for that. But he didn't slow down on his, either. Between the kids who had snuck alcohol or paid older friends with fake IDs to buy them alcohol, they'd combined quite an assortment of liquor and beer. No one was concerned about how much they'd consumed. No need. There wasn't a single threat of anyone coming home or breaking up the party. The party was lit, all that, that's for sure, everyone on social media said so!

It didn't take long before one of the beer pong games was interrupted. Josh fell onto the makeshift table and knocked all the drinks over. Should have been their first clue to shut it down, but it wasn't. The boys were getting rowdy and the girls were getting crazy. The partying and laughter didn't seem to slow down. A game of hide-and-seek broke out, but as soon as Stacie realized they weren't listening to the rules and going too close to the bluff, she ended it. Too bad, because that was fun!

Reece grabbed Payton's hand and led her toward the tent that he had put up for them to crash in that night. Cody and Aubrey were sitting outside the tent, but that didn't stop Reece and Payton from moving past them and crawling inside. Neither one of them had been keeping track of how much they'd drank. Consumed with the party and hanging out with their friends, with zero supervision or the worry of a curfew, they both had more than they thought they'd had. Reece pulled open the canopy, letting the breeze flow through the mesh netting of the roof. The air was cool, which felt good on Payton's face as she lay down on the makeshift pallet he'd made out of sleeping bags. Muffled voices outside could be heard, but they suddenly sounded so distant. Reece lay next to her and moved her long dark hair that had fallen over her face to one side. Grasping her face in his hands, he leaned forward and kissed her. She kissed him back just as eagerly.

Within minutes they both forgot that they were at a party at all, lost in each other. Hands roaming, mouths barely breaking apart from each other's, the two teens found themselves in a position they had never been in before. They were alone, in love, and worst of all, without understanding it, totally impaired. Neither one of them was thinking clearly; intoxicated, having the time of their lives, they felt invincible. Feelings, emotions, and being wrapped up in each other, they had no reason to stop a single thing that they were doing; every touch felt amazing to both of them as their hormones raged. Zero threat of anyone walking through a door, and in that moment, if they had, they wouldn't have heard them anyway. Payton's heart was pounding as she continued to reciprocate each and every move that Reece made. Between the two it was a disastrous, heated, unstoppable situation, until Payton finally gasped for air.

A glimpse of the dark blue sky through the window of the tent above her, the stars scattered as if just for her, the muffled voices, the smell of the fire, and then all of a sudden the alcohol that she had consumed hit her like a freight train. It was like an oven in the tent; no longer cool. So hot that condensation had formed on the sides. Her head was spinning, and she couldn't breathe. Nauseous, she felt as if she might throw up right then and there on Reece. She tried to push him off her body, but her arms felt like jelly; no strength in them at all. Reece's mouth clamped once again over hers, still in the moment and unaware she now felt ill. He kept touching her and kissing her. She tried to push the nauseous feeling deep down inside, and moved her head to one side to avoid Reece's kisses. Reece kissed her neck, as Payton tried to locate any cool air that might blow through the tent. Unaware of what was going on, his hands continued to roam her body. Uninhibited, she no longer knew where her safe zones were. Pushing the limits without thinking, Reece tested the waters with his wandering hands and Payton didn't think to stop him. Spinning out of control, both of them, faster and faster with no time to think. When cool air finally hit her leg, Payton realized her clothes were half on and half off. Shouldn't she have felt her buttons being undone or her zipper go down? But she didn't remember them being undone. She did remember trying not to puke. Reece's pants were about the same, half on and half off. Had she done that, taken off his clothes, or had he assisted? Suddenly embarrassed, not knowing what she'd done, fear and panic swept over her. She turned her head, but he turned his with hers, thinking they were merely changing positions, not knowing for a single second that she wasn't prepared for the unexpected situation that they both found themselves caught up in. Turning her head again, this time with force, she muttered the words she thought would make it all OK.

"I need some air," Payton mumbled. "Not yet."

Her voice so faint, he didn't hear her. The weight of his body, suddenly like a ton of bricks on top of her, no longer felt loving but suffocating, and the cozy comfort of the tent became confining, as it seemingly spun around and around as she gasped for air. Trying with all her might to push him off her chest was impossible; she was tiny, and all of a sudden he seemed like dead weight. Continuing to kiss her and softly whisper kind things to her, including how much he loved her, she tried to swallow the vomit that was crawling up her throat. Swallowing, she pushed it back down into her stomach and hoped that she wouldn't puke on him. For some bizarre reason, her eyes caught sight of a drop of condensation on the side of the tent, and she watched it drip down the wall. Feeling violently ill, trying to talk, but realizing he couldn't hear her, she felt helpless. He couldn't hear her, and she could barely talk anyway.

"I need some air," she repeated for what seemed like the hundredth time.

He loved her, he said. She knew that, but in that moment, she didn't care. She felt sick, incredibly ill, and needed some cool, fresh air. Where was the cool air? And why weren't the words that she wanted to say forming in her mouth and coming out?

"I love you, baby," he said again.

She couldn't say them back and she didn't care right then. "I'm going to puke."

He hadn't heard her; her voice was barely a whisper. For all he knew, she'd said she loved him too. She had no idea her voice was so muffled. Slurring her words due to the amount of alcohol she'd consumed, she was making no sense at all. Looking down, Payton could tell by the way they were positioned what they were about to do. Panicking, she kicked her legs, but they barely moved. Why didn't her body respond to what her brain was telling it to do? She was scared and her arms pushed Reece as hard as she could, but she had no idea her strength wasn't there, and Reece, impaired as well, didn't pay the attention that he normally would have to her petition to stay away from areas that she was uncomfortable with at that time.

"I'm not ready," she thought she'd said out loud. "Not yet."

"I'm not ready," she said again and again. "Not yet."

But he hadn't heard her earnest pleas. Fumbling with their clothing and lost in clouded judgment, her voice was truly muffled and barely audible. Both slurring words, in love, he kissed her again, and didn't even notice that she hadn't kissed him back. Barely able to breathe, as she concentrated on not throwing up, Payton wasn't prepared for what happened next. What started out as the best night of her life was turning into a horrific nightmare. It felt like an eternity, but within seconds the entire situation had gotten away from her. Reece looked her in the eye before kissing her lips, and that's when the excruciating pain that she felt told her that they had done it; pain, penetration, they'd done it. IT! Between the pain, fear, and panic, Payton let out a gasp that sounded like a scream. Reece, fearing she'd startle others, placed his hand momentarily over her mouth and whispered words that she couldn't remember saying.

"It's OK, baby, it's what we wanted. Remember?"

But not yet, Payton thought, but didn't have the energy to say. Her head was spinning around and around and so was the tent. The sound of Reece's voice and the words he usually said brought her no comfort at all. His hot breath hit her face as his muffled words poured out of his mouth, but she didn't care. She wanted him off her, as the vomit travelled up her throat and pooled in her mouth, she could hold it in no longer.

"I love you, you know that, right?"

Frozen. In shock, sick to her stomach, and blaming herself, Payton didn't know what she was supposed to do. *What* had just happened? Images flashed through her mind, but she couldn't process the horrific scene. A familiar voice brought her back to reality.

"You all right?"

She wasn't all right; she was anything but all right. Reece stared at her for a second, then stood up and pulled up his jeans. Too much for Payton to comprehend, she rolled over and threw up in the tent.

Chapter 23

Aftermath

Reece stayed with Payton until she fell asleep. Carefully, so not to disturb her, he made his way outside. He needed some fresh air, get his head together. He wasn't feeling great about the way things ended; not his ideal first time with his girl puking in the tent afterward. A few people were still standing around talking, and a couple of Reece's friends were still up. But most of the partygoers had finally crashed. Some of them hadn't bothered finding their tents, hitting the back of their trucks, blankets making pallets, and coats thrown on top of them to stay warm. Taking a last glance at his phone, Reece noticed it was four-thirty in the morning. Trevor and Cody were planted on the porch steps.

"What's up?" Trevor asked as Reece approached.

"Nothing," Reese responded, realizing for the first time he was exhausted.

Trevor's phone was being passed around. Shot after shot of the party had already hit the social media scene. Pics were on snap stories and everyone was talking about the party. As soon as the drinking had kicked in, all inhibitions had disappeared. Stacie, despite her best intentions, had no way to control it as kid after kid pulled out their phones and started to take group photos, selfies and worse, sneaking photos of unsuspecting couples hooking up. Funny, they said, as they snapped away. The sneaking around part became a game, but the end result was the same—out on the net for the world to see. Stacie landed in a few of them; it was a move that she would later regret. Mouth dry and dehydrated, Reece grabbed a soda and downed it. It didn't taste good, too sweet. Cody suddenly grabbed Trevor's phone out of his hand.

"Who took that?" he asked.

Trevor leaned over, peeked at the photo, grabbed it, and deleted the pic before anyone could see it.

"Man, I have no idea!"

"What was it?" Reece asked.

Cody didn't say anything, and Trevor looked like a deer in headlights.

"Some girl acting stupid, that's all," Trevor replied.

Cody nodded. His stomach growled, reminding him he hadn't eaten anything all night; too busy drinking. Starting to feel sick himself, he needed to eat.

"I'm starving. Anything left to eat?"

Trevor pointed to a bag of chips. "Here, bro, you can have these." He handed Cody the bag, but not before grabbing a handful of chips first.

"So you and your girl snuck off for a while, taking care of business," Trevor playfully shoved Reece.

"Something like that," Reece laughed.

He didn't add to the conversation, but he didn't deny it, and that's all it took. Boy talk, locker-room style, took over. Admired by his friends, the conversation about his actions in the tent with Payton gave him additional bragging rights. The fact that he didn't deny any of their speculations about what they'd done in the tent fed the fire. Only thing he did right in that moment was to keep his mouth shut. The truth was, if he were going to be honest with himself, it wasn't exactly the way he wanted it to go down. Starting off fun, ending with his girl puking afterward. Nice. Not exactly something he was proud of.

"You and Stacie?"

"Nah, man. Like a zoo around here, keeping up with who was doing what and where. Don't touch this, don't touch that, I'm freaking tired!" Trevor took a swig of Coke. "I hope we get this place put back together in time before she has to be back, I mean. Can you imagine facing Coach after his lake house had been trashed?"

Creeping back into the tent, Reece laid next to Payton. He left the flap open to circulate the cool air, which helped with the stench of alcohol puke. She was out of it, which was likely for the best. She was going to feel like crap the next morning. Not having a clear head himself, he continued to push the entire thing out of his mind. Do-over. Do-over. Do-over! They'd redo that night. Even Reece wanted a do-over first time with his girl. Tired. Not feeling well or good about himself, Reece wished he were home in bed. He closed his eyes, but the tent started to spin. Lying on his back with his eyes wide open, Reece tried to fall asleep. It seemed to take forever, but finally he drifted off. The sound of people moving around alerted him that morning had arrived too soon. He felt like crap and could only imagine how bad Payton must feel.

Payton reached for her phone, but felt a person next to her instead. Rolling over, she came face-to-face with Reece. Images of the night before flashed through her mind and feelings of embarrassment and panic set in. Before she could compose herself or her thoughts, vomit rushed up her throat and into her mouth. Jumping to her feet, tripping over Reece, this time she managed to puke outside the tent. To her horror, groups of people stopped and stared. Reece suddenly appeared at her side.

"Still not doing good?"

What a stupid question, she thought. But was grateful her words hadn't popped out of her mouth. Payton shook her head and walked over to the picnic table and sat down on the bench. Despite how hard she tried not to, her eyes filled with tears and she started to cry. Reece slid his arm around her back, but to his surprise she jumped like a cat out of its skin. Even Payton noticed her own reaction.

"I'm sorry. I feel like crap."

The shocked look on his face hurt Payton, but not as much as it had surprised her. He pulled his arm away, embarrassed, and headed to the cabin to find a cool washcloth for her face. Confused by her sudden anguish from the night before, Payton didn't know how to feel. She racked her brain for answers about what had taken place. Did they have sex? Yes. But had she said yes? She didn't think so, but wasn't sure. She had asked him to stop, right? Had she? She couldn't remember, but she did remember saying she didn't feel well and could have sworn she'd said the words "not yet." She remembered that Reece had mentioned they'd talked about it that night. But despite how hard she tried, she just couldn't remember discussing the issue of having sex with him that evening. Was it really possible she didn't remember such a conversation—or worse, they didn't have one? Her head was throbbing, her stomach nauseous, and the flashbacks, combined with rapid-fire questions, wouldn't quit coming. Faster and faster they came. But the question that haunted her most was horrific; it was about the person she loved the most in the world, Reece. Why didn't he listen to her and wait? How much did they drink? Confused beyond belief, not knowing what to do or how to feel, ashamed and scared, Payton's body started shaking uncontrollably.

"OMG! Stop thinking," she whispered to herself. "Please don't overthink this thing; not here and not now!"

"Can I get you anything?" Reece asked as he handed her a cool cloth. "Are you OK?"

"I'm trying not to puke again," Payton replied. "But we probably need to talk."

Reece picked up her hand. For the first time ever, she wanted to pull hers away from his. That had never happened before. How had twenty-four hours changed everything? She felt dirty and confused, and wanted nothing more than to climb into a hot bath. Her hand hung limply in his, which he noticed immediately. Squeezing hers, trying to get a response, he leaned in toward her and kissed her on the cheek. Her long dark hair fell over her face, and Reece, as always, moved it to one side. Payton didn't flinch, but it felt weird. It would take her a moment to process. She didn't realize that *she didn't know how*. Even though her whole life her mom had said she could tell her anything, Payton felt she couldn't confide in her mom now. It wasn't true, but she wasn't prepared to test the waters. The disappointment she could only imagine she'd see in her mom's eyes: lying, drinking, and going to the party had put her in this mess in the first place. Not to mention her parents would hate Reece forever. She didn't want that; she loved him, and she wasn't convinced it wasn't both of their faults.

"I brought you a Sprite for your stomach." Aubrey handed her a cup of ice and soda. "They don't have any crackers."

Payton sipped the cool liquid and actually kept it down. She wanted to talk to her friends, but didn't dare tell them her first time hadn't gone according to her life plan. Maybe she wouldn't have to discuss it at all. Ever. Maybe they'd just think she was sick and that was that, hanging, too much punch. A thought popped in her head, and she almost had a panic attack on the spot. Fear swept over her. Did they use anything? She certainly wasn't prepared. Was he? Was she protected at all? Did he think about that, did they? Was anything about this really OK? Nothing was! White as a sheet and scared to death, Payton needed her mom.

Payton: Got your text. Love you too, can't wait to see you.
Mrs. Phillips: Did you have fun?

Payton: Yes

Mrs. Phillips: See you soon

"Babe, can I get you anything? Something to eat?" Reece asked.

Payton shook her head. "No thanks. Guess I know now why teens aren't supposed to drink." She took a deep breath. "I'm never drinking again. Ever!"

He nodded sympathetically. Hangovers. It would take at least a few more hours before she felt any better. Reece gently rubbed her back as she sat with her head hanging between her knees. Payton tried to act as normally as possible, but all she wanted was for him to leave her alone. Before last night, if she were sick, the thought of him taking care of her would have been the sweetest thing in the world. Now, if he would just leave her alone, she could actually breathe.

He kissed her softly on her forehead. "I love you," he said. "I want you to be OK."

As if forcing the words out of her mouth, she managed to say them back. "Love you too."

Reece took down their tent and loaded up their stuff so they could go home. Stacie walked the property with Sophie and Trevor. The damage was worse than she had feared. Trash. A broken bench, two fire pits that needed to be emptied or her parents would know they'd been there, unmade beds, bathrooms that needed to be cleaned, as did the kitchen. She'd received a text that her parents were on their way back into town. Trevor started gathering as many people as he could who weren't feeling like crap to pitch in and help clean up the place. There were a lot of teens who had overdone it and were feeling as ill as Payton, all vowing to never touch a drink again—that likely wouldn't last. If you arrived in a truck, bags of trash were going home with you; how you disposed of them was your problem. He pointed to Reece's truck; Reece nodded. That was fine. Load it up, he'd find somewhere to dump it on his way out of there. Aubrey, Maddie, and Payton were starting to get messages from their parents, as were most of them. Stalling for too much longer was going to be a problem. Stacie opted to allow her parents to believe random trespassers camped out on the broken bench, or weather had worn it down. She knew it didn't look weather-worn, so was going with random trespassers. The likelihood of them buying it, slim to none, but it was all she had to go with. The key would be getting the inside of the house to look as pristine as it had upon their arrival, and that was proving to be problematic. Overall it looked somewhat passable, if her mom didn't purposely inspect it, but to say it looked the way it had upon arrival was a stretch. It was clear that someone had been in the house; that's all there was to it. Stacie had a plan. The next time they went to the lake house, she would take a few friends and hopefully they could head up there early. Let her friends pick rooms; that way her mom wouldn't enter them. It just might work— doubtful, but possible.

Maddie, being a sweet friend, offered to drive Payton's car home. In her mind, she thought Payton would ride with Reece, and Aubrey would ride with her before meeting and switching drivers. She was shocked when Payton turned her down. Even more surprising was that Payton asked Maddie not to mention her offer to Reece.

"I won't," she promised. "But what's going on? Did you guys have a fight?"

Payton shook her head. It was the first time ever she wished that they had. Fights were easy. You got mad and you got over it. Hurt and confused, and she didn't know how to deal with that yet, especially the confused part. Something else she didn't know how to deal with: the situation or mess she was in. If she objected to having sex with someone she loved more than anything or anyone else in the world, did that count as being defiled? She couldn't even think the words, let alone say them out loud, that were trying to pop into her head. *Did that count as rape? She had said "not yet," hadn't she? But she didn't use the word "no."* The waters were muddied. Impaired judgments, both parties, and he loved her and she loved him. Confused. Scared. Ashamed. Payton struggled to say her goodbyes. A forced, swift kiss was all she could manage before she climbed into her car with her friends.

"OK, babe, follow me," Reece instructed.

"Got it."

"Love you," he said.

"Love you too," she barely spat out.

Payton didn't have the answers that she needed, and she didn't know half of what to expect from the consequences of the situation that had taken place the night before. Emotions she'd never felt before ran through her, and she wasn't mature enough to know what to do with them or how to feel. Fears she didn't know existed consumed her mind. Damage beyond repair had only just begun, and she hadn't even made it home.

Chapter 24

Payton

Small talk filled the car on the drive home. Aubrey and Maddie didn't pressure Payton to talk. She was still feeling puny and besides, she slept most of the way back. They said their final goodbyes, and Payton had never been so relieved to walk into her house and see her mom in her entire life. Claudette had no idea what was weighing on her daughter's mind, but one look at Payton and she knew something was wrong.

"What's wrong with you?"

Payton shook her head. "I feel like crap. I've been throwing up this morning, felt fine last night, but got up and didn't feel well at all."

Her mom put her hand on Payton's forehead. She felt clammy and looked awful. Pale. And she knew she wasn't faking. Something was definitely not right.

"I just want to take a hot bath and lay down."

"I think that's probably a good idea. Are you hungry?" her mom asked.

She thought about it for a second. It was late in the day, and she hadn't eaten a bite.

"I wouldn't mind a bowl of soup if you have some, tomato maybe, with a cheese sandwich?"

As her bath drew, she stared at her naked body in

the mirror. She looked the same; no one would know what had happened. When she was ready, she'd tell her friends, but Payton had already decided she would leave some of the details out. She felt humiliated about them anyway. The way that her first time doing that had gone down, and where it had taken place, not exactly how she'd pictured it in her head. Her phone buzzed as she dipped her toe into the steaming bath. Usually checking her phone and answering every text the second it came in, she ignored the notification and slipped into the water. Limply, her body soaked in the tub. The steam fogged up the entire bathroom, but Payton hadn't noticed. Washing off her mistake, it would seem, but it wasn't going away. Not knowing if protection had been used, the waiting game of her period visit had started. Worry and anxiety consumed her mind, and the fond memories of earlier that evening at the lake quickly disappeared. Her phone vibrated over and over; a quick glance indicated Reece was trying to call. Finally another text; she read it, but so unlike her, she didn't respond. As the water cooled down, she started to shiver. Reaching for a towel, she climbed out of the tub and dried her fragile body. Glancing at the texts, she could tell how worried Reece was.

Reece: Are you doing OK?
Reece: Hope you're feeling better. Please call me.
Reece: Are you doing better?

Tears were rolling down her cheeks as she read the texts. Horrified at her own actions, disgusted with herself, how on earth could she blame just him? She'd let herself down. He should have protected her; he should have listened. It was too much; within seconds Payton was beyond tears running down her face, she was full-blown sobbing and had no idea her mom had just walked into her room with her soup and sandwich.

"Payton, what's wrong?" Her mom set down the tray. "Tell me what's going on."

Mrs. Phillips wrapped her arms around her daughter. She rocked her while Payton broke down and sobbed like a little girl. Stroking her daughter's hair and speaking softly, her mom continued to ask her what was going on. Questions kept coming, but Payton refused to talk.

"Did you and Reece have a fight?"

"Are you and the girls OK?"

"Something happen at school?" She tried to look at her daughter's face. "Did you have a fight with Aubrey or Maddie?" But Payton wasn't budging.

"Payton, baby, you have to talk to me." She kissed her face and wiped her tears. "I can't help you if I don't know what's going on."

Payton's head, still throbbing, was telling her to keep quiet, but her heart wanted to confide in her mom. One excuse after another rolled off her tongue, and even she knew they weren't believable at all.

"It does involve Reece, but not a fight. I don't think, but I'm not sure because we haven't talked about it." She sat up from her mom's lap and wiped away the tears streaming down her cheeks with the back of her hand.

"Payton, you're not making sense. Just tell me

what this is all about," her mom pleaded.

Don't you understand? I desperately want to tell you what this is all about, trust me! But I can't because I'm kinda confused about how I'm supposed to feel about what happened. And if I do tell you, you will hate the person I love more than anything else in the world. And while we're at it, let's not forget about the fact that I lied to you in the first place, broke your trust, and got trashed. How about that? So as much as I want to tell you what this is all about, I can't! Payton thought.

And as soon as Payton thought about all of that, she burst into full sobs all over again. It took a while, but her mom finally calmed her down. Exhaustion, too many late nights, not eating right—numerous things could be contributing to Payton's emotional state, in addition to whatever was going on, her mom thought. She kept saying that when Payton was ready to talk, she was there to listen. Payton wanted to talk, but there was no way she would. Her mom calmed her down and talked her into eating some soup; it took less than an hour for Payton to crash. Sleep came easy; blocking everything out of her head, disappearing in her dreams, Payton couldn't wait to drift away.

The sound of her phone dinging a message alert woke Payton up. She had no idea how long she'd been asleep. It was Reece, but Aubrey and Maddie had left messages as well. Reece was checking on her again, and told her how much he loved her. She typed the appropriate response from a girlfriend in love: thank you, feel better, love you too, and will call later. Her heart loved him just as much as before, but her head was arguing with her heart. She felt icky about the entire situation. Let down. Betrayed. Responsible for the position she put herself in; she knew better than that, but it wasn't supposed to be that way. It was going to be a blast, and had been for most of the night. She felt stupid, irresponsible, but above all, Payton felt ashamed of herself for disappointing her parents and jeopardizing her entire future. The discussion she would have to have with Reece, she had no idea how to begin. She could barely allow her mind to think the words, let alone say them out loud. But there didn't seem any other way to describe what happened. How do you ask the love of your life if he accidently had sex with you or accidently raped you? There was *no* such thing as accidental rape, so was it accidental sex? What happened? Too much reality to think about, too complicated too quickly, Payton moved down to her next text messages.

> **Aubrey**: How you doing girl, OK?
> **Payton:** Yeah
> **Aubrey:** Looks like you had fun ☺
> **Payton:** Not sure I'd call it quite that
> **Aubrey:** What ☺
> **Payton:** Hey, not trying to be rude, but going back to bed. Still not feeling great.
> **Aubrey:** Feel better. Later

Payton moved on to the next text. Maddie had sent her what seemed to be more than a dozen, but she didn't have it in her to read any of them. Turning off her phone, she climbed back into bed to retreat from the real world. Sleep was the best comforter she had. If she was asleep, she didn't have to think. If she didn't think, she didn't cry. If she didn't cry, her mom didn't get concerned. If her mom weren't concerned, she'd leave her alone. Payton wanted to be left alone. Pulling the comforter over her head and saying the words *go to sleep, just sleep* over and over, she eventually slipped off into a world with zero reality at all.

Chapter 25

Reece

Reece texted Royce and filled him in about the night before. "Coach's lake house, well you'd have to see it to believe it," he'd said. He told Royce almost everything, leaving out some of the details, including the disastrous tent event with Payton. Pushed that memory right out of his head and moved on as if it had never happened. Guy thing. It happened. It's over.

> **Reece:** Bro, one word. Lit!
> **Royce:** Glad ya'll didn't drink and drive. That was semi-responsible, but remember if you get busted, we never had this conversation!
> **Reece:** Got it. Never talked to you.

Royce had done his fair share of partying over the years, but little bro wasn't supposed to follow in those kinds of footsteps. Reece's phone was blowing up, just like Payton's had been. Trevor, Cody, Shane, Stacie, Ryan, Duncan, Stacie. He clicked on hers first.

> **Stacie:** Hey, had fun. Heads up. Pics out there, some good, some not so good. Start covering tracs if anyone asks.

Reece: K. Thanks for the heads up. That sucks, pics part. Great party BTW
Stacie: Thanks. Heard you had a *GREAT* time
Reece: Oh yeah.
Stacie: Glad you had fun.
Reece: Thanks.

He knew what she was implying, but his gut told him to keep quiet. He deleted the text and moved on down the line, passing along the message. People were talking and pics were starting to show up; keep your eyes and ears open, he messaged. Cody added to keep everyone informed until things settled down; Trevor and Reece agreed. Finsta accounts happened to be what most had used, but not all. Some were slipping through and showing up on the usual social media sites: Twitter, Instagram, and other popular sites as well. As soon as they showed up, everyone shared. It was a matter of time before the wrong kid or a helicopter parent with a fake account saw a pic and would discover the party and someone, if not all of them, would get busted. No one knew, including Reece, how many photos—or videos for that matter—were floating around. Once the alcohol had kicked in that night, the kids didn't care. Uninhibited, all fear and inhibition was gone. They let down their guard and the drunker someone was, the funnier. Captured on film only intensified the humor. Simple pranks, funny in the moment, destructive once they hit the Internet. Thirty-second clips were easy to capture and post; didn't matter what people were doing, it was all about the likes and shares. Go viral. That was the objective once they let loose.

Reece texted Payton and asked what time she wanted talk via FaceTime. Weirdest feeling, texting the girl he loved but not wanting to talk to her. She'd been acting so weird since the party, and he just didn't get it. She felt sick. He got that. She had too much to drink, thus the reason she felt sick. But he didn't know what else to do. He'd tried to help her: soda, cool rag, and offered to drive her home. Really, it wasn't his fault she got sick. Lying on his bed, staring at the ceiling, he did the same thing that Payton was doing: going over the events of the party, but from a completely different perspective. It had been a blast! Aubrey had looked hot, surprising, and Cody had a great time. He was happy for him. Stacie was awesome, as usual, and how in the hell did Trevor nail her? Still puzzling. Everyone seemed to have had a great time, and he killed it at beer pong, though he couldn't publicly brag about that till he got to school and around his friends. But he did hate that Payton had to ruin the night by getting sick; that sucked. Puking in the tent, gross!

Rolling a football around and around in his hands, he thought about everyone laughing and cutting up. Grinning, he lay down and threw the ball up in the air, catching it in his hands over and over again. His mind flashed back to the moments in the tent, and his make-out session with Payton. Some of it was awesome, how it was supposed to be. He could feel himself getting aroused as he thought about how far they'd gone, and he squeezed the football in his hands to distract himself; no point getting worked up. The party had been awesome, the whole night, until she got crazy and started acting weird, and then of course it went downhill. Payton puking everywhere, well that was kinda gross, but maybe she was embarrassed and that's why she's acting weird, Reece thought. They both deserved a do-over first time, no puke involved. Surely that would make her feel better! It would be their first-time do-over. His eyes got heavy, and he started to fall asleep. Between the long night before, excitement, and drama, it took merely minutes for Reece to crash. His subconscious memory took him to the party. They were by the fire pit making out. Kissing, touching, and at times laughing with the others. They suddenly appeared in the tent, and Payton's voice was resounding in his head as they became tangled around each other. He couldn't make out her words. Her voice in his dream was unclear, distorted. And Reece, in his dream, was watching himself trying to make out the words she was trying to say. He kissed her and became distracted. His hands were wandering all over her body, exploring the delicate areas that he was typically never allowed to go near. Reece, happy, liked this dream. He was kissing Payton and she was kissing him back, but now they weren't in the tent. He couldn't tell where they were. He stared into her face, moved her dark hair to one side, and looked into her deep brown eyes, as he positioned his body on top of her. *I love you,* he whispered. Her voice rang through his head, but it was the words he suddenly heard that haunted him, woke him up with a jolt, and scared him half to death.

"***Not yet.***"

The words sounded oddly familiar, but he'd never

heard them until now. Grateful it was a dream—a nightmare more like it—Reece sat up in his bed. He was sweating and breathing hard, panicked. He reached for his phone, but didn't dial or text anyone. Wracking his brain, he tried to make out the words that she may have said. He couldn't remember. She was too hard to understand, except when she said she didn't feel well. He did know—didn't he?—that she had never said those words. Surely she'd never said those words, he'd never heard them, and thankfully it was a dream. He was napping on his bed, in his room, he reminded himself. Tired from everything, Reece knew his imagination was playing tricks on him. He already felt weird about the whole thing; Payton being sick and acting weird afterward was freaking him out. He forced himself to come back to right then and there, avoiding any more thoughts about *the moment* that he had sex with his girlfriend for the first time. The dream was mistaken; besides, that part, in his dream, didn't even take place in a tent. That proved it: it was a mistake, it had to be! They'd made out too many times to count, and Payton's willingness to be a part of whatever they'd do or had done would have to be part of his deal. Anything less wouldn't be acceptable to anyone: Payton, her family, his family, and certainly not to him! Reece's cheeks flushed bright red, but he didn't know why. Angered, Reece tried to force the words that had popped into his dream out of his head. ***Not yet.*** The worst feeling in the world washed over him as he wracked his brain about the events that night. What if she had said them, and he was just now remembering them in his dream? Deeply embarrassed, confused, and feeling afraid and ashamed, Reece became consumed with fear. Adrenaline often saved for the game rushed over his body, and he uncontrollably started to tremble. He did *NOT* hear those words. He didn't! He convinced himself he was mistaken and right then and there, in his room, he vowed never to be so stupid again. Reece pushed the vague, misrepresented memory out of his head and blocked all the events of that evening from his mind. It was a dream! A terrible dream, but a dream nonetheless. Never again, he vowed. Never again would he drink and put himself in a position where he could forget what he'd done. Stupid on top of stupid! We were all doing it, drinking, hanging out, and having fun, Reece told himself. I didn't do anything. I didn't do that!

Chapter 26

What Are You Saying?

Aubrey and Maddie waited patiently for Payton at their usual table in the left-hand corner of the cafeteria—they wanted details. They thought they knew what had gone down between Payton and Reece, but due to Payton being trashed, they hadn't gotten the full story yet.

"Here she comes," Aubrey said, pointing toward the entrance.

Payton's persona typically took over a room as soon as she entered it, a confidence factor she owned; but today she sauntered into the cafeteria, head hung low, and sat down. Her dark hair fell loosely around her shoulders, but the casual look that she wore suggested she wasn't up to dressing the part for others today.

"Are you still feeling bad?" Aubrey asked, surprised by Payton's demeanor.

Payton shook her head, not realizing she'd portrayed how she felt in her choice of wardrobe and makeup that day. Odd. Makeup, hair, and clothes really did change the way people looked at you.

"Well?" Maddie asked.

"Well what?" Payton responded.

Aubrey snickered. "C'mon. You know."

"No," Payton said softly. "I don't."

"Yes, you do," Aubrey teased. "You don't have to tell us everything, just did you or didn't you?"

Payton knew exactly what they wanted to hear, but she had no idea what she was supposed to say. Truth be told, she wanted to forget about that night altogether. Even her conversation with Reece regarding that, so far, had been limited. Although she knew they'd be discussing it further, likely the next time they were face-to-face, she was dreading it.

"Well, come on. Tell us. What was it like? Was it everything you expected?" Maddie hesitated. "But more importantly, did it hurt?"

Payton's head spun toward Maddie faster than she'd intended, and with narrow eyes and anger in her voice, she snapped at her friend. "Why do you care so much?"

Shocked, Maddie stared at Payton, not knowing what she'd said wrong. She hadn't meant anything by it. It was a girl thing, girl talk. And why would she need to explain that to her one of her best friends anyway? Aubrey was stunned at Payton's reaction. Not like her at all.

"Wow! Well then, that's that. Have a good one!" Aubrey stood up and grabbed Maddie's arm. "Come on, Maddie. Not a good time."

Maddie, still shocked, grabbed her things, and started to walk away with Aubrey.

"I'm so sorry," Payton whined. "Really, please, ya'll sit back down."

Aubrey stared at Payton, puzzled, and asked, "What just happened?"

Maddie hadn't done anything, and Payton knew that. She checked her phone to see how much time she had to explain—enough—and they did deserve an explanation.

"You know most of it, you guys were there. We were all hanging out, having fun. Stacie was buzzing around checking up on everyone and then we were all playing beer pong, only I switched from beer to that punch, remember?"

They nodded. It had been fun, but they hadn't drunk as much as Payton, nor gotten sick. Payton stared at her hands and wrung them nervously. She started to talk, but as soon as her explanation poured out of her mouth, it went terribly wrong. Best way to describe it: it went south.

"I didn't know I'd drank that much, clearly why we're not supposed to drink." Payton rolled her eyes and attempted to make light of the situation, but it was impossible.

"I don't ever want to drink again!" she said.

The girls didn't say anything. Too soon to hold her to that, but they hoped she wouldn't, as well.

"I'm serious!" Payton said adamantly. "It really messed me and Reece up."

"What do you mean?" Maddie asked.

Payton felt numb. Embarrassed, ashamed, and confused about her feelings, she struggled trying to say the words to her closest friends. They started to form in her mouth, but despite how hard she tried, she just couldn't seem to spit out whole sentences. They came out in spurts—parts of what she was trying to say, and none of it made sense. Eventually the conversation went from bad to worse; none of it was coming out the way she'd intended. Maddie and Aubrey, confused, didn't know what to say or how to feel about the entire situation.

"We went to our tent, and it was great at first. I was fine. Things were good. But it got so hot in there, and the tent started spinning." Gazing off and staring into thin air, Payton pictured her and Reece back in the tent in her mind's eye. "Reece had been drinking too, and I don't think he could really hear me."

"What are you talking about?" Aubrey asked. "Hear what?"

"Payton, you're not making sense," Maddie whispered. "What didn't Reece hear?"

"When I said it . . . right before we did it."

"I still don't know what you're talking about, but I knew it! I knew you guys did it!" Aubrey laughed, until she realized Payton wasn't laughing at all.

"What? Was it bad or something?" asked Aubrey.

"I've heard first times aren't good. Painful and all," Maddie threw in for good measure. "Don't beat yourself up over that."

It had been bad, for sure. Painful beyond words, scary as hell, not to mention she wasn't well at the time. Flashbacks once again, plus the weight of Reece's body on top of her chest, his leg sliding in between hers, her clothes carefully being removed, and her voice barely a jumbled whisper; Payton shook her head. It wasn't how it should have been at all, ever, for any girl! She was having difficulty saying the words and tried to calm her breathing. Her face turned bright red, and Payton shocked them to the core when she whispered the words they never dreamed they'd hear.

"But I wasn't ready. I didn't want to do that yet." Payton put her head in hands. She could feel the heat of her cheeks radiate against her palms. "I wasn't ready to have sex, and then I did."

"Wait. What!?!? What did you just say?" Aubrey snapped, grabbing Payton by the arms. "Payton. What did you mean?"

Payton pulled away from Aubrey. "I don't know. Yes. No. Maybe. I think so. I just don't know." She tried to gather herself, but it wasn't working. Tears filled her eyes.

"I just remember saying the words '*not yet,*' but then it was too late. It was practically over."

Payton closed her eyes and went back over the scene. She could see the condensation on the tent, and remembered the tent had started to spin. Her clothes were being removed. Reece's body felt like a ton of bricks on top of her, heavy, so heavy, that she couldn't breathe. She'd whispered the words, she thought, '*not yet,*' and had indicated she wasn't ready and felt ill. She thought about everything for a second. Reece had looked at her, kissed her, repositioned her, and then the penetration and pain. Severe pain. She'd said, "*I'm not ready.*" He'd said something. She remembered trying to speak, but words not forming. And then it was done. The rest was a memory of her humiliating herself while she puked in the tent. Nice.

"Oh my God. I think he said 'it's almost over,' but

I'm not sure. He could have said, 'it only hurts the first time.' I just don't remember." Payton lowered her head. "But I do remember saying *not yet.* The problem was, I just don't think he heard me. I wasn't well and I don't know how coherent I was . . ." She started to cry. "I just don't know."

Then, to everyone's horror, Maddie asked a question that under normal circumstances would have seemed totally absurd.

"Payton, did Reece rape you?"

Shocked by the word, stunned it was used in the same sentence as her boyfriend's name, Payton became angry. She had wondered if that was the right term, but this was her boyfriend; she was allowed to be concerned, not them. Hearing someone else refer to him and that word, well, Payton just about lost her mind.

"Are you serious right now? Did you really just ask me that question?" Payton snapped.

Payton was admittedly confused about how she felt; but "rape" when Maddie said it out loud was such a strong word, and even if it had crossed her mind, how dare her friend voice such a thing!

"This is Reece we're talking about . . . it's, it's, I don't even know what it is! I don't know exactly what happened because it all went wrong. But he wouldn't hurt me, he wouldn't!"

"But he did," Maddie whispered.

Maddie slid her phone to the center of the table.

"Look, I'm not making any accusations here, but I am trying to understand what you're telling us. And I get how horrific that word sounds, because it is, but if you read the definition, what you described becomes blurred." Maddie pointed to the phone. "Just saying . . ."

According to Dictionary.com: *Rape definition: unlawful sexual intercourse or any other sexual penetration of the vagina, anus, or mouth of another person, with or without force, by a sex organ, other body part, or foreign object, without the consent of the victim.*

What was Dictionary.com saying? Weren't there exceptions for situations like this? And that's when the struggle within Payton got even worse. It wasn't exactly like that, was it, the definition Dictionary.com described? Reece was *not* a rapist. Reece was her boyfriend. Reece loved her. Reece had made a mistake and so had she! There had to be another definition for this type of mistake. That definition, rape, surely was reserved for predators, violent criminals, or anyone who purposely set out to hurt other people, right? One thing weighed on her heart heavier than anything else: it was the question that she was sick of asking herself and knew she would have to eventually ask Reece face-to-face. Why hadn't he listened to her? Why didn't he just stop and wait? That night he took the one and only thing that belonged solely to her: her virginity, the one thing that she was willing to freely give to him when the time was right. It was already his. But not there, not then, and not like that, in a tent while she held vomit in her mouth. Payton cringed. She could never get that back, and she knew it.

She wiped the tears that had rolled down her cheeks away with her sleeve. Of course he hadn't raped her; that would be ridiculous. But he hadn't listened to her, for sure. He loved her, he was her boyfriend, and Reece would never hurt her . . . *but he had*. But how could that be the definition of—she couldn't even say the word. It was an accident, she told herself. *Was there such a thing as an accidental first time, because one person can't hear the other object?* Asking herself that question seemed so absurd. What did that say about her? She knew that the only logical answer was no; but when she thought about the boy she loved, the family he came from, she knew he'd never hurt anyone, especially her, on purpose. But it didn't change the fact that she was angry, hurt, and confused. Maddie was right about that, the lines were blurred. Blaming herself was easy; blaming him was hard. She got two things right: alcohol had impaired both of them, and where they were that night was exactly where they shouldn't have been.

"We shouldn't have been drinking like that," Payton bawled. "We shouldn't have stayed the night and none of this would have happened." She wiped her nose and took a breath. "I wish I'd never gone. I wish I'd bailed. I'm so stupid. So stupid!"

Her shoulders shook and her chest heaved as the tears rolled down her face. Aubrey held Payton's hand in hers and chose her words carefully. She couldn't begin to imagine how Payton was feeling and didn't dare try to pretend that she did.

"Have you talked to Reece since all of this?" she asked. "What did he say?"

Payton nodded and shook her head. "Yes and no.

We've talked, but not at length. We still need to do that." She hesitated and then said, "It's gotten really weird. Like that quick, that weird."

"I'm so freaked out right now." Maddie said. "He seemed so normal and caring Sunday morning. Getting you a cold rag, offering to drive you home. I didn't know anything was wrong between the two of you." She handed Payton a napkin and without thinking said, "Technically, by law, he could be labeled a sex offender or a rapist."

Payton freaked. "Maddie, please, I'm asking you to not say such terrible things, ever!"

Maddie apologized for being so cold. She'd never been in such a weird position before; defending her friend's boyfriend, at her friend's request, who could have possibly done something terrible to one of her best friends. She grabbed Payton's hands and forced her to look her in the eye.

"That came out harsh, and I am sorry. What I meant was in a courtroom, to a stranger, what you described could be defined as rape. Which could, not saying it is, but could put him in a sex offender category for the rest of his life. And that's after his sentencing and time served."

Maddie half-smiled and added, "But I'm not an attorney. My information is mostly from court TV. But damn, girl, this could end up bad. Especially if you weren't nice like that, defending him and all, because we're all taught 'no means no.' Or, in your case, *'not yet.'* Reece could be in serious trouble, even though you said you were both at fault. This could be bad."

The conversation was getting out of hand and had to be resolved. So many mixed emotions were running through Payton's mind: anger, betrayal, love, and defending her boyfriend, Reece. The only way to put it behind her was to address it head on. Payton needed some air, and as much as she was dreading it, she needed a face-to-face with Reece.

Chapter 27

We Have a Problem

Working out relieved stress, especially lifting weights; it was Reece's favorite thing to do if he wasn't playing football. Coaches walked around spot-checking the boys and making sure they were actually working; they were. But it didn't stop the boys from talking about the weekend, and they had plenty to talk about. Several of them, including Reece's friend Ryan, were trying to out-do each other for bragging rights. If the girls only knew, which they didn't, surely they'd never speak to them again. The details that they shared among themselves were embarrassing and likely embellished. Talking in code at times, not as careful at others, they tried to avoid the listening ears of the coaches who walked the floor, listening to their conversations.

"Trev, props to you, bro! You've got the hottest, coolest girl for sure!" One of the boys hollered across the locker room.

Others agreed. Stacie was the bomb. How he got her didn't seem to matter anymore.

"Epic party."

"Po Po weren't called!"

"Got laid!"

"Just kidding, Coach, *IF* you heard that . . ."

followed by laughter.

"Man, Cory got with this one girl. Not bad!"

They all had something to add. Guy talk: to them it was just locker-room conversation and no harm done. Even the kids who weren't at the party managed to join in. The unwelcoming descriptive details heightened once the coaches went back into their offices. The boys, not once thinking for a second they were hurting anyone, laughed and made fun of the girls they'd been with. It made it easier that the girls they were all talking about weren't anywhere in sight.

"Our boy Reece, here," Trevor put an arm around his friend, "finally got the deed done with his girl, if you know what I mean." He started laughing. "Hell, took long enough! What's it been, nearly two years?"

"Well damn, about time, don't ya think?!" Danny yelled across the locker room.

Reece didn't agree with nor deny the accusation. Another voice backed up Trevor's claim, so there was no point denying it anyway.

"We barely saw him all night," Josh said.

"Well, someone did. Lookie here!" Taylor responded, admiring his friend Reece and pointing to his phone. "He's a superstar!" He hit play on his phone.

"Here's Reece, mid-action, in the tent." He laughed hysterically. "Which boys, as you know, we call proof."

"Wait, what?" Reece yelled, grabbing for the phone. Horrified, he watched himself on video, in the tent, with Payton. "Where did you get this? Who did this?"

It was kinda fuzzy, but clear enough to see what Reece and Payton shouldn't have been doing. Shocked,

Reece went to hit delete, but looked at it again. Who would have done something so stupid? How didn't he know the person had been there? OMG . . . Payton!

"Oh hell!" Trevor freaked. "This is bad! Really, really, bad!" He looked at Reece and said one word. "Coach!"

Reece, fuming, yelled, "Who took this?" And then he demanded, "Delete it. Delete it right now!"

"Dude, I will, watch, gone. But it was sent to me."

"By who? Who sent it?"

Taylor showed him the phone and allowed Reece to watch him delete the footage and then clear his delete file. It was gone . . . from his phone anyway.

"Who sent it to you?" Reece asked again, frantically.

"Man, I think it was Joey, but I'm not sure. I've seen several today."

"WHAT?" Reece snapped. "Several. Oh my God! Oh my God!"

His heart was pounding practically out of his chest, palm sweaty, and nerves shot. Reece didn't know what to say.

Danny held up his hands. "Whoa, wait a minute, Reece! Not just of you, but of the party. A couple of other videos going around as well."

"This is bad. This is really, really, really bad!" Reece sat down on the bench. "Dude. What am I going to do?"

Trevor sat down next to him and flipped through his social media sites. "Yeah. Not good. Stacie is going to kill me. Supposed to help monitor that stuff. But I didn't know people were sneaking in tents, you know what I mean. And why would someone do that anyway?!"

"Man, it ain't your fault," Justin said sympathetically. "You didn't take them. Other idiots did."

Trevor sent a text and warned Stacie. She responded right away. She'd already seen a few of the pics and fear had rightfully set in. She had not seen Reece's video, but had heard there was video of the party floating around.

> **Stacie:** How did this happen?
> **Trevor:** Don't know, babe, but it will die down.
> **Stacie:** If my dad finds out, I'm dead and so are you!
> **Trevor:** Thanks. I know. But I'm more worried about you.
> **Stacie:** Thnkx babe, love you.
> **Trevor:** Love you too.

"Damn. I didn't get laid, get drunk, or spend much time with my girl at her own party. We monitored a lot of this stuff, but if these pics get to her dad, we're both dead." Trevor's face was white as a sheet.

Reece was worried. At least Payton didn't go to his school, but that didn't mean much in the world of social media; everyone was connected. He was hoping Payton wouldn't see the pics that actually included them. And he certainly didn't want her to see the footage of them in the tent. The clip, though short, didn't leave much to the imagination, and Reece swore once he found out who took the footage, they'd wished they'd never met him.

Payton's face was crystal clear: that damage was irreversible. Their clothes were half off, and it was painfully obvious what they were doing. You didn't even need thirty seconds to clarify that; they were dead. No one was fessing up to who had taken it, and those who knew about it weren't volunteering the information. Reece knew he had no choice; he'd have to meet with Payton and tell her about the video floating around. Maybe he could leave out the pics; they were mostly hanging-out pictures anyway, but he didn't have a choice regarding the video.

Trevor texted Stacie and told her to instruct everyone to shut down any footage or pictures they saw. Delete them on the spot, and do not share with anyone. Delete, delete, delete anything incriminating that they had in their possession or came across. No problem there, she wanted them all gone! He was trying to contact the service providers of certain feeds to see if the videos could be removed, but that was going to take some time. It must have seemed hilarious in the moment, sneaking footage of kids hooking up, and capturing provocative scenes that could be used against each other in the future, but it wasn't funny now. Reputations ruined, friendships destroyed, trusts betrayed, and that was just scratching the surface of what was about to unfold.

Whispers were spreading like wildfire through the hallways. Texts, Snapchat stories, tweets, Finsta—all the social media sites were being used to post videos from Stacie's party. According to the rumors, two types of people had emerged from the epic event over the weekend: the heroes and the whores. If they fared well or not depended on who delivered the information and how well liked the person involved was. Some would come out unscathed, and it was inevitable that some would find themselves totally irrelevant for the rest of their high school years. Teen girls had a way of deciding whose reputation they'd ruin and whose would remain intact, brutally unfair.

Payton didn't attend their school, and though popular at her campus, she was known as Reece's girlfriend at his school. Without her knowledge, she was about to be judged and destroyed by people she didn't even know. Reece, all things considered, wasn't coming out too badly. Popular kid got laid, has proof, well-liked . . . ha. Good party! Jealously contributed to the destruction of Payton. She didn't go to their school, was with one of their popular boys, and look at what she did . . . skank! The video Payton had no idea existed was making the rounds to people who had been at the party and people who knew nothing about the party in the first place. The unflattering pictures and the thirty-second footage of her having sex with Reece circulated faster than any other because he was Reece Townsend. In a world full of mean girls, particularly teens, Reece came out looking like a conqueror and she was labeled the whore. Sad, because before the party had started, they were both good kids.

Chapter 28

We Need to Talk

As much as Reece was dreading it, he knew he couldn't put it off any longer. He had to talk to Payton. She was as nervous as he was, but he hadn't talked to her long enough to find that out. Dodging serious questions when they had talked, purposely keeping conversations light, and subconsciously avoiding seeing her when he actually had the opportunity, all made him realize he was dreading the face-to-face more than he originally had thought. He'd mentioned hanging out with friends and Payton hadn't objected, but that was before he found out about the video. Reece knew he had no choice; he had to tell her before she found out on her own. Aubrey had been spending a lot of time with Cody, and it was only a matter of time before Cody would tell her he'd seen them or worse, show her. Time wasn't on his side; she was going to find out sooner or later. How did one approach their girlfriend about something like this? *By the way, babe, not only was your first time a disaster, but there are pics floating around as well. Oh, and did I mention you're a star? A movie star!*

Reece's cheeks burned at the thought. Hanging his head, he contemplated calling Royce for advice. He pushed that idea out of mind. No point going down that road yet. With sweaty palms, his fingers tapped the message on his phone. He waited for Payton's response. It took longer than usual, but finally came back asking when and where. He sent back the details, the usual place. Meet at the dam and they'd drive to their tree. Payton agreed. Relieved, he shoved his phone back into his pocket and tried to put the entire situation out of his head. After all, the pics weren't his fault, he told himself. And like anything else, things would die down as soon as there was something or someone else to talk about. That was it! They needed someone else to act like an idiot and the heat would be off them. Once he convinced himself of that, Reece felt better. That's exactly what he'd try to convince Payton of as well. Things would die down with time. A text came in. Thinking it was Payton, he pulled out his phone. It was Trevor.

Trevor: Hey man, what's up?

Reece: Make headway deleting pics?

Trevor: Think so.

Reece: Good. Whew!

Trevor: Last ones I saw, I didn't recognize any of the people in them. Not sure how they were even at the party or who they came with.

Reece: Cool.

Trevor: Think things are dying down dude, hoping we're in the clear.

Reece: Man, that would be good news, in the clear.

Trevor: Will let you know if I hear anything different

Reece: K
Reece: Thnkx

As nervous as Reece was about facing Payton, he was ready to smooth things over about the night in the tent. He wanted a do-over night, but didn't know where to start. Settle that, and then sweep the video situation under the rug. If he were lucky, he hoped to completely bypass the details of the video floating around. Not exactly lie, but avoid telling her the whole truth, if at all possible. Reece thought the perfect explanation would be to mention that there were videos floating around, which there were, but fail to mention that Payton was the star. That way he'd have told her the truth, kind of, but hadn't crushed and humiliated her totally. Plus, he was one hundred percent convinced it was all going to blow over anyway! They just needed a little more time, that's all. It was going to go away!

To his surprise, Payton was already on site. She was sitting in her car, window rolled down, waiting for him to arrive. As soon as he pulled up next to her, she rolled up her window and climbed out of her car, as usual. *Off to a great start,* Reece thought. *Nothing out of the norm here.* He was wrong. Payton climbed into the truck. Usually laying a great big kiss on his lips, she sat on her side of the cab, buckled up, barely smiled, and greeted him coolly. Fearful that she knew already, Reece tried to act normal and feel her out.

"Hey babe, scoot over here."

He tapped the seat next to him, and reluctantly she scooted over and sat by him. Managing a slight smile, she motioned with her hands and indicated he should start driving. He put the truck in reverse and nervously headed to the lake and their tree.

"Dang. You must really be mad at me. You OK?" Reece asked.

His beautiful smile, which always made her melt, had disappeared. He looked worried, and it saddened her to see him look that way. Eyes faced forward so she wouldn't cry, she scolded herself for feeling so stupid. Was this really worth bringing up? But she knew she had to talk to him about it or she'd never be able to move past it. Payton had no idea how he'd receive what she had to say, and looking back, she certainly wasn't prepared for what he'd say in response to her feelings about what had happened that night at Stacie's party.

Payton nodded. "I am. But we do need to talk, glad we're here, I just don't know how to say what I want to say."

"Well, just say it," Reece replied. "We can't talk about it unless I know what it is, right?"

She nodded, but glanced downward, and Reece noticed her eyes had filled up with tears. He also realized her face was pale, and it wasn't because of her natural-look applied makeup; she didn't look like her usual perky, happy-to-see-him self. She looked different. Panicked she knew, he didn't know what to say.

"What's the deal?" he asked firmly.

Payton wanted to wait until they were at their spot, under their tree, lakeside. It felt safer to talk there: quiet, private, and familiar. But he wasn't going to let that happen. She couldn't blurt out that she blamed him; worried and nervous, she started trying to explain her feelings.

"I feel really weird about what happened at the party the other night."

"Which part?" Reece asked. "Cause I had fun for a while, then it got weird round about the time you got drunk and sick."

Payton's cheeks burned with heat; she felt embarrassed. She had no intention of getting drunk, nor sick, and all of a sudden his tone didn't seem as sympathetic or understanding as she'd hoped. Trying not to sound defensive, she continued.

"I hardly intended to get ill, Reece." Payton pulled her hand out of his. "I was having a good time as well, I think, until I started to feel sick."

Reece nodded. "I bet it was the punch. Never drink the punch!"

Payton didn't want to talk about the punch or the fact that she shouldn't have drank it at all; she knew that, she wanted to talk about their conversation—or lack of one it would seem. The one that she'd played over and over in her head. The words she couldn't shake and the ones she was convinced she'd said right before what happened between them took place. Reece waited for her to speak, not knowing exactly what he was supposed to say. Payton sat in the truck, not knowing how to ask the questions that she needed answers to in such a way that she wouldn't hurt him. She wanted him to answer the questions about that evening, and the only way to get the answers was to act as if she already had them. Had she consented or did she ask him to wait, as she remembered? If she had voiced those words, as she believed that she had, why didn't he listen to her, especially if he loved her as he claimed?

"What's going on, Payton?" Reece asked, frustrated. "Spit it out already."

He picked up her hand and looked her in the eye. She wasn't making sense and looked like a stranger in that moment, not like the girl he loved and had come to see that day. Her dark eyes were watery and distant. Her skin was pale, and her lean body looked thinner than usual. Frail. She looked frail. Her demeanor was off, to say the least. She wasn't acting like his Payton.

"Have you been eating?" he asked.

Payton nodded her head. Truth was, she'd barely picked at her food all week, worried about the conversation she was trying to have right then. Her hand went limp in his, as he tried to get her to respond to the things he was asking. His phone vibrated; a text came in. He didn't answer it, but glanced and quickly read it. Payton struggled, but managed to string a sentence together.

"I'm bothered about the other night. I wasn't ready, to do that, and I think that I asked you to wait." She couldn't look at him. "But you didn't. Reece, why didn't you listen when I said '*not yet*'?"

Reece sat in the truck, stunned and uncertain of what to say. She'd lost her mind. Her recollection of that night was slightly different than his. Though he would admit she'd gotten sick, and maybe said the words "***not yet***," but he wouldn't swear to that because he hadn't heard those until he woke up in his room. But the fact remained that it was over and done with, right? So why was she talking like that? He waited to see what she'd say next, not sure if he should defend himself or comfort her. He didn't have to wait very long. Payton started to unload her feelings regarding that night; it was as if a burden was lifted that weighed ten times more than she did, allowing her to think clearly again. Reece sat in the truck, speechless.

"I know I said the words *'not yet'*. I know I did." She looked into his eyes, but for the first time couldn't read them. "You didn't listen to me; you didn't stop." She fought back her tears. "I just need to know why. Why didn't you listen? Why didn't you wait?"

Despite how hard she tried, tears welled up in her eyes. He didn't wipe them away; she did, with her hand. Reece looked at her as if he didn't recognize her; who was this girl sitting beside him, and what exactly was she trying to say? Was it possible his girlfriend was implying the most awful thing imaginable? He heard her words, but couldn't believe they came out of her mouth. He shook his head as anger fueled within him. She was crazy! Absolutely crazy; the girl had lost her mind. If he wasn't mistaken, she was implying he did it all by himself.

They were in it together . . . Stacie's party—they'd planned to spend the night in the tent together, gone to great lengths, and now this! The words Payton said embarrassed him, tugged at his heart, and at the same time angered him more than he thought possible. Blame. It dawned on him that Payton was blaming him for having sex with her that night. How dare she! Tears now rolled down her face, and part of Reece wanted to reach out and wrap his arms around her and comfort her, but the fury he felt within at the words that had spewed from her mouth left him paralyzed in shock. Payton's voice shook, and her hands trembled as she tried to make her point. She wasn't trying to hurt him; she needed answers. To Reece's horror, she kept going, and he was trapped in the cab of the truck with her and couldn't flee.

"Reece, did you hear me?"

He heard her just fine. Her words stung. Uncomfortable, in shock and not knowing quite what to do, Reece sat there and let her say what she needed to say. But he didn't hear every word. His mind couldn't process it. He heard some of it, but not all of it. All he heard were accusations and blame. Payton still needed answers; he could hear the pain in her voice, but how was he supposed to answer that when she had been there as well?

He started to speak, but now the words wouldn't form in his mouth. Frustrated and wanting to get out of there, he shook his head in disbelief. *What the hell was going on here? Had he heard her correctly?* He had. Payton, cutting him deeper than she even realized, delivered her closing comments.

"I just wanted to be a part of that experience with you, but I feel that night you took it from me when I wasn't ready. It should've been special. Our moment. Our night." She hesitated, took a deep breath and said, "Reece, it shouldn't have just been yours, but it was. That's all . . . it should have been *ours!*"

What he wanted to say would have hurt her and

caused additional damage. Trying to defend what he may have or may not have heard while he wasn't thinking clearly himself didn't seem to matter right then anyway. They were both trashed, beer on top of beer, and being persecuted based on actions neither of them could remember clearly sucked! It wasn't the perfect scenario; he never dreamed his girlfriend would puke afterwards or worse, turn on him like this. Surely she wasn't thinking clearly, right? Her words rang in his ears, and for a second his dad's face flashed before his eyes and that brought him comfort, seeing a face he recognized. Did he hear the words she was talking about, *"not yet"*? He wasn't sure anymore. He did in his room, for sure, but he was asleep. Was that a recollection of that night, he didn't know; but he did know it scared the hell out of him to think that it could have been. His dad had raised both of them, him and Royce, and taught them that **NO MEANS NO**. He'd heard it for years. But what she was implying, Payton, here and now, made him sick to his stomach. How could she say such a thing and why would *she* think it happened the way she described it?

Reece glanced across at her, but he couldn't look at her, and his face immediately turned back toward his window. He was convinced, especially now, that he hadn't heard the words *"**NOT YET**,"* or if he had, they hadn't registered. One thing was crystal clear: her version versus his weren't the same at all. Reece couldn't get away from her fast enough! He needed time to think and some fresh air. It sucked because, up until that second, she was the most important girl in the whole world to him. Consumed with fear, guilt, and now confusion, Reece felt sick to his stomach. He was going to have to put a call into Royce. He needed someone to talk this over with; but for now Payton was still sitting in his truck, staring at him.

"I didn't recall your words, literally, until I woke up from a bad dream. I thought it was a nightmare, but looks like I'm living it!" He couldn't look at her; a combination of anger and frustration overtook him. "You'd drank so much you got sick, remember? But I'd been drinking too, everyone had."

How could she forget? "Sick" didn't begin to describe how miserable she had been. Puking inside and outside the tent—lovely.

"But mark my words, that won't happen again. I'll never drink again after this mess!" Reece stared out the window, tempted to turn his keys and drive his truck back.

"This is a mess to you? I'm trying to explain how I feel," Payton snapped.

"Yeah . . . it doesn't feel like that," he responded. Taking a deep breath, he added his final thoughts about that night. "That night was planned. You might not want to admit it, Payton, but it was. It might not have gone according to your plan, but we planned it. And yes, now we have this mess." He clenched one hand around the steering wheel and reached to turn the key. "But what you're implying, Payton, I don't deserve, and you may not believe it, but that's not exactly how it happened."

His face was somber, and he offered no form of

solace to her. Green eyes dull, he wanted to flee. This conversation certainly hadn't been the one he'd anticipated. Forget mentioning the video; this was absurd.

"Well, that's how I remember it and I'm not trying to hurt you or fight. I'm just trying to talk to you and explain how I feel about it."

He wasn't sympathetic or understanding. He was furious that she was accusing him of something so terrible. Had she forgotten how much he loved her? They sat in the truck, ice cold toward each other. A stranger wouldn't have recognized them as the same teen couple from a week ago. Reece knew he wouldn't hurt her or go against her wishes in any way. Blindsided by the horrific nature of what it sounded like she was trying to imply: nonconsensual, date rape, Reece drove back in a silent rage.

Chapter 29

OMG . . . Did You See It?

Rumors had spread to both schools. Who got trashed? Who hooked up with whom? Did anyone bring party drugs, which surprisingly no one had, and of course the photos and videos came up. It didn't take long for the gossip to turn malicious at Payton's campus, as well as on social media, especially between the girls and people who didn't even know the kids involved. The consensus between most of the teens seemed to be if kids had been dating a while, no one cared what they were doing. Sad. Things had gotten so casual. But if they didn't know you or if you didn't meet up to their standards of what a popular hot kid was supposed to look or act like, the comments had turned into bullying. It went back to the heroes versus the bitches, sluts, hos, whores, and skank categories. Payton, still unaware she was the topic of several conversations, mostly by other girls, had unknowingly become the butt of their jokes and nasty comments.

"She's such a skank!"
"What does he see in her anyway?"
"Right! She's not even that pretty."
"To be honest, Reece is hot."

"What a slut!"

"He'll move on now. They all do."

"Who makes a sex video in a tent!"

"Right. Tacky!"

The laughter drew attention from the teacher. Warnings were given, but that didn't stop the whispers, and the boys got wind of what the girls were talking about: Payton.

"That's Badger's handiwork," one of the boys laughed. "He captured Reece getting him some."

Finally a name attached to the video damage. Badger. What an idiot!

"Still, who does that . . . in a tent . . . while Badger's filming?" a redhead with an agenda asked.

"They didn't know." Jessie laughed. "Badger shoved his phone into tents, shot footage, and looked to see what he had later. Just so happened he captured some prime-time material!"

Jessie pulled out his phone and sent word to Reece.

Jessie: Girls in class watching your movie

Reece: Nice

Jessie: I told them to delete it

Reece: Thnkx man

Jessie: Not sure they did

Reece: Appreciate the attempt

Reece's demeanor seemed calm, but it wasn't. He hadn't slept well since his conversation with Payton. They'd barely talked since, neither one knowing what they were supposed to say now. He'd picked up his phone at least a dozen times to talk to Royce, only to put it down again, hoping it would all blow over. He wasn't trying to minimize how Payton felt. He was confused too. But had he really handled it as awfully as she said? It sickened him to think that he had. He'd gone over that night and their conversation in the truck a million times. Her tears and the sound of her voice, absolutely chilling. Telling her about the video, well that just might be the last straw. Reece hung his head and tried to calm his nerves. Surely it was a matter of time before someone else would do something worth focusing on besides Stacie's party. Not soon enough for him.

Reece's phone vibrated in his hand. He read the message and his heart jumped into his throat. She knew!!!! Not knowing what to say, and dreading another fight, Reece didn't answer her text. Another one came in. He still didn't answer. And another. Finally he responded.

Payton: OMG. Did you see it?
Payton: How did this happen?
Payton: OMG OMG OMG!
Payton: Reece WTH! OMG! Call me now or text, OMG.
Payton: Did you SEE IT?

He lied.

Reece: Haven't seen it, don't want too. Will call at lunch. DTB
Payton: WTH! DTB at a time like this . . . wow . . . talk at lunch. Screw you!

And there it was: he'd done it wrong. He knew he was an idiot, but he just didn't know what to say, and he was headed to AP Physics. Not wanting to deal with it, Reece blocked it from his mind. Payton broke down and allowed her friends to rally around her. As feared, Aubrey, thanks to Cody, was the one who had shared the information.

"Get Cody to find a copy," Payton demanded. "I have to see it. I need to know what they're looking at. OMG!"

"Do you think that's a good idea, really?" Aubrey countered. "Do you need to see it? He said it wasn't very long, and we probably just need to get rid of them."

"He's seen it? Oh my God!" Horrified Aubrey's boyfriend had seen her in that predicament, Payton wanted to die.

Payton insisted. "I have to know how damaging it is, what it is." All of a sudden she let out a chilling cry. "Oh my God. My parents! How did this happen? And why is Reece acting like he doesn't care?"

Aubrey's fingers tapped away on her phone as she desperately tried to track down Cody. Finally he answered and the messages started going back and forth. She had no idea that Cody was passing them to Reece for review. Reece, horrified and dreading his call at lunch, could only shake his head. Maddie did her best to try and comfort Payton, but it wasn't working. Panic had turned into fear. None of them knew what to do. Tell someone? Who? Barely able to breathe, Payton felt like she was dying. Humiliation on a level she'd never experienced before consumed her, and she hadn't even seen the footage yet. Hurt, confused, angry, humiliated, and in love, she felt as if she was on the verge of a mental breakdown. Anxiety took over her body as her pulse raced, her head hurt, and she desperately needed to throw up. How could one night of so-called fun jeopardize everything important to her? Her relationships, reputation, family, and future had all been threatened from one idiotic mistake. People were talking, teachers kept asking questions, and she had no choice. The lies started to roll off her tongue in order to avoid the truth. It didn't help. She was making everything ten times worse. People were looking at her as she walked down the halls, whispering and pointing. Her face flushed, breaking out in hives, Payton felt like every person in the school knew what she had done. She felt dirty and cheap. Asking the teacher to be excused, Payton found a solitary stall in the restroom and sobbed her eyes out. Not sure if she could gather herself in time to go back to class, she called her mom.

"I've started and bled through. Can I go home?"

"Awe. You didn't take anything with you?" her mom replied, having no idea the state her daughter was in.

"No, Mom, I didn't. Can I go home?"

"What's wrong?" Claudette asked, picking up a sob on the other end of the phone.

"Nothing. I just need to change, but I'm cramping so I'd like to go home."

"Well you sound as if something's wrong, like you're crying."

"I'm fine. Can I go?"

"Yes. But you'll have to go to the nurse, they won't let you just leave."

"OK."

Payton convinced the nurse the cramps were that bad and she left campus. The girls agreed to grab her things, and Aubrey said she'd forward the video as soon as someone could retrieve it. It was difficult to see through tear-filled eyes, but she made it home. She had less than twenty minutes before she'd be able to talk to Reece. Payton had never been so glad that she walked into an empty house. Her mom being at work was a gift; there was no way she could face her and keep it together. No sooner had Payton walked in the door than her phone vibrated. The text message alone sent chills down her spine.

> **Aubrey:** I don't think you should watch it but here it is. I'll call later

Payton sat down in the middle of the staircase. Her hands were shaking. She texted Aubrey and Maddie in a group text.

> **Payton:** About to watch it, get over here a.s.a.p. today
> **Aubrey & Maddie:** Will do. No problem.
> **Aubrey:** I really wished you wouldn't watch it, but I support your decision
> **Payton:** K

Payton hit "play." It was the worst thirty seconds of her existence. And there was no doubt that the person on the screen was Payton Phillips. And guess what, she didn't look like she wasn't having a great time! No telling when those thirty seconds were shot, not at the exact time of the now-debatable words that had been voiced: "***not yet.***" Face, neck, and chest beet red, Payton grabbed her stomach and let out a gut-wrenching scream. Uncontrollable tears flowed. Fear, panic, embarrassment, having no idea what she was supposed to do or where to turn, Payton buried her face in her hands and sobbed hysterically. She couldn't lie her way through it, she couldn't cover it up, and she had no idea how many people had seen it. She watched it again, and again, and again. And then, as if it would make it all go away, Payton hit "delete." Her phone rang and she almost didn't answer it. Noticing it was Reece, she took the call. Reece could barely understand a word she was trying to say.

"How did this happen?"

"I don't really know how it all got started."

"Have you seen it?" Payton asked.

"Yeah," Reece replied hesitantly. "Just a few minutes ago," he lied.

Payton got quiet; the silence was deafening. Reece tried to carry on the conversation.

"I heard Badger was going around taking videos of everyone as a joke. Ours, well, ya know. He thought the videos would be funny." He hesitated. "But they got out. They weren't supposed to, but they did. You know how that stuff spreads."

"Funny," Payton said. "Are you kidding me right now? Freaking funny! I'm devastated."

"I know you are, so am I."

"I don't think you do, Reece. I really don't!" Payton snapped. "My reputation's ruined over a split-second decision we supposedly made in the midst of fun."

She couldn't think clearly. She had to blame someone for the video, and he was the perfect target.

"Look, I didn't do it, and I'm as embarrassed as you are, pissed. But we've got to figure out what we're going to do here."

She didn't respond. He was so calm, and she didn't know if his demeanor relieved her nerves or if she was angered by it. She wasn't calm. She was scared to death. Reece was scared, but his ways of handling things were a tad different than hers. Her tears drowned out her voice, and he couldn't understand her when she tried to speak. Talking to her seemed impossible in that moment, and thinking he was being helpful infuriated her even more.

"Well I'll let you go, and we'll talk later, OK?"

Overwhelmed with fear, guilt, and shame, she unleashed on Reece.

"That's your freaking answer? Hanging up?! You need to fix this mess. This is your friend and your mess. All of it!" She paused for a moment. "Tell me what we're going to do when our parents find out? Tell me how you're going to fix it!"

"They're not going to! They can't!" he snapped.

"Are you defending me with those people? Are you?" she screamed.

"Defending you from what? You're my girlfriend and Badger is an ass for doing what he did in the first place."

"It's not that simple, Reece, and you know it! It makes this situation a hundred times worse than it already is. My parents will die!"

"As usual, you're overreacting. I'm going to let you go before we both say things we can't take back."

"Overreacting, really?"

"Love you, bye." And he hung up.

She didn't get to finish her vent. She didn't get to tell him that, despite all of this, she did still love him. Payton felt worse after she'd talked to him. Texts started to hit her phone, one after the other, and some from numbers she didn't recognize.

> Girl, is that you on that video?
> Really?
> OMG what were you thinking?
> Do your parents know?
> Skank
> Seriously!
> Your boyfriend's hot.
> Want to go out?
> Slut
> Got 30 secs? ☺ ☺ ☺
> I've got a tent, want to party?
> Nice bod.
> Haven't seen you like that before
> Didn't know you liked to party . . . like that, I mean

Payton wanted to die. There was no way in hell her parents wouldn't find out about this entire thing. She was dead!

Reece was pissed. When it came to Payton lately, every time he opened his mouth he said the wrong thing. His fingers tapped away on his phone. Group message to his boys: find Badger, track down as many videos and photos as you can find and keep trying to get rid of them. He had to try and fix it, make it all go away. Digital fingerprints, making it disappear completely, was impossible. But Reece knew for both of their sakes that Payton was right; he had to try.

Chapter 30

Stacie

You couldn't have met a sweeter teen to her parents than Stacie Wiggins the week following her lake party. Every word out of her mouth was polite, she was cooperative when asked to do something, and answered any and all questions. She'd even been sticking around the house for plenty of family time, but the most shocking thing that her parents noticed was that she wasn't glued to her phone. Cautiously thrilled to have their teen daughter hanging around, they weren't holding their breaths that it would last long. They wondered if Stacie and Trevor had been bickering, but that theory was squashed when Stacie asked if Trevor could come over and hang out with them as well. It was her way of monitoring the damage control after the party, since things were unstable.

"Sure, Trevor can come over. We love it when you're home," Pattie Wiggins said, dying to ask why they were staying in, but not wanting to jinx it. "How about a movie night, or do you prefer a game night?"

Stacie had been worried sick about all of the photos and screen shots that were floating around; plus, she was in several of them. The location of the party would surely be revealed, leaving no room for a lie to cover it up if she got busted. How was she supposed to say she was at another party if the photos clearly showed her parents' lake property? Sticking close to home allowed her to monitor her parents' behavior. And even if Stacie would never admit it, being home made her feel safe. She was starting to regret throwing the party at all, wishing more than anything she'd just gone with her parents or truly spent the night at Sophie's house. When would she learn? Always the one to push the limit, not understanding why she felt the need to do that; it occurred to her there might be something wrong with her. *Note to self,* she thought, *ask Mom if she did that when she was a teen as well.*

"I'd really just like to watch a funny, mindless movie. Popcorn. Blanket. Crash." Stacie dug her hands into the back of her jean pockets. "Will that work?"

Her mom couldn't help but grin. Stacie looked so sweet and young, standing with her hands behind her, hair pulled back into a tight ponytail, no makeup, and her big blue eyes bright as usual. She looked like her kid again, and not the young lady she was turning into.

"I think that's a great idea. A night in, perfect; you look a tad tired."

"I didn't sleep well last night, not sure why."

"I'll fix finger foods for tonight, snacks for the movie. Your dad should be home soon, but let's let him wind down a minute. Tell Trevor about seven-thirty."

Stacie was receiving updates from her friends. She found herself defending Payton. She was shocked at some of the things that were being said, though admittedly she had laughed at a few of them.

Remembering that they were supposed to have been semi-friends, Stacie intervened.

Stacie: It's not like that, they're dating.

Michelle: Reece is way too hot for her.

Stacie: She's actually really pretty. Bad pic.

Lauren: Ya think . . . LOL . . . OMG . . . Get dressed already!

Michelle: They didn't act like they were dating on Sunday. Awkward.

Stacie: Payton was hung over.

Lauren: Don't you remember? Girl puked on Reece!

Michelle: Seriously?!?! OMG gross already!

Lauren: Yeah, nasty. Not sure he'll want to go back to that, you know what I mean.

Stacie: Stop. You're killing me. LOL. She didn't throw up on him. Just in the tent.

Stacie: At least I think that's what happened.

Michelle: Still gross!

Lauren: Bitch shouldn't drink if she can't hold her liquor.

Stacie: Wished none of us were drinking NOW! Delete anything you have, please. Don't feel like dying.

Michelle: K

Lauren: Already did.

Stacie: Thanks. Later.

Stacie deleted her messages, took a deep breath, and scanned her social media to make sure nothing was lingering. There were a couple of questionable photos, too close for comfort for her, and she immediately put in the calls. After promising to invite those who had posted over to meet her dad once the photos were removed, they agreed. If she could monitor the social sites until someone else did something stupid and they were in the limelight, she might just scrape through this mess unscathed. But that wasn't to be the case; Stacie was about to meet her fate.

"Hey babe, I'm running late," Coach called and said sweetly to his wife, Pattie.

"Everything OK?" she asked.

"Yeah. Well, I think so. Meeting the dad of one of my recruits for a quick pint at Jerry's Pub. He said he had to talk to me regarding some issues with his son. Not sure what they are, but the kid has great potential, and I don't want them to feel as if they've committed to the wrong school."

> **Mrs. Wiggins:** Dad's running late, but we can start without him if he takes too long.
> **Stacie:** Seven-thirty still good?
> **Mrs. Wiggins:** Yes. Why don't you come down here and join me?
> **Stacie:** Where?
> **Mrs. Wiggins:** Seriously, not answering that . . .
> **Stacie:** LOL You just did!

Stacie joined her mom in the media room. Scrolling through the new releases, she picked three movies that she thought everyone would enjoy or at least be interested in enough to make it through the entire thing without complaining. Mrs. Wiggins, plate in hand, started asking Stacie the usual mom questions. How was Trevor? How were her studies coming? Did she have anything she wanted to talk about? OMG, was that a trick question? Was her mom fishing for answers that Stacie wasn't prepared to share? Head down, picking at her food to avoid eye contact, Stacie simply shook her head no. It was enough. Clearly, thank goodness, her mom was still in the dark. Trevor should arrive any minute. He'd texted and said he was on his way, but little did Stacie know he'd never enter the house. He'd arrived minutes earlier, but so had Coach. The interaction between the two wasn't the usual pleasantries; in fact, the exchange was far from it. Trevor had parked his car, stepped out, and walked toward Coach, hand extended as usual. But Coach declined to shake Trevor's hand as he normally would. Coach's arm was extended, but he was pointing back toward Trevor's car. Fear suddenly surged through Trevor's body, as he realized they had just been busted. Trevor opened his mouth to speak, but the rage in Coach's eyes forced him to close it tight immediately. Coach grabbed Trevor firmly by the shoulders, turned him around, and pushed him toward his car, forcing him to move. Trevor started walking quickly, keys in hand, and as he reached for the car door he said the worst thing he possibly could say.

"Sir, I think I can explain."

Coach's eyes flashed toward him. "You think you can explain. Son, let me tell you something: you're going to explain, but not right now. Because if I look at you a second longer I'm going to say something I can't take back or worse, lay hands on you, and I don't feel like going to jail. That's hardly the example I'm supposed to set."

Trevor slunk into his car, backed out of the driveway, and left. As soon as he turned the corner, he pulled over, grabbed his phone and texted Stacie. He had no idea if she'd get the message in time, but he had to try. His hands were shaking as he tapped away. Never so scared in his life, he couldn't imagine what she was about to face. Two words.

Trevor: He knows.

Stacie didn't text back. All Trevor could do was sit and wait. His next text was to Reece.

Trevor: Bro call when you can.
Reece: At dinner with the fam. will later
Trevor: It's bad. Coach knows.

The front door slammed too loudly. Pattie Wiggins jumped out of her chair and walked into the foyer to greet her husband. Clearly the meeting with the recruiter's father hadn't gone well. As soon as she laid eyes on her husband, she knew something was terribly wrong. He was livid, absolutely fuming. His eyes flashed toward the stairs, his fists clenched tightly, as if he were ready to throw a punch, and his jaw was rigid. He spoke first.

"Trevor will not be joining us this evening."

Stacie stood in the doorway of the media room, scared. She still hadn't checked her phone. Her mom looked puzzled at her husband's statement, except for a different reason. He had said it with such certainty that she was positive that whatever had upset her husband involved Trevor.

"Are you going to tell me what's going on?" she asked, and then turned to her daughter. "You might want to stick around."

Knowing beyond a shadow of a doubt that whatever he wanted to talk to her about had something to do with the party, Stacie started to panic. Not knowing what information he had, or where he had gotten it, was terrifying. Mad didn't begin to describe what he was feeling at that time, and Stacie couldn't remember a time in her life that her father had ever looked at her that way. He pointed to the media room.

"Sit down, now!"

"Why?" she asked.

"Don't talk," he boomed.

Both Mrs. Wiggins and Stacie jumped half out of their skin. Pattie's face turned grey, and she looked at him as if he'd lost his mind. He shook his head, as if begging her not to say a word. Silently counting to ten, he took a deep breath in order to calm himself. Finally turning to his wife, he started the conversation.

"You're not going to like this. You might want to sit down as well."

He started to tell them about his call and conversation from his recruit's dad. Evidently the father was concerned, and with good reason, about the coach he'd be entrusting his son to. His son had told him about a party that everyone was talking about at school. It had been a hit. Lots of kids, booze, possibly drugs, and definitely lots of sex, no parents, obviously, and questionable footage and pictures had been floating around. Pattie's head turned toward her daughter. One look and she knew Stacie was involved.

The boy's dad had confessed that when his son first told him about some of the things the crazy kids had supposedly being doing, he actually laughed: beer pong, hide-and-go seek, the kids cooking and partying. But then the seriousness of the events started to unfold. Sex. Drinking. Unsupervised all night. Videos. Kids puking. Coach stared into his wife's eyes, not once being able to look at Stacie while he talked about it.

"Very serious issues started to evolve or come to light."

Stacie recognized a look that she hadn't seen in a very long time. Disappointment. Her mom said one word.

"Stacie."

Stacie sat silently. It killed her, but the silence confirmed her father was right and the events did involve her.

"Oh, I'm not done," Coach stated.

"Go on," Pattie demanded, her arms folded across her chest, eyes fixated on her husband.

The boy's father asked if his son had been at the party. He said his son said that he was not, but that he had viewed many photos, Facebook posts, storylines, tweets, and even several videos from kids who had been there, and that's when he showed his dad a few. There were many to pick from.

"It was after viewing some of them that the father realized this party seemed more mature than a teen party should have been, and he felt the need to call me," Coach said. "The shocker was when he brought proof." He looked at his wife. "None of it is good."

"Why? Why did he have to call you?" Stacie yelled, storming toward the kitchen.

"That's what you have to say? Why did he call me? Are you kidding me right now? Sit down!" Coach yelled.

Desperate for answers and grasping at straws, Pattie threw out a scenario. "Trevor threw the party, right? He was in some of those questionable photos. Is that why you sent him home? Was he with another girl or drunk? What did he do?" She was screaming, desperate to confirm her daughter wasn't involved.

"No, Pattie! Our lying, thieving, manipulating daughter, whom we can't trust ever again, not only was in many of the questionable photos, but also was the mastermind behind the party." He didn't wait for his wife to respond. "Yes, you heard me. She," he pointed at Stacie, "threw the party. Do you want to tell your mother where?"

Pattie Wiggins stormed toward Stacie and screamed at her. "TELL ME WHAT YOUR FATHER'S TALKING ABOUT!"

Looking around her house as if trying to spot something, anything out of place, Pattie shook her head: no one, let alone a ton of teens, had been in their house. Doug Wiggins, furious, embarrassed, and nervous, was shocked that his daughter would not only be a part of something so foolish, but that she had been the actual mastermind of the entire plan!

"Not here, Pattie. Think!"

The light bulb went on as soon as he said those words.

"Oh my God, Stacie, no. Not at the lake house!" She ran her hands over her face. "That is so dangerous—the lake, the bluff, and that drive, oh my God!"

Stacie, sick out of her mind with fear, burst into tears. This infuriated her father on a level she'd never dreamed. How could she cry when she brought all this on herself?

"Don't do it! How dare you sit there and cry! Do you have any idea what you've done?" He didn't wait for her to answer as he unleashed his rage.

"You lied. You put your life and the lives of others at risk. Minors in possession; they could have gotten alcohol poisoning or died. The lake—what if someone had drowned? The bluff, that's like a cliff. I understand several kids got sick. Nice! And let's not forget the infamous videos."

Stacie shook her head. "Not several, just a few."

"Stop it. Just a few, really, that's your answer. I'm a coach. A parent. Responsible for other people's kids, and you put kids in danger at my house. You lied to us. Manipulated us. And are you aware of the situation with your friends?"

Stacie froze. The only situation he could be referring to was Payton and Reece. She was scared to respond, and Pattie Wiggins was anxious to hear the truth.

"Do you know what he's talking about?" Her mom pointed at her in rage. "Answer me!"

Stacie nodded. It could only be one thing that was as bad as her dad was referring to, the thirty-second damaging footage of Reece and Payton. Coach was raging. Furious. His daughter was trembling and seeing her that way broke his heart, but in that moment, in his anger, she had caused the entire mess. Stacie Wiggins had unwittingly destroyed several people's lives, and the damage done was a blessing in disguise. She could have actually inadvertently killed someone had they drank too much, gotten alcohol poisoning, wandered off and drowned in the lake, pool, or hot tub. They could have stolen back their car keys and left, could have been in a wreck, died or killed someone on the roads. Grateful that no one was injured was the only positive outcome. Reputations had been trashed, and his reputation as a parent, coach, and caregiver to other people's kids could be at stake, his livelihood and his whole life. Everything they worked for could be lost if a parent sued them. Stacie hadn't thought about one single thing other than being accepted by her peers, which she didn't need, and having fun. She would have to be the one to tell her mother about the videos.

"Tell her," her father demanded.

Stacie's tears streamed down her face. Her words weren't audible at all, and her mother made her repeat them; painful to say out loud, for the first time Stacie couldn't imagine what Payton and Reece must be going through.

"Reece and Payton were together, in a tent, and

someone thought it would be funny to sneak up and capture them doing stuff. They took some, not much, footage, but it went all over several social media sites."

Pattie paced the floor. "Doing what? What I think they're doing?"

Stacie didn't answer, but that was a mistake.

"STACIE!" Coach screamed at the top of his voice. "Tell your mom what was happening on our property in addition to the lying, drinking, and likely trashing of the place!"

Two inches from her face, eye to eye, she'd never seen her dad so furious with her, his hot breath hitting her skin as he spoke. Dipping her tear-filled eyes downward, knowing that trying to lie at this point was useless, she mumbled the words she knew her mom didn't want to hear. There was no need to repeat them. Shocked, furious, stunned, and disappointed couldn't begin to describe how the Wiggins were feeling about their daughter in that moment.

"They were having sex," Stacie confessed. "That's what they look like they were doing."

"LOOK LIKE THEY'RE DOING?!" her father screamed. "Did you watch the video? Don't answer that, I don't care if you did or didn't. I, unfortunately, did. And guess what, princess—you caused this mess!"

Coach stormed toward the kitchen only to march right back toward his daughter. He wasn't done with her, and rightfully so.

"I'm not done with you, mark my words! But you will never stay home alone or with a so-called friend again when we have an away game. You will go and sit at every one of the games, and that's a lot of ball. I go, you go, we go! You will go on every road trip without a word. You have proven you are untrustworthy."

He stopped to catch his breath, and then said the words that killed her most. "I am ashamed right now to call you my daughter! You, being in this family, with my position, should have known better. How dare you be so irresponsible! You lied to us. You jeopardized the safety of other kids, for what? Don't answer. I don't care!"

Pattie slid down the wall and sat on the floor in the foyer, still processing the words that her husband had said. What if that had been their daughter having sex on tape? All of a sudden, in the midst of the arguing, Pattie said something that made Stacie want to vomit.

"They were having sex, in a tent, on our property, while we were gone." She jumped to her feet and stared at her husband. Now she was yelling at the top of her voice.

"Damn it, Doug, Payton's a minor. The tapes, the damn tape, the footage of their daughter. You know what we have to do."

He stared at her, confused, waiting for the answer. "What? What are we supposed to do now about that?"

"You'll have to call and warn her parents."

Then, as if in slow motion, she turned toward Stacie and yelled, "Look at what you've done!"

Chapter 31

The Dreaded Phone Call

Looking back, between the rumors, whispering, photos, and videos that had been shot that night, it was inevitable: parents were going to find out. But the last thing that Coach Wiggins ever wanted to do was a make a phone call based on the actions of his daughter that led to the destruction of someone else's kids. He'd contemplated waiting, cooling off, and gathering his thoughts, but he was afraid he'd lose his ability to make the call. Stacie was still his daughter, and he felt bad about how he'd yelled at her; he knew he could potentially rationalize not placing the call at all, especially if he focused on his heartbroken daughter, who sat sobbing at the bottom of the stairs. He dismissed Stacie, but as she turned to walk away, he called out her name. *Where had time gone? She suddenly looked like his little girl again.*

"What if that was you on that tape?" he asked. But he didn't want nor expect an answer. "What would you want her father to do?" He looked away from her and down at his feet. "I'm surrounded by great kids, raised two amazing boys, athletes. The kids I'm responsible for are great students, have good work ethics, and have been raised right. But do you have any idea Stacie—

any—what even kids like *that* would do with the kinda footage you guys took?"

She didn't try to object; she hadn't known or approved of it and tried to explain that, but he raised his hand to stop her from talking, and she knew better than to argue. She may as well have shot the video herself at that point.

"Your friend Payton seemed like a really nice girl," he hesitated. "But do you really think that matters now? Those kids, the malicious ones, they're just looking for someone to burn."

The words were harsh, but she knew he was right. The texts had already started; she'd actually intervened several and Payton *was* getting burned. No one seemed to care that Reece was in the same video; he wasn't looking too bad, yet. As much as it pained her, she nodded her head. Coach Wiggins, her dad, had no choice; he had to make the phone call. He put in some calls and got the numbers.

Sitting in his office, he stared at the number on his desk for the longest time. Pattie walked past his office, but despite her best efforts couldn't bring herself to go in. Sick to her stomach, a mixture of shame and grief, she too felt sick over the call he was going to have to make. How did they not know their daughter? It had never once occurred to them that she'd lie to such a degree. Be a teen, yes. White lies maybe, but something of this magnitude, she simply couldn't comprehend that Stacie had pulled it off. Pattie couldn't go inside the office, but she sat down to listen within earshot.

It seemed to take forever, but Coach finally tapped

the numbers for Mr. Phillips' cell on his phone. The pleasantries were kept to a minimum, and he could tell that Mr. Phillips was stunned that Coach was calling. Everyone in town knew who Coach was; the call itself made Mr. Phillips uneasy. He couldn't have begun to imagine how uncomfortable the call was about to get.

"There's just no easy way to say this, Mr. Phillips."

"Perry, just call me Perry."

"Perry. It's just going to be easier if I just tell you the main reason I called."

There was an awkward silence, but Perry finally nodded his head. Realizing Coach couldn't see his actions, he managed to verbalize the words for Coach to carry on. In his mind he was trying to remember the events of the day, as if that was important in the moment. He would realize within seconds it wasn't. He could hear the words Coach was saying, but he couldn't process them. He wasn't angry, yet; he was stunned, shocked, sad, disgusted, freaked out, in denial, and wait a minute, now furious.

"So let me get this straight. She was supposed to be at her friend's house, but they ended up at a party at your house, thrown by your daughter?"

Coach interjected. "Actually we were out of town, at a game. They had a party at our lake property, a couple hours from here; of course, we didn't know anything about it, Mr. Phillips, Perry."

Coach hesitated and, as if choking on the actual words, said, "My daughter deceived me and her mom. Said she, like yours, was going to a friends and didn't. She lied. I don't know yet if she orchestrated this party on her own. I don't think so, it was pretty well planned, so I believe she had help, but the location was our lake house."

Mr. Phillips, in shock, digested the information. "Well, I appreciate the phone call, Coach, and rest assured we'll be having words with Payton."

Coach interjected. "There's something else, and it pains me to deliver this information. But the reason that I am is because we have a daughter, and despite this horrendous situation, we still love her, as you love yours. If what I'm about to tell you involved Stacie, I can only hope that someone would warn me as well."

Dead silence. What was he talking about? Unsure if he could handle any more politeness, Mr. Phillips asked Coach to spit out what he had to say.

"There's video floating around. It's short, but it's damaging, reputation-wise, and unfortunately involves Payton."

He spoke softly, with empathy, as he delivered the terrible news, knowing how horrific it could be for this man's daughter. "If you move quickly, and I mean swiftly, you have a shot at limiting how many people share the video I'm talking about."

"Wait. Payton's on some video?" Mr. Phillips voice was elevated.

Coach didn't answer; he knew by the tone of Mr. Phillips' voice that he knew the answer.

"You have my word, Perry. I will assist, as best I can, with shutting this thing down."

As soon as Coach hung up, knowing what the man was about to go through on behalf of his daughter, he could barely hold back tears of his own. One call down, one to go.

Mr. Phillips stared at the phone in his hand. He'd heard the words, but none of it made any sense. Coach had no reason to lie, but on the other, it was possible Coach had the wrong kid. There was only one way to find out—Payton. Frantically he jumped into his truck and headed home. Calling ahead would've been a mistake. His wife, Claudette, wouldn't have believed it anyway. Suddenly a grotesque thought popped into his mind: had it gone viral? Surely not! He couldn't have looked even if he wanted to verify it; the thought made him want to puke. Anger, disgust, frustration, and a sense of embarrassment surged over him as soon as he thought about Payton in full view for the world to see. He never dreamed she was a perfect kid, what teens were, but this was off the charts!

His hand beat the steering wheel as he drove. Sick to his stomach, he rehearsed his lines, but there was no point; as soon as he walked into the door, his rage took over. Raised voice, slamming doors, Perry Phillips screamed for Payton to get down the stairs that very second. Trembling, she stood before him and within seconds Claudette Phillips stood between the two of them.

"What's going on down here?" She looked at him for an answer.

"Well, why don't we ask Payton?"

Payton's eyes grew huge, and panic took over her already trembling limbs. What was he talking about? Realizing it could only be one thing, she went sullen, not daring to breathe a word. Claudette turned to her husband, eyes pleading for answers, but his eyes were stone cold. He reached over his wife and grabbed Payton's arm, turning her toward him. Never having seen him act in such a way before, Claudette, his wife, panicked.

"What is wrong with you? Someone better tell me what the hell is going on," she screamed.

Terrified to speak, not knowing exactly what he knew, Payton clammed up. It didn't last long, as her mom begged for someone to tell her what was going on.

"Tell your mom. Tell her, Payton."

"I'm not sure what you're mad about," she responded, hoping he would start talking.

It was a stretch, but she'd settle for anything. No point in spilling everything yet if there was no need. Her mom interjected. Ushering everyone into the sitting room, she suggested they all sit down and talk about why he'd walked in so mad in the first place. Start there, she'd suggested, and then let Payton explain. Payton had run out of her bedroom without grabbing her phone; she had no backup or support from her friends. Sick to her stomach, she waited. She didn't have to wait long. Her dad sat down opposite her; his demeanor had softened slightly.

"I got the strangest phone call today from Coach Wiggins. You know who he is?"

Claudette looked shocked.

"Stacie's dad," Payton managed.

"Ah, yes, Stacie." Her dad didn't want to talk about Stacie, not yet anyway. "Not really concerned with

Stacie right now . . . you, on the other hand, you are my concern."

Payton's stomach crawled up her throat, and she felt as if it were sitting in her mouth, just waiting to fall out onto the floor. Whatever information he had, it wasn't good. All she could do was wait; there was no bluffing at this point. Searching his face, Payton realized her dad had a yearning in his eyes. Misinformation. He wanted her to tell him that what Coach had said was wrong; but she knew that she couldn't. Now she had to figure out what information he had. If there were anywhere else in the world she could have been right then—anywhere—she would have rather been there than the hot seat she was sitting in. If only a hole in the ground would open and swallow her up.

Clearly they'd been busted about the party. But why was Coach calling her dad? Maybe he was calling all parents; that had to be it, she told herself as she waited. Coach was making the rounds. As she was about to find out, that wasn't the case.

"Where do I start, since you won't?" Too angry to discuss the obvious—lying, drinking, and deceiving her parents—hurt and scared for his daughter, he went straight for the kill and said words he'd regret forever.

"How about your disgusting little tryst on tape?"

The look on Payton's face was one he'd never forget. At that moment two things occurred to him. One, he'd said the most disgusting thing he possibly could to his daughter to hurt her, and secondly, she'd likely never forgive him. On top of that, it was clearly true.

There was a video floating around of his precious daughter having sex at a party in a tent. As soon as he could, he wanted to lay his hands on Reece Townsend!

"PERRY!" Claudette screamed, shocked and angry that he'd said such cruel words.

"You're screaming at me? Scream at her!" He pointed at Payton.

Payton's face said it all. Fear gripped her body as she scrambled for words to justify what had happened, but there weren't any. The thought of her dad seeing that tape humiliated her to such a degree that the simplest words wouldn't form; hoping he'd heard about it, but hadn't seen it, was the only thing that kept her feeling sane in that moment. Horrified, tears rolled down her face, and she found herself gasping for air as anxiety took over. Body shaking, not knowing where to turn, she wanted to die on the spot. Jumping to her feet, she tried to flee, but her mom yelled her name with such alarm in her voice that Payton froze in her tracks.

"Don't you dare move!"

Claudette walked toward her daughter; wanting to comfort her, but needing the truth, she waited to see what Payton would say. "What is he talking about?"

Payton didn't answer. In that moment her mom frightened her, as Payton confused anger for concern.

"Answer me, Payton, damn it! What is he talking about?"

Between sobs, an unrecognizable explanation started to roll out of Payton's mouth. Her mom, unable to stand it any longer, finally stopped her and put her arm around Payton, walking her to the couch so she could sit down and catch her breath. Her dad stood by and watched. They couldn't understand a word she was saying, and Payton needed to gather herself so that she could explain what had happened. Her mom dashed to the kitchen and grabbed a glass of water and handed it to her.

"Take a sip of this, then breathe, and then talk."

Payton, afraid of the answer, asked her dad. "Have you seen it?"

He shook his head, furious that there was anything to see at all. "Reece?"

Payton nodded. Mrs. Phillips's placed a hand over her mouth, shocked at what she was hearing. Her daughter had not only lied, but also had sex with her boyfriend, and was foolish enough to share it with the world. Who did that these days, knowing the dangers of social media? Supportive of their children by nature, anger and hurt suddenly took over Payton's parents.

"How irresponsible can one girl be?" her mom yelled. "What in the hell were you thinking?"

"She wasn't thinking about anyone but herself," her dad answered on Payton's behalf.

Crying, her mom started asking rapid-fire questions. "Why weren't you where you were supposed to be? You lied. Was there alcohol involved? Who filmed it? How many people have seen it? Why wouldn't you tell us about this?"

Payton's head was spinning. The look of disgust on her mother's face made Payton even more ashamed of herself. Her parents had never looked at her that way, and yet through the pain in their eyes, she could see hurt. Hurt meant love. They were hurt! They still loved her. Angry, yes, and disappointed, but somehow she knew they cared. Her mom, though not realizing it, kept interrogating her, kept pushing. She needed answers for why Payton made the choices she had that night. Feeling as if she'd done something wrong as a parent, letting her daughter down, trusting her with a friend, Claudette felt furious with herself. Kids had sex, she knew that, but not hers, right? And shared on social media—this was too much for any parent to digest; did she have any idea, Payton, what she'd done to herself?

"You're a minor, Payton, a sixteen-year-old kid. You're not emotionally ready to have sex or deal with the emotional turmoil that comes with that, even though you may think you are. Sixteen. And now you've shared it with the whole world. They don't care about you; they'll terrorize you over this. Why do you have to grow up so fast?" she asked, head in hands. "What if you get pregnant, did you think about that, not to mention SDTs floating around out there?"

She looked her daughter in the eye and asked her a question, but nothing in the world could have prepared her for the words her daughter responded with. "You're sixteen. Why there, why then? Was it just because you could?"

Terrified and under duress, Payton had no idea what to say except to tell the truth.

Emotionally drained and in hysterics, Payton cried, "But I didn't, I mean I did do that, but I didn't really want to do that yet, right then." She buried her face in her hands and said, "Mom, I wasn't ready."

And that's when all hell broke loose.

Chapter 32

Two Sides to Every Story

They say there are two sides to every story, and somewhere in the middle lies the truth; there is no exception to this one. Payton's version of events and Reece's version of the incident that occurred in the tent didn't quite match up. Both were about to have an opportunity to tell their side, but neither of them were prepared for the storm that would take place afterwards.

It took a few seconds for the bombshell that Payton dropped on her parents to sink in. Claudette, Payton's mom, stared at her husband in shock. Had they heard their daughter correctly? Was she sure? Instantly disgusted by the very thought of such a question, Perry jumped to his feet and raced across the room, scaring both Payton and his wife half to death. Two inches from her face, but trying to remain calm, he asked her to explain exactly what she meant by that comment. This kind of accusation was detrimental to all concerned. Unacceptable if true, damaging if not true, and practically a death sentence if it had happened to HIS DAUGHTER!

"What happened, Payton? Tell us right now exactly what happened!"

Realizing what she'd just put in motion, Payton could barely speak. The weight of the situation she'd been carrying around with her, not to mention the confusion and strain on her relationship with Reece, combined with the humiliation and destruction of her reputation, had finally taken its toll. Payton couldn't handle any more in that moment. Her words weren't audible when she tried to explain. She didn't look like a teen, but a young kid who had no business being anywhere but safe at home.

Angry, hurt, destroyed as a father for his daughter, Perry couldn't see the state that his daughter was truly in, fragile at best. As a father, he needed immediate answers. Claudette rushed to Payton's side. Holding her daughter in her arms, rocking her as if she were an infant, she noticed for the first time in a long time just how tiny her daughter had become. Slipping away with worry, it was clear that Payton hadn't eaten properly in days. Skin and bones, she was frail, stressed, and emotionally exhausted. But they still needed answers. What had happened? Were they really talking about Reece here? The boy they'd welcomed into their home and trusted their daughter with for all this time? Did this just happen?

Claudette stroked Payton's hair and sat her straight up on the couch. Wiping great big tears from Payton's face, she asked her to think. Payton's hands were trembling. Confused. How could she explain exactly what had happened and protect the boy she loved? And worse, was she supposed to protect the boy she loved? Undecided if it were an accident, knowing

245

there was no such thing; Payton didn't know what to do. Reece wouldn't really talk to her, and when he did, she couldn't pull it together long enough to be herself.

Wiping her eyes and blowing her nose, taking a sip of water, Payton was ready to talk. Her opening statement made Perry, as a father, want to blow his own brains out.

"Before I start, I'd just like to say that I'm not convinced that Reece heard me when I said I wasn't ready. I don't think he heard me, but I don't know for sure."

"I can't believe you just said that," Perry yelled so loud that Payton jumped to her feet and the tears started over.

Claudette glared at him, a warning for him to calm down and listen. He took a deep breath, apologized, and gathered himself. Payton described how Stacie and her friends had planned and organized the location of the camping party, but everyone had brought alcohol, food, and tents to sleep in. Rolling his hands to get her to speed up, Payton moved onto later in the evening.

"We had talked about being together when I was ready, and Reece has never ever been disrespectful or crossed the line regarding any of that. Ever!"

Payton was terrified to tell them about the drinking part, knowing how many times they'd told her not to do it, but she knew she had to tell them. Knowing she had to say it and seeing their reactions was the worst.

"I had a couple of beers and some punch, but I don't know what was in the punch or how much I had.

Too much. Reece was drinking as well—everyone was."

Her dad paced across the room, shaking his head. "Kids and booze don't mix! And like it or not, Payton, you're still a kid."

Payton sat on the couch, shame like a covering over her skin. Not believing she was having this conversation, disappointed in herself, she waited for him to allow her to proceed.

Her mom inched in and sat down next to her, squeezing her hand and encouraging her to continue. Payton wasn't exactly sure what to say next. It was something she'd never, ever intended to share with anyone, let alone her parents.

"Tell us exactly what you mean by you weren't ready, but you did it anyway, and now you're on video. You're going to have to explain that."

Heat rushed to her cheeks. Embarrassed didn't begin to describe how she felt. They'd been drinking, and after a while headed to the tent that Reece had brought for them to sleep in. Making out and having fun led to a heavier progression of things, though Payton struggled with her descriptions. The temperature inside of the tent, mixed with the alcohol, and the sudden intensity of the situation with what was happing with Reece, caused Payton to panic. It was then that she realized she felt sick and wasn't prepared nor ready for what was about to take place. It was at that time she thought that she'd started to protest by saying she wasn't ready. She remembered saying *"not yet."* But that's when it all got complicated, and nothing would be the same ever again.

"It was so hot in there, the tent, I couldn't breathe, and I started to feel sick," Payton said.

She hung her head and continued to describe what had happened. "When the tent started to spin, and Reece was kissing me and my clothes were half off, I knew I wasn't ready."

Perry turned his back to his daughter and paced the floor, hiding the tears that now filled his eyes. Rage turned to sadness as he listened to his daughter.

"I said '*not yet.*' I may have said 'I'm not ready.' I know I thought it, but I'm not sure it came out." She burst into tears. "I don't know if I said 'I'm not ready,' but I did say, '*not yet*'."

They could hardly make out her words in between the sobs; she sounded pitiful. Torn. Emotionally torn.

"Reece had been drinking and I don't know if he heard me." She took a gasp of air. "I said it at least twice, but he was heavy and I couldn't get him off me." She looked up. "I honestly don't think he heard me; but I know I said it because I truly wasn't ready. The beer, he didn't hear me."

Her mom started to cry, feeling disgusted with herself for not knowing what had happened before now, and for not giving her daughter a safe place to fall. Why hadn't Payton come to her? She felt as if she'd let her daughter down on so many levels. Cradling her once again in her arms, she didn't need to ask Payton to continue; she did on her own.

"All I remember next is it hurt, and Reece saying something, but I'm not really sure what."

She told them afterward she threw up and Reece

took care of her. But the video was taken unbeknownst to them by a kid who thought it would be funny; they had no part in it, and it had been a nightmare ever since.

"It's not good between me and Reece right now," Payton sobbed. "I'm confused and not sure how to feel."

Then Payton looked at her mom and dad and said, "I don't believe he meant to hurt me, but I'm mad that he doesn't see it the way I see it."

"And exactly how do you see it?" her dad asked.

"That he drank too much and didn't listen."

Perry jumped in. "You know you're right, this is a mess. Depending what side of the fence you're sitting on, it could be seen as a date rape situation. Because NO MEANS NO. And if I'm not mistaken, you said '**not yet**'."

Payton's heart sank. She didn't want any trouble for Reece, and it didn't seem that way to her. Claudette didn't know what to say. She was as furious as her husband, and as brokenhearted as her daughter. Kids were drinking, both made bad decisions due to being impaired, and now both lives could be ruined. Tragic, any way you sliced it, and they'd barely discussed the video.

"I'm so scared. The video rumors, that's bad, yes. But I love him, and I'm going to lose him over this. It's all messed up now. I can't be myself around him, and he can hardly look at me because I'm so angry. It's my fault. I just know it, because I shouldn't have been there in the first place."

As soon as Payton said that, her dad interjected;

he would have the last word.

"Let me be clear, this is not your fault!" her dad insisted. "You had a part in it, you all did, but you are not to blame."

***

Roger Townsend, Reece's dad, slid his phone into his pocket. Sick. He felt sick to his stomach. He spoke to coaches all the time, had for years, but he'd never once had a conversation like he'd just had. Walking into the kitchen, he opened the fridge, pulled out a beer, and sat down. Reagan, his wife, stopped in the doorway and stared at him, glancing at the kitchen clock and then at the beer in her husband's hand. She stated the obvious.

"Little early, isn't it?"

"Yes!" was his unapologetic response; it was too early for a beer.

He wasn't quite ready to discuss with his wife the conversation he'd just had with Coach Wiggins. He needed a minute. Time to compose his thoughts. None of it made sense. His kid wasn't that brainless. But Coach wasn't a liar either, that he did know.

"Where's Reece?" Roger asked.

"Why?" she asked protectively.

"Where is he?" he asked firmly.

"What's going on?" she demanded to know.

"Is the boy in the house, yes or no?"

Reagan shook her head. "He left earlier, said he was going to the lake with the boys. Fishing." She hesitated for a second, then pushed him. "If this has to do with Reece, you better start talking."

She sat down at the table next to him. He relayed

the conversation that he'd had with Coach Wiggins. Stunned, they sat at the table in silence. Every now and then she would ask, "Are you sure it's him? Are you sure?" Her husband only nodded his head and reiterated that there was footage regarding the whole, in his words, "disgusting scene."

"I never did like that girl, I didn't," Roger Townsend stated.

"Don't say that," Reagan said softly. "You're angry. I'm furious, but that's not right. We do like Payton. This is their mistake. *Their* stupidity, not hers!"

Roger finished his beer and went toward the fridge, but stopped himself. Hardly the answer, and he knew that, so he grabbed a mug and poured a cup of coffee instead. His mind was racing, and he only knew half the story. If he had any idea of what was being said in Payton's camp, he would have been hysterical.

"This could ruin his football career, do you realize that?" He took a sip of coffee. "My God, Reagan, what in the hell was that boy thinking?" He sat back down at the table. "He was drinking, but he wasn't driving. Glad he had enough sense not to do that, drink and drive. But granted, I hope he didn't get stupid and drink too much."

"Drink too much?" his wife objected. "Roger, he shouldn't have been drinking at all!"

"I'm not saying he should've been drinking! I'm saying he did and I hope it wasn't too much. Oh hell! I don't know what I'm saying. Where's Reece, get him on the phone and get him home now!"

It seemed to take forever for Reece to return home.

His parents were sitting at the kitchen table, anxiously waiting for him. His mom's face looked weird; not mad, just not like herself. His dad looked mad.

"What's going on?" Reece asked.

"Why don't you tell us?" His dad stared at him from across the room. "I'm waiting, son, and my patience is wearing thin."

"Coach Wiggins," his mom said. "Why don't *you* tell us why we'd receive a call from Coach?"

Reece felt a knot form in the pit of his stomach. The party he could handle, but why was Coach calling? Reece's mind flooded with possibilities. He had found about the party, the drinking, lying, teens doing what they shouldn't be doing, the damaged seat at the lake house—the possibilities were endless. He stood and listed them in his head.

"What did he say?"

"Wrong answer," his dad responded.

"I went to a party over there, well, at his lake property, that Stacie threw." They had blank faces. "Stacie's his daughter, remember?"

"Got that," his dad said firmly. "The rest of the story."

Reece came semi-clean. "We were drinking. I was drinking. I'm sorry. I know I shouldn't have, but I didn't drink that much."

That might not have been the right thing to say, or was it? Reece didn't know. His dad wasn't given anything away. His mother didn't know the whole story yet, and just about fell out of the kitchen chair when his dad blurted out his next question.

"Any particular reason you thought it was a good idea to have sex on tape?"

"WHAT?" his mom yelled. "What did you just say?" Evidently she hadn't realized that concerned her son.

"What did you think I was talking about, Reagan?"

And then his father flew into a rage. "Son, are you freaking kidding me? Do you have any idea what this could do? All you've worked for—any?"

Reagan Townsend stared at her son. The words that her husband yelled were going in one ear and out the other. Sex. Footage. Tape. Her son a senior and Payton a minor, and now the whole world knew they were having sex.

"How long have you two been doing this?" his mom asked.

"What do you mean?" Reece played stupid.

"Sex, Reece. How long?"

Reece shook his head. "Mom, it's fine. It was the first time." But the more he spoke, the worse it got. "We had planned to hang out that night since it was the one night we were going to be out all night, but that part wasn't necessarily planned. We talked about it, sometimes, but things got heated in the tent."

His parents stared at him, not surprised. Kids. Seclusion. No adult supervision and alcohol: it was a recipe for countless disasters. But his version, though he didn't realize it, was making him look like a real jerk.

"We were all drinking. When we went to our tent, things kinda ended up going that way, and we sorta did that by accident. I think. I mean, we planned to spend the night out there, but ya know." He could barely talk about that to them. "I didn't think much about it at first, but then Payton acted real weird."

His dad interjected. "What the hell you talking about, boy? You either had sex with the girl or you didn't."

Reece couldn't believe he was having this conversation in front of his mom. Bashfully he said, "Yes, we had sex. I thought that's what we were doing; I mean, that is what we were doing, kinda, yes." He put his head in his hands and took a deep breath. "But then it got weird, like afterward."

He took a second and thought about what he was trying to say, but it didn't matter, it didn't come out right.

"Payton said she hadn't felt well or wasn't ready yet, or something like that, about it, I can't remember. But she'd been drinking, it hit her, and that's when she threw up. It was just plain gross."

His mom's face suddenly filled with anguish as the reality of the situation became apparent. Her eyes flashed toward Reece as she jumped out of the chair and ran so fast toward him that she startled her husband. Grabbing Reece by the shoulders, forcing him to look at her, she stared him straight in the eye.

"Reece, son, do you hear what you're saying? Do you hear yourself?" She was frantic, practically screeching. "Did you or did you not have sex with Payton? Son, damn it, did she tell you it was OK?"

As if a light bulb suddenly went on, Roger jumped to his feet as well. "Oh my God, son, think, you little ass! Think! Think! Think! What did you do?"

Chapter 33

Payton

Silence had never seemed so deafening. Payton had finally dried her tears, but every now and then a sniffle came from the spot on the couch she was curled up on. Shocked and angry by the words they'd just heard, her parents had momentarily dismissed the video. Payton's mom moved across the room and sat down at her side, devastated that her daughter had gone through such an experience and then felt that she had nowhere to turn. Her dad, about to fly into a rage, tried to gather himself long enough to process what he'd just heard; confused, he moved to the other side of the room. This was a boy they liked, a kid they welcomed into their home and trusted with their daughter! Her boyfriend. They'd been drinking, yes, and it would appear things got out of hand . . . a polite way of saying, "What the hell happened?" But why did Reece take her there in the first place? And why hadn't he listened to her pleas? He took her to the party, damn it; he should have protected her! And then her dad's own thoughts came back and haunted him: who would have thought that she'd need protection from him, Reece? His mind flooded with the whys and what ifs, and his anger turned to rage.

"I don't ever want to see that boy in this house

again!" Turning toward his wife, he added, "Do you hear me, ever again! I don't know what I'd do if I saw him. I just don't know what I'd do to him."

Payton grabbed a cushion and buried her face in it. Her mom tried to comfort her and calm down her husband. Hands in the air, she begged her husband to calm down, eyes redirected at Payton, hoping he would see the state she was in. He needed to back off and give her a minute. Payton was at her wit's end. Courageous enough to speak, what she stated weren't the words they wanted to hear. Jumping to defend her boyfriend, Payton glared at her dad and screamed that she wouldn't stop seeing Reece. It was clear he didn't understand, but how could he, neither did she. Voice strained, she pushed her confusion aside and defended the boy she loved, hurt and all. Still uncertain of exactly what had happened that night, one thing she knew for sure: she still loved Reece Townsend.

"None of this is coming out right. It wasn't supposed to be like that."

Her eyes darted toward her mom for help, but she wasn't getting any sympathy or help from her mom. Defending the person who hurt her daughter, intentional or not, was a tough sell and made absolutely no sense to either parent as they watched their daughter crumble before them.

"You know better than this, Payton," her mom yelled. "Regardless of what you think or say happened, this situation isn't right."

She stood in front of her daughter. "If you weren't in a frame of mind to say yes, it was a no. If he wasn't in a frame of mind to remember, it was a **NO!** Try to defend that!" She lowered her voice and, as kindly as she possibly could, whispered, "And let's not forget that you're a minor."

Payton, defiant, held her ground and, despite the fact she had no idea what to believe anymore, she continued to protect Reece.

"I was there, Mom. And what you're trying to say happened, didn't happen like that."

Torn between love and being afraid of saying the wrong thing, she fiercely tried to divert the attention from Reece to her. She didn't know if he'd heard her. She didn't know if she had spoken clearly. The thought of him lying about something so serious was incomprehensible to her, and the sound of Payton defending him was incomprehensible to her parents. He loved her; he'd told her that at least a hundred times or more.

"I know that we both wished we hadn't gone to Stacie's that night, and we shouldn't have been drinking. But I also know that Reece wouldn't hurt me the way you're trying to say that he did." She could barely talk. "But I don't know how to describe it other than as a horrible accident."

Her head was spinning, and her heart was breaking. Defeated didn't begin to describe what she was feeling. It sounded ridiculous—an accident—and she felt shame and humiliation even in her own home. The sight of her parents torn and anguished killed her inside. She misunderstood the most obvious thing of all: they were sad and heartbroken for what had happened to their little girl.

"The truth is, I don't know what happened, but I know we're both to blame and it shouldn't have happened. If you force me to say that Reece raped me, I can't do it. I couldn't classify this as what you're trying to call it, date rape—that's not right for people who truly experience such tragic things. But it has to be my fault as well because I was the one who drank too much when I know better. I shouldn't have been drinking at all." She couldn't look at them. "I shouldn't have even been there, and as much as you hate it, that isn't his fault, it's mine."

Her parents blamed themselves for not protecting her, and disagreed with the words that she was spewing, but not daring to shut her down in the state that she was in, they told her that forcing her only to have her dispute their claims was pointless. A crumpled pile on the floor, not resembling their daughter at all, Payton sobbed her heart out as she said her final words for that night.

"I love him, and now I know because of this he won't love me."

Perry Phillips, tears in his eyes, sat down next to his daughter. He held out his hand, silently praying she'd reach out and hold his, and thankfully she did. Claudette, crying uncontrollably, sat down on the other side of her little girl, a young lady to the world. After a few moments, her dad managed to speak. As softly as he could in the moment at hand, through his own tears he comforted his daughter.

"You are an amazing girl—beautiful, smart, and

one of a kind! No one in this world is just like you. No one! And none of this is your fault. None of it!!!!" His strong hand wiped her face, and through his tears he added, "But I do blame Reece. I do blame him for taking you there, for not waiting until you were ready, and putting you through the humiliation of what you're about to experience because of that damn video. I can't help it; I love you, and I blame the boy for hurting you."

Payton raised her head and opened her mouth to object, but there was no point. He was still talking anyway.

"I must make one thing very clear, Payton, one thing. Call it what you will and I will call it what I will, and to me, you said the words '*NOT YET*', and to me and the rest of the world, that is a definite *NO*. Forcing you to file a report is pointless, but I'll ask you to think about it, that's all."

Overcome with grief, he couldn't possibly finish the rest of his sentence. Claudette reached over Payton and squeezed his hand. Through his tears, he finished what he had been trying to say.

"I want to be very clear regarding what I say next, very clear, do you understand?"

Payton nodded.

"This will never be your fault. Ever. You did a lot of things wrong that night, but this wasn't one of them. You lied. You were drinking, and I can't trust you any time soon, for obvious reasons. But Payton, this isn't your fault."

He waited for her to make eye contact, but the tears that had filled her eyes brimmed over and rolled down her face. His big, kind hands reached over for the last time that night and wiped them away, but they continued to flow. Gingerly choosing his words, he wrapped it up, trying to enforce his thoughts without driving her completely away.

"This is a prime example why teens shouldn't drink. It impairs their thinking and decision-making; it's just a fact. And then binge drinking—you could've gotten alcohol poisoning and died." He managed a smile. "And why kids want to grow up so fast is beyond me. There's so much to wait for. Payton you're worth waiting for, do you realize that?"

Payton nodded. "I get it, I do. And I won't do that again, drinking, it's not for me. But I'm begging you, please, please don't hate Reece."

Without hesitation her dad responded. "Nope, I can't promise that!"

***

Payton's phone had been blowing up, but not with texts from Reece. He was lying low, which was likely for the best. But she missed talking to him, wanted to hear his voice, and was desperate to know he was all right during all of this mess. It seemed to have gotten bigger than either of them had dreamed. As much as she hated to admit it, she wondered if he was as worried about her as much as she was worried about him. She'd sent him messages, but his responses were short and to the point. She couldn't decipher if she were reading too much into it, or if he was really becoming distant and blowing her off. She felt sad and abandoned.

Aubrey: What's going on?
Payton: Parents know.
Aubrey: Know what?????
Payton: Everything.
Aubrey: OMG
Aubrey: You OK?
Payton: No
Aubrey: Want me to come over?
Payton: Yes
Aubrey: BTW are you still deleting texts?
Payton: Yeah. Getting nasty.
Aubrey: People we know?
Payton: No. Don't recognize the numbers. Stuff like whore, slut, skank. Oh and my favorite, want to come to our party?
Aubrey: It will go away.
Payton: Not soon enough ☹

Payton used to love notifications on her phone; now dreading them, she barely glanced at the screen. Eventually she'd have to go back to school and act as if the name-calling, looks, finger-pointing, stares, and giggles didn't bother her at all. It did. Crushed her, but she could fake it, right? She only hoped she was strong enough to act like the words didn't hurt; they did. Days leading up to the release of the video, being the topic of conversation, had been bad enough, but now everyone knew it was her in the tent. The verbal bullying was horrific. Although still well liked by most, this didn't stop people from joining in from afar. People she thought were her friends couldn't help but comment, when all she wanted to do was move on and forget.

Blocking all that out of her head, Payton focused on trying to mend her relationship with Reece. She couldn't understand why he wasn't calling her back and his texts were so short. Disappointment turned to fear, fear turned to anger, and anger turned right back into hurt. Hurt made her imagination run wild, and anger started to set in all over again. Reece had no idea that one conversation with him, a real conversation, could have put her mind at ease. But what Payton really wanted more than anything else in the world was to go back to the night before the party—that night everything in her life was perfect. That was never going to happen, and Payton realized she was going to have to deal.

Aubrey showed Payton several texts before deleting them; they were at least positive and defended Payton in regards to some of the nasty comments being spread around school. She had a few allies, nice—she needed all the support she could get. Hesitantly, Aubrey asked about Reece.

"What did he say when your parents found out?"

Payton showed her his response. It wasn't what she thought it should be, but then again it was a text. She was trying not to read too much into it, but that wasn't easy, especially at this time.

Reece: Great. That's all I need.

Noticing the disapproval on Aubrey's face once she read the response, and despite the fact she felt the same way, Payton still tried to defend Reece. His messages were always short, she'd said. He was being drilled at home and Royce was on his way, which meant the whole family had been called collectively to talk to Reece. That's what young, inexperienced love did—made you lose your mind or at least common sense.

"He's busy with the family and guys hate to text." Aubrey did her best to sound supportive.

Payton nodded, grateful that Aubrey agreed. But even she knew that Aubrey wasn't buying it. For whatever reason, Reece wasn't acting the way that she felt he should right now, but continually defending his actions was taking a toll. The emotional strain was far worse than she dreamed. Her mom walked into her bedroom and greeted Aubrey. The conversation was light, and she barely managed small talk.

"Aubrey, glad you're here. I hope you all learned something from the other night?"

Both girls nodded. Claudette wasn't about to ask if Aubrey's mom knew; no point in going down that road, but she did ask if she could speak to Payton alone.

"I've made an appointment for you to go to the doctor, for a checkup, to make sure you're all right."

"You did what? Oh my God, Mom, no!" Payton resisted.

"The answer is yes, and it's for your well-being, not mine."

Horrified at the thought of her first real young woman's well-visit being over something like that, Payton hung her head.

"Don't feel like that," her mom said softly. "You're at that age anyway, but after this, it's really important for numerous reasons. Don't ask me to list them."

Payton shuddered, shook her head, and quit

objecting. She wasn't in a position to argue, compromise, or negotiate anyway. She'd have to go to the doctor and even the doctor would know she'd had sex. *OMG,* she thought, *could this situation possibly get any worse?* Little did she know the answer was yes!

Chapter 34

Reece

Royce had words with his coach, who generously allowed him an extra day plus the weekend to spend at home, family crisis. During the drive, he tried to figure out what was going on, but his dad had insisted they discuss it in person. Texting Reece wasn't getting anywhere either; little brother didn't want to talk about it, and quite frankly didn't seem to grasp the potential trouble he'd caused for himself. Royce was fully aware of his parents' concern for Reece. Reece was blocking it all out. It was, after all, Payton they were talking about, his girlfriend; why the panic and sudden overreaction to a date that, in Reece's mind, had gone south? Surely she'd calm down.

Lying on his bed, tossing his football in the air, Reece read his text messages from Payton. Part of him wanted to call and talk to her, but part of him was afraid she'd rehash the night of the party. Tired of fighting and defending himself, and wanting more than anything for things to get back to normal, he decided to wait a while longer. A quick text would have to do.

Reece: This is jacked up for sure.
Payton: Will you call me please?

Hesitation set in. He could barely respond, knowing she deserved a call, but dreading making it. It wasn't that he didn't want to call her; he didn't want to have the conversation he knew they'd have. He wanted to talk about picking her up at seven, and where would they go? And how he couldn't wait to see her, but now he was dreading seeing her, and it wasn't because he didn't care about her, because he did. But facing her now had become a complicated mess. Parents, brothers, hurt feelings, insinuations, accusations, rumors, video, OMG the video, not to mention the pending talks with his coach. It was a disaster.

Reece: I'll try to call you later.

He hit send and his heart sank, only imagining what hers did. His fingers tapped the phone screen again, knowing his answer was too vague.

Reece: Royce coming.

Payton sent back a text saying OK. Throwing his phone down onto the bedside table, he picked up his football and started tossing it back and forth in his hands. A knock on the door startled him; his mom walked in and sat on the bed. She looked worried.

"Everything OK?" he asked.

"I don't know, son. Is it?"

Puzzled, he shrugged his shoulders. What was he supposed to say to that? How was he expected to know if everything was going to be all right? The silence between the two became awkward, the first time ever in his life that had happened. She finally stood up and walked toward the door. Looking around his bedroom as if he weren't in it, glancing at each football team photo, pictures with friends, and things he loved, she said something that would haunt him forever.

"Son, we love you and stand by you no matter what; you're our son. But do you realize that, depending on how Payton feels about that evening, what took place between you and her, you could have just ruined your entire life and ours?"

Shocked that his parents actually thought there was a possibility he'd done something to Payton against her will, Reece started to panic. He misunderstood: they weren't accusing him of doing something so horrific, but trying to look at it from Payton's perspective. They were hoping against hope that Payton would verify Reece's story and that they had both made terrible decisions while being impaired. But being in a modern world, technology and protective laws rightfully in place, the thought of those laws being abused terrified them. A senior in high school having sex with his girlfriend, disputed, could still, under the right circumstances, mark the boy as a rapist or sex offender for the rest of his adult life. If that happened, everything he'd worked so hard for—athletic scholarship, education, plus his reputation—would have been for nothing.

His family understood the severity of the situation regarding the debate *he said, she said*, but Reece didn't seem to have a clue. Surely Payton would admit to her parents that they were both intoxicated, stupidity at its finest, and everyone could agree that they'd obviously lied about where they'd been, but had learned a valuable lesson. The key would boil down to the "he said, she said" if it ever got that far. Hanging her head, Reece's mom turned and walked out of his room.

"Get down here, boy, your brother's home!" Reece's dad hollered up the stairs.

Usually waiting at the door for Royce to walk in, Reece dreaded facing his brother. He had no idea what he was supposed to say. His dad was acting semi-normal, but his mom was acting weird. Roger pointed toward the game room.

"I'll be right there, getting a drink."

"Grab me something, Dad, anything," Royce hollered.

As Reece walked by, Royce grabbed him and hugged him, just as he normally did. This helped put Reece's mind at ease. It was possible it wasn't going to be that bad. Royce fell onto the couch; Reece grabbed pillows and flopped onto the floor by the fire. Roger sat down next to Royce and asked his wife, Reagan, to join them.

"Family meeting, let's do this!"

A couple of chuckles broke out, but his mom didn't laugh. His dad tried to lighten up the situation by telling a joke, but not even Royce could manage a grin.

"Fine. Let's get it over with then," Roger stated.

"Bro, tell me what happened. All of it, and don't hold anything back." Royce looked at his parents, then at Reece. "Do you want them to leave?"

Reece shook his head; no point, they'd already heard most of it and would likely ask him again anyway. He started from the beginning. The party planning stage, how they all got their stories straight, the idea of everyone camping instead of staying in the house, which his mom felt was considerate, though she emphasized she didn't agree with any of it. He told them how everyone, including Payton, was having a great time. When he talked about how they went to their tent, all eyes moved away from Reece, and his mom left the room. They waited for her to return, since his dad insisted she hear the story in case they had to defend him in court.

"Do you think it will come to that, Roger, really?" Reagan asked nervously.

"I don't know. I just know we have to be prepared. We don't know what Payton's going to do, really what her family is going to do. I just know that this idiot, no offense son, didn't make it sound good when he first told us."

Reece blushed. "Guess I had that coming and I never once thought, until this very second, we'd be talking courtrooms."

"This is where it gets really complicated," Reece said. "Because I didn't remember her saying those words, '**NOT YET**', until I woke up here, in bed. Like the next night. I swear it was like a nightmare. I'd fallen asleep, actually remembered the words in a dream—a nightmare it seemed like."

Royce, startled, asked, "You mean when you were sober and the alcohol had cleared your head?"

"I guess. Sober, yes. But I was asleep when those words popped in my head." Reece put his hand over his mouth, shocked himself by what he'd said. "It was the worst feeling I've ever had. Ever. I felt sick. Physically sick, when I heard those words in my head. But that was the next day, in my room."

Head hung in his hands, disgusted with himself, he added, "I would never hurt Payton on purpose, or anyone else. We had planned that night, planned to spend the night out there together and sleep in the tent. And that's where it gets complicated again. We have always said that when we were ready, we would do that. But that night with the party, everyone having fun, all our friends, drinking, one thing led to another, and then we were in the tent and eventually that happened. And of course then she was sick. And now it's bad. And weird. It's a mess."

The young teen who sat before them looked like a scared little boy, their little boy. The one they'd baked cookies with, took fishing, watched play T-ball and get his first touchdown on the flag football field. The one Royce dragged around because Reece adored his big brother, the one his mother tucked in bed because he couldn't sleep until she read him a story, and the one whose dad taught him to hunt with his first .22. And here he was sitting in front of them, scared to death. As horrible as the whole thing was, and it was horrible, they didn't know what to think or who to blame. It seemed as if both kids had put themselves in a terrible situation that had ultimately ruined everything. It was, without a doubt, a tragedy of misjudgment on both parts.

His mom hugged him. He was still her boy,

regardless of whatever could happen next. She was begging whoever would listen—God, the Universe, or anyone—that they would spare her son and give him a do-over. *Let Payton verify his story, please, let her see it the way he did.*

"I think you guys need to take a break," Royce suggested. "Let this stuff cool down. It's for the best. Trust me."

"Your brother's right. You're about to go to college, if this thing doesn't blow up. But if it doesn't cool down, it's going to get messy, and it's too big of a weight for you. Consider this a lesson learned. We don't know what lies ahead yet. You'd be wise to let things cool off between you and Payton. No lying, drinking, and getting in situations that can get you in any more trouble, and focus on you! Sports and your studies and get through the rest of the year," his dad agreed.

As scared and empty as Reece felt, a break didn't sound like a bad idea. He loved Payton, but they were young, and this had shaken him up pretty bad. If they took a break, maybe they could start over or just clear their heads. Not to mention dealing with her parents, letting her down—it was just all too much. He had no desire to deal with any of it. He could stay busy with other things; this trouble he didn't need and ditching all of it for now sounding tempting.

"I'll think about it. But we've got to see what happens next."

"Well, speaking of a break, Hank doesn't really want you talking to her a whole lot until we see what's going on," his dad added.

"Hank, your attorney? Why did you call him?" Reece asked.

"I didn't call him. He's my bud, and we were talking. He suggested you lay low and wait and see what they do." He looked at Royce and Reagan before saying, "But he did say the ball is in their court right now, till we know what they decide to do, and that under no circumstances are you to talk about what happened between you and Payton."

"But I'm not sure I did anything, other than what you know about. Did I do something wrong? Cause I couldn't remember something she said? Is that illegal?"

Reagan jumped in. "It could be, by some, perceived as wrong. If she doesn't verify your story, if her parents move forward with this legally, she's a minor, son. If she says she wasn't ready and you still had sex, it could be perceived as date rape." She softened her voice. "I hope, I beg, that Payton verifies your story and they don't move forward legally. But son, do you understand, really understand, the situation you could potentially find yourself in?"

It was becoming increasingly clearer, and it all depended on how Payton and her family felt about the same situation. One night of fun, a bad decision regarding his girlfriend, and he could be in more trouble than he knew how to handle. He was nervous, scared, and at that point he was certain his parents were right; following their *friend's* advice, Hank the attorney, was probably for the best. Lay low. Take a break. Later came, and he didn't call Payton.

Chapter 35

Parent Meeting

It was inevitable: the Townsends and the Phillips were going to have to sit down and talk. Roger Townsend made the decision, despite Reece's objections, to make the call. *Take the offensive and not the defensive position,* he thought. It was awkward, to say the least, but it wasn't as if they hadn't talked on the phone before. A location was designated and plans were made. Reece shot Payton a text.

> **Reece:** Can you believe this?
> **Payton:** Bet your parents hate me now.
> **Reece:** No they don't. Bet yours hate me though LOL
> **Reece:** Sorry about the LOL crazy right now.
> **Payton:** I get it. No problem.

She didn't say they didn't hate him. It was the most she'd talked to him in a while, usually only one line at a time, and no responses after that. They both waited on pins and needles, but no word from their parents. They had no idea how it was going. Payton, sick to her stomach, scrolled through the nasty messages about herself. She shouldn't have done that; it only made her feel worse.

The restaurant wasn't crowded, and they sat at a table in the corner. After placing their orders, the uncomfortable conversation began; no point in small talk. Roger thanked the Phillips for meeting them and asked how Payton was doing. He was complimentary, but subtle in his comments. Perry nodded, but kept his comments to one-word answers. Finally Roger addressed the elephant in the room.

"I hate that we're here under these horrific circumstances, the party, and the circumstances revolving around that night." He hesitated, took a sip of water and carefully proceeded. "Do you mind, please, telling me Payton's version of the events that evening?"

The look on Perry's face wasn't a good one. Roger added, "And then we'll do the same, of course." He went one step further. "Do you want me to go first?"

Perry shook his head. He stared at the Townsends across the table as Claudette shifted uncomfortably in her chair next to him. As a mother, she had so much to say, but the words were sticking in her throat. Confusing the entire situation was the fact that this boy, *their* boy, had been a part of their family and their lives for the past couple years. She reached under the table and held onto her husband's hand. She squeezed his hand, letting him know that she would go first. She started to recount Payton's story. To the Townsends' relief, the stories matched. Suddenly Claudette stopped talking to hold back tears. She had come to the part in Payton's version where the lines were getting fuzzy, blurred, and crossed. It wasn't that the teens didn't have the same account of the incident in the tent, it was the recollection of when the words **"NOT YET"** were said, and it was unclear if they were heard and ignored, or simply unheard at all. The Townsends froze.

Gathering her thoughts and composing herself, Claudette continued.

"It's not that my daughter denies being there, she was, and drinking, yes. And in today's constant fight for so-called equality, those were her decisions, not Reece's. But she's a minor. She chose to drink when she knows it's illegal, and we do not approve of or support that. That was her decision and unfortunately a damn bad one. Not only for the obvious reasons, but because it put her in this situation where she's not sure if he heard her. Admittedly these were her words, *I'm not sure if he heard, but I think he did, but I don't know.'* And therein, you see, lies the problem. She's not sure. But that said, in her own words, Payton does not believe that Reece would ever intentionally hurt her—"

Before Claudette could finish her sentence, a wave of relief swept over Reagan as she burst into tears. Pain only a parent could feel, relief, and gratitude that Payton had verified the version that her son had told. She reached over and grabbed Claudette's hand, but Claudette didn't return the gesture, and Reagan immediately let go. Wiping her own tears, she sat and listened to what Claudette had left to say. Tears of her own ran down her face as Claudette spoke, but Claudette persevered and spoke on behalf of her girl.

"I know that she loves Reece, that young teen first-love thing. But I do believe her, or God help me I want to, when she says that he has always been respectful of her and her body and her wishes every time they're together. And I'm glad. Because to entrust someone with our daughter who wouldn't be respectful, well, that falls on us." She wiped her eyes. "He's been in our home. We know him. We don't think this is a kid who would hurt her like that, but we don't ever want her in this situation again. Ever. I blame him for taking her there. I can't help it, I just do."

The Townsends didn't defend him. They simply listened. She blamed Reece for allowing Payton to drink so much, since he was older. Reece's parents desperately wanted to point out that he was an idiot kid as well, but they didn't. Claudette blamed him for keeping her daughter out all night; Reece's parents understood that as well, even though they didn't have a daughter. But they were relieved that he wasn't drinking and driving. The Townsends continued to bite their tongues, keeping their thoughts to themselves, fearful Payton's parents would change their minds and force her to change her story. Perry cleared his throat. Roger sat straight up, hoping it wouldn't come to raised voices, but prepared himself just in case. It was Payton's father's turn.

"She's making us believe her, swearing by it, and we want to believe that Reece is a good kid. But if he hadn't been, if he had hurt her intentionally, meaning disregarded her words, so help me, I just might have killed him. If not literally, damn close."

Roger Townsend looked Perry straight in the eye. "Sir, that is my son. But God forbid, if he had hurt her intentionally—or any girl for that matter—I would've helped you."

"Thank you for believing that he's not a monster. That they both made horrible decisions, and thank you for coming here this evening." Reagan's hands were shaking, and she was emotionally wiped out. She took a sip of her wine. The food came, but no one could eat.

"How is Payton?" Reagan asked.

"She's confused, and I don't blame her. It will take time. She can't remember, due to the alcohol, exactly what happened, which is confusing, hurtful, and emotionally traumatizing. The video, well you know all about that. The bullying and harassment has started. So she's humiliated and quite frankly she doesn't want to go back to school, but she can't avoid that forever." Perry stared at them as he spoke. "Guess she'll have to deal with the consequences; punishment enough I think, don't you?"

There was nothing left to say. Their son's future wasn't going to be thrown away, but there were still consequences for everything he'd done. Grounding. Humiliation with the video, time on the bench for drinking, almost suspended by Coach, to name a few. How he was going to deal with Payton, well, that was his decision anyway. They could only advise him, but they really felt a break was needed. Reece was torn. It was impossible to go back to the way things were, and he didn't know how to move forward. Payton's parents would never think of him in the same way and she, despite her words, didn't look at him the way she used to. It sucked being a teen sometimes!

Chapter 36

Where Do We Go from Here?

Sleep had eluded Reece Townsend for days. Payton was weighing on his mind; he loved her, but his dad had a point. Getting ready to go to college, he needed to focus on his studies and football. It was going to be hard to keep up with both, especially with a girlfriend back in high school. And after this, it might be damn near impossible. He was dreading facing her parents, and for a split second contemplated dragging Trevor along, but talked himself out of it. Texting her now had become a chore. She was constantly upset about the harassment of the video. She was getting it a hundred times worse than he was, he knew that, but it wasn't his fault. And his lack of sympathy regarding the nasty bombardment of texts, snickers, and comments were taking a toll on the two.

> **Payton:** Did you read that screen shot I sent you?
> **Reece:** Yeah
> **Payton:** Who is that?
> **Reece:** Don't know.
> **Payton:** Well?
> **Reece:** Well what?
> **Payton:** Seriously. OMG . . . Forget it!
> **Reece:** I don't know what you want me to say.

Don't read them. They suck and you know they're not true.

He didn't want to deal. He wanted to play football, hang out with his friends, and let everything get back to normal. Payton would've loved that too, but she wasn't that lucky. All eyes were constantly on her, and she could feel her skin crawling as people whispered behind her back.

Slinking down the hall, trying to blend in unnoticed, Payton struggled with being back in school. Aubrey and Maddie couldn't be by her side every second, and the confident, beautiful girl everyone knew her to be was slipping away. Rumors, whispers, texts, video replay, and shares on social media had turned Payton from one of the popular, well-liked students to the girl everyone had a joke about. At first she held her own. She had a comeback for everything that people were brave enough to say to her face; but worn down, embarrassed, and tired of trying to defend the impossible, she gave up.

Zero support from Reece was the worst. She felt used and worthless. If he loved her, why didn't he understand how awful this was for her? Why didn't he take up for her? She felt alone and afraid. She was losing the boy she loved and it was his fault! Most of the nasty, snarky comments were being said behind her back, but she knew they were talking about her. The girls were bitchy and the boys were obnoxious and rude. She couldn't even get relief by crying anymore; too many tears already shed. Her confidence shaken, the light in her eyes gone, and with Reece distancing himself, she didn't know where to turn. It killed her to constantly reach out to him, but she did. It went against everything she'd been taught. If a boy loves and respects you, he will treat you right and keep you in his life. Reece wasn't keeping her in his life. He was barely registering that she was a part of it. It blew her mind to think this was the same person from merely a few weeks ago. This was the boy she thought she'd spend the rest of her life with. She didn't recognize him, but she hung on.

Payton: Are we hanging out tonight?
Reece: Got practice, but we'll talk later.

Her heart sank; his response was code for "don't bother me." Payton tried to hide the disappointment that was written all over her face.

"Hey, I've got an idea," said Aubrey.

Payton stared aimlessly at her friend. "What's that?"

"Let's have Maddie do something really stupid and take the heat off of you. Sound good?"

Payton managed a slight smile. She took a deep breath and focused on the kid at the front of the class. Every time she tried to think about something else, Reece popped into her mind. Driving herself crazy with worry, she tried to focus on something else. Aubrey thought he wanted to see someone else, but she didn't dare say it out loud. Why else would he act like that? Maddie thought he was just being a jerk, and she did say that out loud, half expecting Payton to defend him, but she didn't. It was worse than they expected; their friend sat there stone-faced and showing zero emotion.

Payton's heart was breaking. From mad at Reece to blaming herself, she had no idea what to do or how to feel. Oh, and not to mention, her reputation was mud. Reece's not that badly; everyone in his circle seemed to be moving right along, as if nothing had happened. How was that even possible? Her life had been destroyed, and he kept plugging along. Adding insult to injury, Cody texted Aubrey and said they'd all gone to lunch. Reece went, and Stacie rode with him.

"Are you kidding me right now?!" Payton snapped. "Where was Trevor?"

They could talk after school and all would be well. They had to figure out how to get back on track. Payton knew two things: she loved him, and she missed him. The rest they'd figure out, but Reece never called.

Chapter 37

Bitter Betrayal

At seven thirty she could stand it no more; firing off a text, angry that Reece hadn't called when he said he'd call, she let him have it! The text ticked him off. He'd been busy. Weight room. Homework. Not to mention trying to get back on his parents' good side meant extra chores around their place. Could he have taken two seconds to text her earlier, yes, but she wanted a call and he didn't feel like it. He didn't want to fight. Payton fired off another text. Anguish and fear had turned into rage. She wasn't coming across well on text at all.

> **Payton:** Could you give me the courtesy of answering my texts?
> **Payton:** You promised you'd call, but you didn't.
> **Payton:** Helllloooooo
> **Payton:** You're being a jerk. Answer your texts. Rude.

Reece's behavior was frying her mind. A simple text would have put her mind at ease, but not knowing what he was doing when he was usually with her, and not knowing what was going on between the two of them, was driving her crazy. Payton was acting moody, emotional, and lashing out at those around her. Her mom walked into her bedroom, lay clean clothes on her bed, shook her head, and walked out. The girl was unraveling and her mom blamed Reece. Finally a text notification came in.

Reece: Chill

Furious but wanting to talk to him, Payton tried to calm herself down before replying. *What an ass,* she thought. Answering the text and pinning him down to a phone call, she waited for the phone to ring. The call was brief, but plans were made. He would be there Friday evening at seven-thirty. If she could keep it together until then, Payton knew once they saw each other and talked, they'd be back on track as a couple. Or at least that was her goal. Reece ended the call and, unlike Payton, put the whole thing out of his mind. He had two days to forget about it, minor texts in between, then he'd come face-to-face with her parents again. For now, he'd watch some TV with his family and text Royce later.

Friday evening rolled around too quickly for Reece, a first. He knew his dad was sick over the semi-accusation alone and struggled with thinking about Payton the same way. Sliding on his boots, his dad asked if Reece was going to pick her up.

"I don't mind going with you, son, to pick her up. We can come back over here and have a movie night."

As tempting as that was, he knew he had to go alone. If his dad could face Payton's family for him, talk to her and handle this, that would have been awesome, but he knew that he had to be the one to do it. Conflicted about how he felt now himself, and having no idea how he would be received at the Phillips' house, Reece climbed into his truck and headed over to Payton's.

Payton had been watching the clock since she'd gotten home from school. Showered, dressed in Reece's favorite outfit, despite how thin she had become, and how dull her eyes now seemed, she still pulled off *beautiful*. Begging her parents to be nice, she waited for the sound of his truck to pull into the neighborhood. Perry and Claudette were struggling. Claudette hid it for her daughter's sake better than her dad, Perry. His face was rigid and at times he caught himself with clenched fists. Noticing this, he slid his hands into his jeans pockets. As soon as he heard Reece's truck, he looked toward the door, and Payton was already standing there waiting. He shook his head, and gently pulled her backward by the arm.

"This isn't up for debate. I'll meet Reece today."

Opening the door, he stepped outside. Her dad was about to make everything worse! Her mom, Claudette, ushered her into the kitchen, assuring her it was going to be fine.

"Your father has a right to say his piece," she said. "You should respect that; I can assure you that if he had his way, Reece wouldn't be over here today."

Payton didn't care. She didn't want Reece to be upset. Claudette was shocked that the only person she was worried about was him, not even herself. As much as her mom wanted to understand this, it infuriated her. She knew her daughter was smarter than that, but then again she had to remind herself that Payton was thinking with her heart and not her head.

Reece wanted to turn around and leave as soon as he saw Mr. Phillips standing in the driveway. For a second he wasn't sure if he was even supposed to turn off his truck, but he parked and climbed out. Taking a deep breath, he walked toward her dad.

"Sir. I'd like to apologize for everything that's happened."

Mr. Phillips analyzed the boy's face. It felt like an eternity, but he finally reached out and grasped Reece's hand. He didn't shake it. Just held it firmly in his. He placed his other hand on his shoulder, and Reece knew they were about to have words. Everything inside him told him to keep his mouth shut, a wise decision. Perry Phillips unloaded.

"Not sure where to start, Reece, so I guess I'll just say my piece."

Reece nodded his head. His stomach was doing flips, and his heart was beating out of his chest.

"I'm sick that you took her there, to the party. There's a difference between a party and an overnight. That was your fault and I flat out blame you!" He stared into Reece's eyes.

Reece didn't say anything.

"If you were a man, and I'm just being honest, one of us would be in jail and one in the morgue. But you're not quite a man, are you, I mean age-wise." He let go of Reece's hand. "But you know that wasn't smart."

Payton paced the kitchen floor, begging her mom

to break up her dad's awkward conversation. She could see the look on Reece's face, and he was dying.

Mr. Phillips stepped backwards, as if to take a good, long, hard look at Reece. Reece's cheeks were flushed; he was nervous and scared. But he stood there and waited to see what else Mr. Phillips would say.

Reece wished he wasn't in that driveway. He loved Payton, but right now, a senior, leaving to start the next phase in his life, he didn't love her enough to have her father look at him that way, with hate in his eyes. He knew immediately what he had to do. They were going on a break, permanently.

"Sir, I understand. May I talk to Payton?"

Mr. Phillips stepped aside, and Reece walked toward the door. Payton answered it. She asked him in, and he asked her if she'd come outside. Not wanting to move, knowing in her heart it was going to be bad, she asked if everything was OK. He didn't answer.

"Why don't you come in? We can talk in the kitchen if you like."

"Let's go for a drive. To our tree, by the lake, and talk?"

It was possibly the last ride she'd take with him, and for some reason she could feel it. But what if there was a possibility that she could make him see that this was going to be OK? Her mom didn't dare walk past her daughter; the desperation in her girl's eyes and face broke her heart. She was better than that; she'd just temporarily forgotten. Payton grabbed her jacket and followed Reece to the truck. Usually she'd bounce, literally, up into the cab, but right then she felt as if he she were driving to the end of the best chapter in her life. One night, a horrendous event, mistake after mistake, and it had ruined everything.

The drive seemed to take forever. The silence hurt her head. It was more than obvious he was going to say something she didn't want to hear, but she didn't know it would be delivered as terribly as it was. Parking the truck in their usual spot, Reece avoided all eye contact.

"Look at me, please," she pleaded. "If you have something to say, please give me the courtesy of at least looking at me."

It was harder than he dreamed. Breaking her heart in front of his eyes. He didn't want to look at her; he wanted it over. Reece wanted to move on, get rid of the nightmare and never have her look at him with such disdain again. If he could put that whole night and every night since out of his head, he would, but he couldn't while he was tied to her. The words didn't come easily, gagging on every one of them, but he managed to spit them out anyway. He held onto his dad's words, but in the back of his mind he couldn't help but wonder if he was making the biggest mistake of his young life. He did love her, but obviously not enough.

"I just think with everything that's happened we should take a break. It's crazy for you; it's crazy for me. You're constantly pissed off. Your parents are mad, mine are too; it needs to cool down. Plus I'm getting bombarded all the time about the video thing; it's just too much with school and everything." He didn't dare glance her way. "If we take a break, we can see what happens after that."

Payton couldn't stop the tears from flowing down her face. Shattered. He had completely shattered her. He reached out to hold her hand, but that infuriated her and she pulled it away.

"Don't. Don't do that. You're getting bombarded. I'm getting terrorized. I'm called a whore, slut, skank, party-girl, you name it, and that's by everyone. They've written crap on my locker. They whisper in front of me and behind my back. I get texts, phone calls, and offers . . . yep, offers." She talked through her tears, angry, hurt, and disappointed. "I'm angry with you because you will not take the time to listen to me, to hear what I'm trying to say. I defended you this whole time. And likely always will. I said '*NOT YET*'! I don't know if you heard me, you say you didn't, and I believe you. I choose to believe you, Reece, but that doesn't mean that I was ready. Or that I don't regret everything about that night; it means I love you enough to forgive the mistakes that we made that evening. To handle the garbage I'm going through at school and still defend you—to everyone: my parents, friends, and even myself."

He turned and stared out the windshield. Hearing her words, but having no idea what to say or do, he just sat there, wishing he wasn't in the middle of the storm he'd created.

"But that's just it. You shouldn't have to defend me to yourself. It's changed you and me, together. I can't help that."

Payton couldn't believe what she was hearing. He still couldn't hear her.

"I'm left to deal with this mess and you're dumping me. Nice. Ending it now so you can go off to school and do whatever you want." She grabbed his arm and tugged it, forcing him to look at her.

"Look at me! Look at me!!!!!! Do you realize what you've done? Do you?" she asked as he stared at her blankly. "You've made me completely disposable. I'm a disposable person; someone you get rid of when you're done."

"Payton, stop," he whispered. "That's not true. It's complicated, that's all."

Funny, he didn't look as beautiful in that moment. Those green eyes, not so much. The toll of the situation had come to a head. Broken. He'd broken her. There was nothing left to say; his mind was clearly made up. He was ending it, and she was shattered.

"Well, Reece Townsend, I hope you're proud of yourself, you've absolutely devastated me. Thanks a lot! Sixteen years old and disposable. Take me home!"

Chapter 38

Time Heals All Things

Reece dropped Payton off, but didn't walk her into the house as he normally would. He felt two things: like crap for hurting her and relieved it was over. He loved her, but believed she would never be able to look at him the same way, and the aftermath of the mess they'd created wasn't worth dealing with to him. Her parents hated him, and his parents were still scared. Her words ran through his mind as he drove. She was wrong; but the fight wasn't worth it to him anymore. He took the long way home and cried himself. Hurting her sucked. But staying would have been worse. It wasn't the same, and there was no going back. He couldn't help but look at his phone to see if she had sent a text, and he wondered if he should check on her. He didn't. If he was making a mistake, he didn't know how to fix it anyway.

Payton climbed the stairs, completely drained. Her mom heard her sobs from the second she walked in the door. Her dad, half expecting what had happened, put his head down and buried it in his newspaper. It killed him to see her hurt; but no boy deserved to treat his daughter like that. Throwing herself on the bed, burying her face in her pillow, wails came from Payton's room. Her whole body shook. She felt as if her heart was physically breaking; pain like she'd never experienced in her life pierced through her body. One night, a series of events, and her whole world had come crashing down around her.

She couldn't breathe. Her head hurt. Her heart was shattered, and Reece was a jerk. But worse, she still loved him. Her mom sat on the bed and rubbed her back. She bit her tongue and, as much as she wanted to, she didn't offer her daughter one ounce of false hope that Reece would come back. After several minutes, Payton's sobs eased and her mom whispered in her ear.

"You are the most beautiful, valuable girl in the world. Valuable. Worth loving and worth being treated with respect. This pain that you're feeling will eventually ease, but it will take time. But one day, I promise you, it will subside."

She stroked her daughter's hair, kissed her cheek, and held back her own tears. "The person who is supposed to love you forever has not found you yet, nor you him. But when you do find each other, that person isn't supposed to leave when things get tough, and he certainly isn't supposed to hurt you." She patted her back. "Payton, this is going to hurt, likely for a long time, but then you will heal. You will heal. Time heals all things; it will heal this as well."

Payton sat up, her face tear-streaked, as frail as her mom had ever seen her. She nodded her head. "I just can't believe how badly it hurts. I can't believe he broke up with me over this, and I can't believe I was so excited about that night. That night has ruined my life." She looked at her mom, who was holding her hand. "I've become one of them—a disposable person. The ones we talk about at school. Use them and leave them; it's awful, cause now I'm one of them."

Claudette Phillips was shocked. "A disposable person. How dare you call yourself such! You will never be disposable to anyone, certainly not to me."

Payton was exhausted, heartbroken, and worn out. Sick to her stomach, half the person she was a week before, she couldn't believe one experience had changed her in such a way.

"I wonder how many girls have experienced what I did."

"I don't know," her mom answered. "Which part— the heartache, the sex too soon, sex under questionable circumstances? Millions. But I imagine they don't want to talk about it."

Payton pointed to her laptop. "I think I'm going to write about it. Write an article in journalism or maybe blog about it. Try to warn other girls that maybe our parents aren't as dumb as we seem to think they are." She couldn't hold back her tears; it hurt so badly, the pain. "Feeling like a disposable person is the worst feeling in the world."

Claudette Phillips could hold back her own tears no longer. She wrapped her arms around her girl, held her, and rocked her, as if she were ten. "You are not disposable. You aren't! I think you should write about it, make it a blog series." She took a deep breath. "I'm sorry you went through this; it shouldn't have happened. But you are not the only one. It's part of life and it's painful for young girls—and boys. You are valuable and one day you will be the person I know you are supposed to be. And trust me, you don't realize it yet, but the person right here, this isn't you."

***

It took a while to start healing, but Payton eventually started a blog series for teen girls. It was part of her healing process. It helped her bond with other girls, heal, vent, and share valuable information. It included information about dating, date rape, date-rape drugs, and where to find help if something were to happen. It also included fun stuff—fashion, music, and celebrity entertainment. She wrote articles for her high school newspaper, and eventually set up live chat sessions with teens. Though she'd never admit it, she thought about Reece every single day; the difference was that the pain eased and it hurt less and less each time he crossed her mind. The amount of times became fleeting, and soon, she considered dating again. She has not yet jumped back into the dating pool.

Reece graduated and took comfort in his friends and parents who supported his decision to take a break from his relationship with Payton. He graduated and went to the college of his choice. Staying busy with sports, studies, and making new friends, he purposely pushes Payton out of his mind when she pops in his head. He often feels guilty about the way he handled the situation and fears he didn't handle it correctly. Every now and then he thinks about reaching out to her, but lacks the courage to do it. Fear, on his part, especially of being rejected, has held him back. A part of him still loves her, and hopes he bumps into her sometime. He has wondered on many occasions if he made the right decision. Time will tell.

Discussion Questions

1) There's plenty of blame to go around; which person do you blame? Stacie, Reece, Payton or a combination?

2) Why do you blame the person you chose?

3) Do you believe this was a date rape situation? Why or why not? List the consequence of lying and the legal ramifications that could have occurred.

4) Who did you sympathize with—Payton, Reece, or both? Why?

5) Which contributing factor do you think destroyed them the most: impaired decision-making leading to the sex that took place, not seeing eye-to-eye about how the sex came about, the anger due to lack of communication, or fear?

6) Boys and girls see things differently. Did you agree with Payton's position or Reece's? Why?

7) Did you agree with Payton's parents or Reece's parents? Why?

8) Social media plays a role in spreading rumors and destroying reputations. Why do you think kids feel the need to share everything they do?

9) If you were Payton, how would you have handled this situation?

10) Did you agree with how Reece handled the breakup?

11) If you were Payton, what would you have done differently?

12) If you were Reece, what would you have done differently?

About the Author

Multiple Award-Winning Author Amanda M. Thrasher was born in England, moved to Texas and resides there still. She is an author of children's books, picture books, middle-grade chapter books, young adult (YA) novels, and a reader's theater titled *What I . . . A Story of Shattered Lives*. She conducts workshops, writes a blog, and contributes to an online magazine. She's a multiple Gold

Recipient of the Mom's Choice Awards for *The Greenlee Project* (YA and General Fiction), and for *Spider Web Scramble,* a Mischief book. As Chief Executive Officer at Progressive Rising Phoenix Press, she assists authors in bringing their work to life, sharing her writing process and her years of publishing experience.

Amanda is a multiple Gold Recipient of the Mom's Choice Awards in YA, General Fiction, and early reader, chapter books. The **Mom's Choice Awards®** (MCA) evaluates products and services created for children, families, and educators. The program is globally recognized for establishing the benchmark of excellence in family-friendly media, products, and services. The organization is based in the United States and has reviewed thousands of entries from more than 55 countries. Around the world, parents, educators, retailers, and members of the media look for the MCA mother-and-child Honoring Excellence seal of approval when selecting quality products and services for children and families.

The Greenlee Project, a book about the consequences of bullying and cyberbullying, also won the first place Young Adult Book Award at the 16th annual North Texas Book Festival (NTBF). The NTBF helps schools, public libraries and literacy programs in North Texas. Since its inception, it has awarded more than $45,000.00 in grants to deserving programs.

For more information, visit the author's website at: www.amandamthrasher.com.

Other titles by Amanda M. Thrasher

The Greenlee Project

Spider Web Scramble

Mischief in the Mushroom Patch

A Fairy Match in the Mushroom Patch

The Ghost of Whispering Willow

There's A Gator Under My Bed

Sadie's Fairy Tea Party

What If ... A Story of Shattered Lives

Coming Soon --*CAPTAIN FIN* ~ A Novel by Amanda M. Thrasher based on a screenplay by Kevin James O'Neill

Progressive Rising Phoenix Press is an independent publisher. We offer wholesale discounts and multiple binding options with no minimum purchases for schools, libraries, book clubs, and retail vendors. We also offer rewards for libraries, schools, independent book stores, and book clubs. Please visit our website and wholesale discount page at:

www.ProgressiveRisingPhoenix.com

Progressive Rising Phoenix Press is adding new titles from our award-winning authors on a regular basis and has books in the following genres: children's chapter books and picture books, middle grade, young adult, action adventure, mystery and suspense, contemporary fiction, romance, historical fiction, fantasy, science fiction, and non-fiction covering a variety of topics from military to inspirational to biographical. Visit our website to see our updated catalogue of titles.